# THE WOMAN WHO
# WENT FOR BROKE

# ALSO BY C.K. CRIGGER

*Letter Of The Law*

*Liar's Trial*

*Lost Girl Lake*

*Madame's Daughter*

*The Yeggman's Apprentice*

*Yester's Ride*

*The Winning Hand*

# THE WOMAN WHO WENT FOR BROKE

## THE WOMAN WHO: BOOK SIX

### C.K. CRIGGER

WOLFPACK
PUBLISHING
— EST 2013 —

**The Woman Who Went for Broke**
Paperback Edition
Copyright © 2024 C.K. Crigger

Wolfpack Publishing
701 S. Howard Ave. 106-324
Tampa, Florida 33609

wolfpackpublishing.com

Paperback ISBN 978-1-63977-355-8
eBook ISBN 978-1-63977-354-1
LCCN 2024933506

# THE WOMAN WHO
# WENT FOR BROKE

# CHAPTER 1

JANUARY BILLINGS CLOSED THE DOOR TO THE HOUSE, HER late husband Shay's house, behind her and called to her old dog Penelope, Pen for short. The dog seemed to sense a wrongness in all the activity that had been happening the last couple days, and she whined as if wanting to go back inside and stay there. The dog's distress was almost enough to make January think she was making a mistake in leaving.

"It'll be all right," January told the dog, though not quite certain of this herself. Her hand rested on the dog's gray, black, and white head. She remembered a time when Pen had been inky black all over. "You'll be back, you know. With me, when I come over to check the horses and cattle. Or to stay with Johnny and Evie if there's someplace I can't take you. But you've been at the new house all through the building of it. Pretty soon you'll be used to it and forget you ever lived anywhere else."

She would never forget, though. She'd become a woman and known a husband's love here. And sorrow when he'd been murdered. And adventure. Not that she couldn't have those things at the new house if she wanted. Except for the sorrow. She could do without that.

After working on the new house for over a year, this was official move-in day, and eagerly anticipated. And yet, it almost seemed as if she were abandoning Shay where he rested in the graveyard on the hill above the house.

Swallowing down sentimental tears and calling herself a fool, January climbed onto the wagon seat, checked the load in the wagon bed was tied down and ship-shape, and slapped the lines over the backs of a pair of matched Belgians. "Come on, Pen," she called again, and glancing over her shoulder at the two horses tied on the back of the wagon, hollered, "Hup, Hoot and Mollie. Time to go."

She had a shed at the new house. More a shed than a barn, only big enough for her cow, and at a squeeze, these four horses and their tack. First thing on her agenda was to start on a new barn. She planned on using the foundation of the old one that had been a couple hundred yards up from the bridge. The ramshackle old barn from her grandfather's day had burned a couple years earlier. She had been inside at the time, under attack by a ruthless madman and his men, and had been lucky to get out alive. Sometimes, January reflected, she felt much, much older than the twenty-five years she actually claimed.

Pausing at the rail fence around the horse pasture, she stopped to tell the horses gathered to watch them leave goodbye and that she'd see them soon. And then they were truly on their way. She traveled two miles, wincing as she heard some inadequately packed dishes clatter, then across her hand-built bridge over Kindred Creek and up the hill to her new house.

January was proud of the house she'd built, mostly with her own two hands. Her father had been a master carpenter, and during the years he'd believed himself a wanted man, he'd kept her close in case they had to run. That meant she'd learned to build a bridge, a house, and just about anything else a carpenter put together. She'd also learned to handle a gun.

When her father died and she came back to the homestead at The Falls, it became a toss-up as to which of those lessons became the most valuable. Last fall she'd come down on the side of the gun, but in all honesty, it varied.

The yard, due to the recent thaws, was churned to slurry by wagon wheels and horse hooves. On her approach, January tried to visualize how it would be come spring when she began prettying up the place. Just because her home was a working ranch didn't mean it couldn't look nice. During her time in Spokane, while the Flowers Trust—a huge surprise to learn she was the Flowers heir—became established, she'd visited some high-toned homes and gotten some excellent ideas. Of course, those people had full-time gardeners, so she'd have to simplify, but...

Her mind filled with plans, she drove around the house and backed the wagon up to the wide service porch. Best to keep from tracking mud all over the front room, she figured, and this way she could stack boxes and items under cover of the wide back porch and bring them inside when she was ready. The books though, she'd have to bring those in right away in case of rain or even some late snow. The day might be bright at the moment, but it could turn in a flash at this time of year.

Sweating, maybe cussing a little as her foot slipped and she felt a muscle in her back protest, at first she didn't notice Pen had disappeared. When she called, and called again, both times receiving no answer, she got a little worried for fear the old dog had set off to return to the other house. But at a third call, she spotted Pen over at the chicken coop. January had moved the chickens, a representative showing of both her own Buff Orpingtons, and Shay's White Langshans over to the new house the day before. Chickens, she sometimes thought, had brought her and Shay together.

It made her smile until she noticed while Pen peeked at her from outside the henhouse, she still didn't come. In fact, the dog turned her head to look over her shoulder.

"What the heck?" January whispered to herself. She had no fear for the chickens. Pen knew better than to bother them. In fact, there was one big old white hen that seemed to be the dog's pal.

January had taken the first few steps toward the coop, a leftover from the days she and the dog had lived in the barn before it got burned over their heads, when she became aware of three horsemen riding up from the road just before it crossed the bridge.

Coming here, she thought, ducking back out of sight. She didn't recognize them as neighbors come to lend a hand with the move. Nor even acquaintances from town. A frisson puckered her skin. Past experience had taught her not to ignore a sign like that. Especially not now, as the woman not only in charge of the

Flowers Trust—read fortune—and the care of two underage, newly discovered family members.

She didn't have her old .38 on her hip today but, as pretty much always, it wasn't far from her. Now, before the men got close, she retrieved the revolver and placed it on a small table and set a stack of books in front of it. At hand, but not obvious.

Satisfied, she waited. With the kitchen door open, if she stood just so, January could see through a window to the front without being seen herself. Although a pretty brass knocker was attached to the door, one of the riders had dismounted and commenced pounding on the door with his fist.

*Idiot. Why doesn't he use the knocker?* The brass knocker helped the sound carry throughout the house, which was of a good size. Family sized.

She didn't move. Let them either come to her or ride away. She knew which she'd prefer.

After a while, as she went on with her work, the pounding ceased. She heard a mutter of voices then, when she inadvertently dropped an apple crate containing some of her woodworking tools, one said, "Hear that? Around back."

They gave her plenty of time to get back to her .38. Pen, January noted automatically, still hadn't appeared, not even when the men rounded the corner.

The one on foot, heavyset with a florid face half-hidden under a crop of grizzled brown whiskers and wearing a brown hat with a tall crown, led his horse toward her. Without greeting, he stepped right up onto the porch, muddy boots and all, without waiting for an invitation. Maybe he could tell one wouldn't be forthcoming.

"You deef," he growled. "Men knock on the door; you're supposed to answer."

He—all three of them actually—made a point of staring at her cheek. More likely than not the raised scar in the shape of an S—a *gift* from her grandfather Schutt —was glowing with color. It always did when she got mad or upset or excited. His rude words had made her two out of the three.

One of her fine, dark eyebrows lifted. "It may have escaped your attention," she said, looking down her nose at them even though two of the men remained mounted, "but I'm a little busy here. State your business." If you have any, she almost added. Almost, but not quite.

His gaze shifted to the open door. He even took a step forward, but stopped as January barred the way with a broom handle.

"This is a private home, not a hotel," she said. "Which, in case you were raised in a livery stable and don't know, means you keep to the other side of the door unless you are invited inside." She paused, then added, in case that didn't sink in. "And you are not."

"Hold on, Gus," one of the other men said, "Maybe we ought—"

But Gus, that apparently being his name, had his hackles raised. "Get out of the way, woman. I'm looking for someone and I'm searching this here house for her whether you like it or not."

"No," she said firmly, "you are not."

January didn't move. Didn't even let her eyes go to the revolver lying only inches from her hand. And the broom, a wide one with a stout hickory handle made special for heavy chores like sweeping the porch, stayed put.

One of the other men dismounted and tossed his reins to the man still astride. "Ma'am, my apologies for my partner here. He's getting a little tired and cranky. You see, we've been searching for a girl. A runaway. Have been for three long days now. Out of the pure goodness of his heart, a rancher from over near Wenatchee hired some young gal and now she's run off. He'd thought honest work in a god-fearing home would be her salvation. Still does, and that's why we're looking for her. To bring her back. Back home. She won't be punished. Not much anyway. Maybe locked in her room—her very own room—and not allowed to eat with the family for a couple days."

"Yeah," said the one he'd called Gus. "And we've followed her here. Right here."

"Yes, ma'am. That's exactly so." The other speaker took over again. "So if you'd kindly let us come inside and take a look around, we'd soon be out of your hair."

Good grief! He wasn't anywhere near being a good liar. Not even a fair liar. January's heart seemed to fill her chest too full to pump blood. She swallowed. "Why on earth would three grown men be looking for a runaway hired girl here? This is a long way from Wenatchee."

The man, taller, thinner, and better dressed than Gus, smiled at her. A single rotten tooth showed plain among a few good ones. "Oh, not so far. Why, excuse me. We should've introduced ourselves. We're deputy sheriffs in Douglas County and are just trying to help out the sheriff."

January kept her face calm, though it required effort.

Should she mention Wenatchee wasn't in Douglas County?

She took a breath and kept the broom where it was. "The girl's name?" She aimed the question at Gus. "Her age? What does she look like? Do you have a photograph? Or even a drawing? Who are her parents? I'd think they'd be the ones looking for their child."

Gus opened his mouth but turned to look at the other man. His smile, January noticed, stretched wider.

"I don't know as that is your business," he said. "We'd like to keep this private, you know, to save the girl's reputation."

"And the 'rancher's,' I assume." January heard herself put quotes around the rancher part. Huh! Rancher, her left pinkie toe. More probably a pimp.

"Yeah." Gus's agreement struck her as a little too heartfelt.

"Well, I'm sorry, but I can tell you she's not here. And no. I'm not opening up my house for a bunch of muddy-booted men to tromp through. You'll have to take my word for it. Just like I'm taking your word that you're who you say you are, and that a young girl has run away from a legitimate job."

"What..." Gus started, but Slick—January had taken to calling the thin man that in her mind—Slick said, real quick, "We've got a warrant."

"Really. A warrant for a runaway?" Her fingers crept forward and touched the butt of her pistol, needing less than a second to pick it up. "Let's see it."

Slick started patting the pockets of his suit coat but came up empty. "Sorry, I must've left it in my other coat."

At that, January, unable to help herself, huffed out a

short laugh. At the three bullyboys, at the incongruous-ness of their speech, at this whole ridiculous episode.

Gus, in the face of her amusement, started forward, tripping a little on the wide head of the broom. Slick scowled.

"Get on your horses and leave," she said crisply. "And don't come back or you'll meet up with an actual deputy sheriff. Oh, and for your information, boys, Wenatchee is in Chelan County, not Douglas."

Of course, they didn't get on their horses. Or leave. As she'd guessed, they took instant umbrage. First, for her calling their bluff. Second, for showing no fear. Third, for calling them boys. All three items she knew, were sure to pique the ire of a certain type of man.

Gus lunged forward, and with his feet already half tangled in the broom's head, when she jerked the handle upright, he fell face down into the box of tools. Some of them were sharp, the chisels and the adze and the rip-cut saw. As Gus howled, Slick, reaching under his coat, had a large revolver halfway out when he came face-to-face with the one January already had pointed in his face.

"Not a good idea," she said.

But maybe it was Pen who truly saved the day from devolving into a shooting match. Finally loosed from her fascination over at the chicken coop, the old black dog had slunk up behind the silent, still mounted rider, and nipped his unsuspecting horse on its heels.

The horse, not surprisingly, set off bucking. The rider, in an attempt to stay on, let go the other horses' reins, upon which they galloped off down the road. Meanwhile, January's Belgians, and of course, her saddle horses, Hoot and Mollie, both still tethered to the wagon, placidly watched. Later, when she thought about it, January had the silly notion they might've been laughing.

Slowly, Gus sat up. Blood smeared his face and trickled into his untidy beard. He clawed at the gun set askew at his side, but a shot not two inches from his fingers deterred the motion.

Instantly, before Slick could do more than blink, January was back to aiming at him. She shook her head. "And now I'll have to patch the hole in my porch which, I've got to say, makes me very unhappy. I've had enough of you. Leave, all of you, before there's blood, a great deal of it, to mop up as well."

They didn't like it, but they went, yelling threats and stalking off down the road after their horses. Gus limped a little, maybe because of where the broom handle had ended up when she tripped him. She kept her eyes on them, calling Pen over to receive a reward of pets and love. January could swear the dog was smiling.

This had made another number to add to their umbrage count, she realized. Number four, for besting three men at their own game. She sighed, thinking she'd just made three more enemies to watch out for.

But all this didn't satisfy her curiosity over Pen's fascination with the hen house. Since she was still shaking, internally if not visibly, she thought to let the reaction settle while she investigated. But she waited until the men disappeared around a bend in the road.

"Come, Penelope," she said then, using the dog's full name, something she only did when things got serious with her faithful companion. Long strides carried her swiftly forward, Pen trotting to keep up. January carried the .38 in her hand.

It was hard to say what she expected to find although she had a good idea. Something, anyway. And when straw rustled inside the small building, it made more noise and raised more dust motes to shine in the sunlight pouring in than the chickens normally did. They were prone to take their dust baths outside. Besides, counting quickly, January saw all the birds were present in the yard.

So. Something larger had taken up residence.

She stepped inside, wrinkling her nose at the distinct chicken smell she always found a bit overpowering until her nose got used to it. At first, the place looked empty, the roosts, the nests empty of any clucking occupants. But a second sweeping look told a different story. A set of bright, cornflower-blue eyes peered over the top of a stack of loose straw.

Human eyes.

# CHAPTER 2

DISMAY STRUCK JANUARY AS SHARPLY AS AN ARROW—AND
she had first-hand experience with that as well as a scar
on her leg to prove it.

"Hello," she said. "I see you've met my dog. You
might as well come away from there and meet me."

She thought the girl was shaking her head, but it
might just have been wobbling from hunger, weakness,
or maybe even fear. January opted for the fear.

"They're gone," she added. "I put the run on those
men. For good, I hope. I didn't like the looks of them."

The straw rustled, but the girl remained behind it.

"I assume you're the *hired girl* they said they're
looking for." From the looks of her, the girl wasn't really
old enough to go into the kind of service those men had
hinted at. Still, January knew some men liked very
young girls. And other men were willing to make sure
those desires were fulfilled.

And not only men, she remembered, the dark
thought pushing its way in.

*Damn them all. The country is overrun with perverts.*

She sighed. "My name is January Billings and this is my house. I am a deputy sheriff in this county. Part of my sworn duty is to protect people, which means I will protect you. Won't you tell me your name?"

The girl finally spoke. "You can't be a deputy sheriff," she said in gruff, but scornful little voice. "You're a woman. I'm not stupid enough to be taken in with your lies."

January couldn't help the spurt of annoyance she felt. This was supposed to be a big day—a joyful day—for her. It would be her first night in her new house. A house it had taken her months and months and months to plan and finally build. And to think her first visitors were a smart aleck, not to mention ungrateful girl, and a trio of men who figured to either run roughshod over her or shoot her dead—whichever seemed most expedient.

"And you are not as smart as you think you are, little girl. Probably the dumbest thing you can do is hide behind some loose straw and argue with me. Come out and we can talk about what you should do."

"I've got a gun," the girl said.

"So do I." January called the bluff. "Also, food, water, and a hot water bath in a real bathtub. I can't imagine you want to go around smelling like you've been living in a chicken coop for days." From across the coop she could see dirty hair and filthy clothes. Wherever she had come from, the girl had had it rough.

Very slowly, as if to prove it was her choice and not January's invitation, the girl stood up. "I haven't been living here. I only came last night."

Well, January thought, she wasn't lying about that. Yesterday evening after supper she had moved some

things over and going by Pen's total disregard of the
coop at the time, the girl hadn't been around then.

"What did you do to—to that man?" The girl inched
nearer. "He screeched worse than a girl."

"Nothing much." January snickered. "Just tripped
him up with a broom handle when he thought to bull
his way into my home." An evil little grin, quite beyond
her to control, slipped forth. "A broom handle between
his legs jerked all the way into his crotch did the trick
and changed his mind quite nicely."

The girl's eyes went big and round as she flung
herself forward. Sort of alarming for a moment, but it
turned out she wasn't trying to attack or take January's
.38. She was trying to shake her hand.

January allowed it to be shook.

Finally drawn outside into an atmosphere
containing less essence of chicken, January got a good
look at the girl. She was a bit smaller than Hattie—one
of the new-found relatives for whom January had
become responsible. But like Hattie, the girl was beginning to bud. January figured them to be of an age somewhere around twelve or thirteen. Those startling blue
eyes she'd met over the straw stack went with dark
honey-colored hair, sort of sweaty looking at the
moment, and porcelain pale skin. A pretty girl under
the dirt, just the kind unscrupulous men would find
appealing.

The girl remained mute when asked her name and
where she'd come from, but finally, enticed with what
January offered as either a late breakfast or an early
lunch, little by little she opened up. Maybe more than
January was comfortable hearing, after she pieced the
parts together. The knowing opened up hard questions

on what she should do about it because, as she well knew, something would have to be done. But not once did the visitor admit to being the girl the men were after.

January frowned. She wished Eli Pasco were here to give advice. He'd promised to help her move into the house when he'd been by last week, but on this, the appointed day, he hadn't made an appearance. And Johnny Johnson, whom she'd also relied on to help, had needed to work for Bo Cobb today as the rancher had calves being born. Bo, being Johnny's other part-time employer, had first call on his services. She and Bo had agreed to share his work, which kept Johnny in a job, even if he wasn't about to become wealthy anytime soon. All of which meant January was on her own today. And now this.

Eli had, for some reason, been called out of town. Or so Johnny, who'd been drafted to carry the message, told her this morning when he stopped off on his way to the Cobb ranch.

"What kind of emergency?" January had asked, feeling a cross between disappointed, worried, and aggravated. She had been looking forward to the tingle of excitement she always felt when Eli came into sight.

"Dunno," Johnny replied. "He didn't say. Just said he had an emergency."

Aside from his help with her move, mostly she wanted to talk with Eli about the present situation. After this morning and hearing the girl's tale, January was afraid Gus, Slick, and the other fellow would return. And, self-sufficient as she might be, three men coming at her were a bit much for one woman to handle. Plus, she admitted ruefully, revenge would not just be on account of their thwarted mission. Gus was bound to want payback for his sore crotch.

Then there was the question about what to do with her unexpected young runaway guest. A child, really, despite the fact, as January soon discovered, she had a vocabulary apt to shock some of the fine folks here-abouts. Truthfully, it sort of shocked her. Roused her curiosity as to where the girl had picked it up, as well.

Anyway, Eli'd know what to do. But then, so did she.

Blue Eyes, as January dubbed her, after slinking into the house like a shy fox, sat at the brand new kitchen work table, a heavy affair of thick maple blocks glued and clamped together. Constructed by January's own two hands over the winter when the weather kept her inside, it was a fine piece. She'd had to import the table's wood from a lumberyard in Spokane, having judged the common fir or pine available from local mills too soft for her purpose. A kitchen needed hard wood, and the maple was her first and best choice. Blue Eyes seemed to like the table, running her fingers over the smooth finish as if playing a piano.

Her chicken coop guest lost no time in polishing off the thick roast beef sandwich and a fine Wealthy apple from Shay's orchard that January had planned for her own lunch. Blue Eyes exclaimed over the apple's rose-tinted flesh.

"Never seen an apple with red innards before. It's damn good." The girl stared down at the object before chomping down on another giant bite.

"I'm glad you approve." It was hard to keep her mouth shut and her gaze averted as Blue Eyes ate. The girl gobbled as if starved. January was sure any minute now she was going to choke and she'd be helpless to do anything about it. Meanwhile, she loaded dishes into a cupboard and kept a watchful eye peeled.

But Blue Eyes didn't choke. Finished with her meal, the girl licked her fingers, making January shudder. Those fingers were none too clean, having spent time not only in the henhouse, but possibly somewhere even worse. In plain fact, they were filthy.

"Would you like a bath now? The water should be warm enough. I got the boiler going this morning first thing." Able to smell the girl from across the room and taking into account quite a lot of accumulated grime, she made the offer off-handedly to avoid spooking her.

Blue Eyes shrugged. "Don't much matter. I ain't got any clean clothes."

"I can find you something to wear. I have a young relative who lives with me. She's at school in Pullman right now, but some of her clothes are here. You can borrow them and wash your own." Unless January managed to turn them into rags instead.

The girl looked at her, suspicion in those eyes. "A relative?"

"Yes. She's about your age, I think. I'm sure she'd be happy to lend you something to wear."

"Yeah?" Staring at her with narrowed blue eyes, the girl shrugged. "I ain't never heard of anybody willing to share her clothes. More'n likely she'd slap me silly."

"No, she wouldn't. Although she might prefer you take a bath before you put them on."

Blue Eyes seemed to think it over, clenched her hands, then spread her fingers wide, passing them over the tabletop as if playing a tune only she could hear. "You won't peek at me, will you? Old Mrs. Gers—" She broke off, her pale cheeks flushing. "Anyway, I sure as shit don't want anybody looking when I ain't got any clothes on."

"Language," January said, frowning, then, "I don't blame you. Bathing is private. Of course I won't peek." And just who, January wondered, was this Old Mrs. Gers... that Blue Eyes couldn't even finish saying her name? Besides a female voyeur. Or a watchdog. She feared she could guess, if not specifically, than in general.

"Promise?" the girl said fiercely. "Promise you won't look."

"I promise." Getting to her feet, January forced a smile, though she felt more like weeping. Not again. Did she have to go through this sort of thing again? She'd had enough of rescuing young damsels in distress. More than enough. "Come with me. The bathtub is upstairs. You can start running the water while I find some clothes."

Blue Eyes was a little wary of mastering the taps. Evidently, wherever she'd come from, she'd at least seen an indoor privy because she seemed familiar with that, but not with the complete bath suite. January, feeling a bit cheated in that she wouldn't be the first to christen the deep, claw-footed tub, nevertheless was gratified by the pure glee in the girl's face as she practiced turning the water on and off and using first the hot, then the cold to temper the flow.

Leaving her guest to splash to her heart's content, January went back downstairs to finish unloading the wagon and getting its contents inside. Not exactly the process she'd meant to use—she'd intended to leave some things on the porch for later—but that was before meeting Gus, Slick and the other. They'd be back. She knew it. Something in the smoldering gleam of the silent man's eyes had told her so.

Probably tonight. And that meant she had things to prepare.

*  *  *

JANUARY HAD DRIFTED into that state where she was neither fully asleep, nor fully awake. It took Pen to sit up and put a warning paw on January's knee. A light sleeper at the best of times, January startled alert.

"Where?" she said, low enough to be inaudible a yard away. Even so, Pen, although she no longer heard as well as when young, knew the question. The dog turned her head toward the door and huffed softly. The back door, as January had expected.

"Good girl. I hear them now," January whispered. Already on her feet, she snatched up the 12-gauge where it sat beside her chair. Too savvy to be taken unaware, she hadn't bothered to undress and go to bed. Likewise, she'd left a lamp burning, the wick turned down low. The mere glimmer of light cast deceptive shadows over by the porch door.

Safely out of sight and bedded down upstairs in Hattie's room, Blue Eyes slept soundly. Or had when January looked in on her a while ago. Earlier, after the bath, which had taken almost an hour but revealed a lovely young girl, Blue Eyes had reappeared in some of Hattie's clothes and, to her hostess's astonishment, pitched in to help with the moving in process.

She didn't ask if she should—or wait to be asked if she kindly would. Just picked up a box. "You got a lot of stuff. Where does this go?"

January, using a small dolly to haul in two apple boxes of books at once, glanced at the parcel Blue Eyes carried. When packing up, she'd marked the destination of each box across the top, plain as day. Couldn't the girl read?

Schooling her features, she smiled. "That's mine. It goes in the room at the top of the stairs."

A pattern followed, the girl asking directions with every load she carried. She was good help though, and by the time they finished, judging by the soft snores coming from the bedroom now, she must've been exhausted. January's anxiety grew. Where had this runaway girl come from that she didn't know how to read? Not even a little, from all the signs.

And why were these men so determined to have her back that they were willing to risk breaking into a stranger's home to get her? An armed stranger's home.

Maybe she'd find out. Beside her, Pen made a low moaning sound deep in her throat as the chunk of firewood January had left in front of the outer side of the door fell over and received a hearty kick. A man emitted an explosive grunt, cursed, and tried turning the knob.

January had made it easy for them to get this far. Best to make it fast and get the fracas over with in hopes of avoiding broken glass and splintered woodwork. She made sure her .38 was loose in the holster and leveled her shotgun.

"Stupid bitch," the one outside said. "Door ain't even locked."

Someone else said, "Keep your voice down. Just get the girl and we'll get out."

"If'n I see that woman, I'll make her pay," said the

first man. Gus. January recognized his voice from earlier.

"Just get the job done," said the other. It must've been the one she'd decided to call Slick.

The door began to open, slow inch by slow inch, as if they expected it to creak.

*Two shadows. There should be a third man. Where is he?*

A dark figure moving right outside the side window provided the answer.

"Look out," the shadow man yelled. "She's got a gun."

"I'll get her." Gus sounded excited and instead of taking a step back, he took a step forward. Shoving the door wide, he and Slick fought each other to be first inside. Gus won, stumbled again over the block of wood, and fell hard.

"Watch it, you oaf." Gus clambered to his feet, looking over his shoulder as Slick accidentally kicked him.

A comedy fit for a belly laugh—if she'd been so inclined. January hadn't stopped with placing the wood chunk outside on the porch for the unwary to trip over. The inside had its own little booby trap. She'd filled a burlap sack with sticks, bricks, and fist-sized stones. The sack, held by a flexible hook above the door, had twine attached. When the door opened, the bag also opened. Not only that, the sack itself fluttered down after dumping its load on the unlucky person who entered first, and then flopped over that person's head.

Gus went down for a second time under the onslaught, yelling something indecipherable. Slick, who had followed right behind, was too close to avoid a collision. He went down as well, landing hard on top of Gus. They tussled, each trying to break free of the other. Gus, with the sack draped over his head, flailed his arms, trying to remove it. He landed a solid blow on Slick who, angry with Gus by now, ripped the burlap away from his partner's head and told him to shut up. They cursed each other, the job, the man still outside, and the wren, whoever or whatever that might be.

Most of all, they cursed January. She stepped back, deeper into the dark front room, where the dimness helped hide her. Pen's growls and sharp barks added to the cacophony.

*Where did the third man go?*

A rush of movement as Pen dashed past her let January know to turn around. Fast. The third man had managed to get into the house behind her, the antics of the two clowns having provided a distraction as he kicked open the front door. She had just a glimpse of him outlined in the opening, and of the starlight glinting off the six-gun he pointed at her.

"Where's the—" he started.

January didn't give him time to finish. She pulled the right-hand trigger on the double-barrel. The roar filled the room, competing with the sound of the .45 as he fired. She felt the sting as the bullet grazed along her side beneath her arm. He went down and didn't move.

Pen rushed forward to sniff and tug at his hand.

January whirled back to the first two victims. They'd gone still as if turned to stone. And as silent. "Drop those guns and kick them over here." She knew she was shouting, the strain of it hurting her throat. Her ears rang from the gunshots. A hot blaze of pain made it hard to lift her arm. And the shotgun.

They didn't move, standing dumbly, staring eyes shifting between her and their downed partner.

A thought flared. If she'd used the scatter gun on them to begin with, this whole mess would be done with. She jerked the shotgun barrel. "Now."

Gus's mouth gaped, not the most pleasant of sights. Finally, Slick found his tongue. "Is he dead?"

"I don't know," January snapped. "Don't care. Probably. And you soon will be if you don't do as I say."

"She'll do it, Gus," Slick said. "She just shot Earl."

"I seen her," Gus mumbled. "The boss—"

"The boss ain't here."

They were carrying on a whole conversation, a deliberate distraction that, as January felt a little dizzy all the sudden, she didn't have patience for. "You're both under arrest," she informed them. "Lie down flat on the floor with your hands behind your back."

Gus snorted. "Whaddya mean. You can't arrest us."

"I can." She hated the dizzy feeling. What in the world was the matter with her? "I can also just shoot you. A good idea, really. That would probably be the easiest."

To prove the intention, she pulled the other trigger. The shot went between the two—a near thing—and out the door behind them. She dropped the gun as the two men bellowed in fear. By then her .38 had made its way into her hand. The bore pointed at them with lethal purpose. Gus's bladder let go, the dark stain spreading down the leg of his pants.

Two pistols landed on the floor with a thud.

Somehow, and she was never quite sure how, January got the manacles on Slick, and used a length of twine on Gus. Prodding them in the back with the barrel of her .38, she marched them outside to the old root cellar, a leftover from her grandfather's day, and set a padlock on the stout door with them inside.

Only then did she give in to the night as it whirled around her. Barely making it back to the porch and sinking onto the cold steps, she thought to rest until the feeling passed. But then everything faded to black. Or maybe just dark gray, a situation that lasted right up until she heard a worried voice calling her name. That, and the fact she had icy cold water sopping down her face.

Shivering, she blinked away water and stared into cornflower-blue eyes.

"Hell's afire," the girl said. "What's the matter with you? I was beginning to think those peckerwoods had killed you dead."

January forced her tongue to work. "Usually, if you're killed, you *are* dead."

"Yeah," said the girl. "Like the mule's hind end that's layin' shot all to hell on your front room floor."

"Language," January muttered.

Shrugging off this rebuke, Blue Eyes tugged at January. "C'mon, get up. You can't sit here on the steps. It's cold. You'll take a chill. I'll help."

"In a minute," January muttered, grateful for the dark. "You go on in and go back to bed. I'm all right. We're all right." What a lie. She wasn't, but she didn't want to let on to the girl. For some odd reason, her lips felt numb. Numb enough she had a tough time forcing the words out. The words sounded odd, too, as if they were made up of letters in the wrong shape. What's more, she knew the minute she stood, judging by the fresh hot trickle of blood already coursing down her side, she wouldn't be able to hide it.

The girl found out anyway when, unbidden, she got behind January, placed her hands under January's arms, and lifted. Started to lift, anyway. But since the bullet wound began just under her left arm, January couldn't stifle her pained cry.

Blue Eyes dropped her like a hot cannon ball. "What the hell?" She gawked down at her hand, stained dark under the night sky. "You got blood all over you. Did that son of a bitch shoot you?" A pop-eyed stare accompanied the question.

January moaned and muttered a little something she hoped the girl didn't hear. "Well, I didn't shoot myself. I've had worse." Though true, for a statement meant to be reassuring, it pretty much failed.

The girl's face set. "Can I light a lamp now?"

January, thinking she'd just as soon stay sitting on the steps all night, managed to get to her feet unaided. "What a good idea," she said, using a tone that caused the girl to squint at her. "Then we can both take a look at the dead man and you can tell me who he is, where he's from, and why the three of them are after you."

"After me?" Blue Eyes stomped into the house and held the door open for her. "Why do yo—"

"Don't bother to lie. Of course they're after you, and I intend to hear why."

# CHAPTER 3

ELI PASCO DIDN'T HAVE AN APPOINTMENT, BUT DRESSED in his best suit of clothes, his boots polished and his chin shaved clean, he supposed he passed muster well enough to get into Delbert Avery's grand Spokane office.

Avery's secretary, legal aide, clerk—whatever title the help went by—certainly remembered him from before, when he'd been here with January Billings regarding the Flowers family inheritance. Seemed to Eli the man turned a shade paler when he looked up from his desk to greet the visitor. Seeing he probably didn't see the light of day often, that meant he went almost as white as an albino.

"Mr. Pasco." The secretary/aide/clerk leaped to his feet. He stuttered a bit, took a breath, and regained his poise. "What can I do for you?"

"Got a question for your boss. A legal question. Him being the Flowers estate attorney, I expect he'll have an answer for me."

The secretary was holding his ground. "Ah. A legal

question. I see. Is it important? May I ask the nature of this question?"

On the verge of saying no, Eli rethought his response. Why not? The man would no doubt soon find out anyway. As he recalled, Avery always made notes and had his secretary record them, plus their answers, on his typewriting machine. Still, January might not appreciate him letting this news spread when she found out he'd been here, as she was bound to do. Still, Jem had asked him to not tell her and he was acting for the boy. The fewer people who knew, the better.

"Does this concern the Flowers Trust?" the secretary asked into Eli's thoughtful silence.

"It concerns Jem Flowers," Eli replied, which was true, although not in the way this fellow might be thinking. Although, he supposed, whatever concerned Jem concerned the trust and ultimately, January, in some way or another. "Yes, it's important. I wouldn't be here if it wasn't."

The clerk gestured to the leather armchairs scattered around the roomy waiting area. Small tables with ash trays sat beside most of them, each receptacle meticulously cleaned after use. Mr. Avery didn't approve of smoking.

"Then have a seat," the clerk said. "Mr. Avery is with someone at the moment, but I'll fit you in the moment she leaves."

*She?* Eli didn't know why, but for some reason the tiny mention of a female client speaking with the attorney raised his hackles. Not that women were immune from needing representation. Why would they be? But something about the emphasis the clerk put on *she* disturbed him. It sounded almost like a warning.

When January, following her grandfather's recommendation, had first signed on to Delbert Avery as her
attorney of record, she had specified he should talk with
Eli as he would with herself. Avery had disapproved—
not that Eli blamed him—but so far matters had
worked out well.

Selecting a chair facing the suite's entrance but not
its exit, he placed his good Stetson hat on his knee and
sat. The clerk returned to his desk where he could
watch the door to Avery's office while keeping a
cautious eye on Eli. Since Eli didn't usually cause a
ruckus in a place like this, he was puzzled. His reputation was built on discretion rather than rash behavior.
Not unless provoked, at any rate. And he wasn't carrying
his Broomhandle Mauser C96 semi-automatic pistol in
its bulky cross-draw holster today. Only the pocket
revolver in an underarm holster, all discreetly tucked
out of sight under his coat.

The wait seemed longer than the five minutes a big,
round schoolhouse style clock measured off. At that
point, the door to Avery's office opened with a slight
click. Voices spoke, hushed and too low to hear the
words. The clerk shot out of his seat and hurried to
meet the client.

"Ma'am," he said, reaching her before she got an
elegantly shod foot into the corridor, "let me help you
out." He bent toward her, effectively, as Eli noticed with
some amusement, barring the view into the waiting
room. Smooth as butter, he took her in the opposite
direction, her silk gown rustling as he murmured something about a bereaved person in the waiting room.

So. Eli smothered a grin. The secretary wasn't above
little white lies when the situation called for it, and he

wondered why it did. Who did the fellow intend to protect? Her or Eli? The pair had already reached the end of the hall when he got a real look at the woman, and this time what he smothered was a rough hitch in his lungs that felt like they wanted to explode.

The woman, astonishingly enough, was Bethany Flowers. Or should he call her Mrs. Joseph Flowers III? What was she doing out of prison? Equally important, what was she doing here?

Eli jumped to his feet and took a step toward her, but the secretary moved faster, hustling the Flowers woman out and calling "good day" to her just as suave as a man could be.

"Changed my mind," Eli gritted when the clerk faced him again. "I don't reckon I need to see Avery after all."

But then, the office door opened and Delbert Avery poked his head out. He looked around. "You sure she's gone?" he asked in a general sort of way.

The secretary nodded. "Just."

"Good." The attorney turned to Eli. "I think you'll want to talk when I tell you what's happened. Mrs. Billings will want—she'll need—to know the details. I assume you're her emissary although I can't imagine how you happened to arrive at such an expeditious time."

Eli's very dark eyes narrowed. "How'd you know I was here."

Avery opened the door wider and motioned Eli inside. "My clerk and I have a newly installed system. Press a button and he's able to warn me when someone comes into the office I need to see." He hesitated. "Or someone comes in that I need to avoid." He nodded, as if indicating the woman who had just left. "Except she slipped in before he got the chance. Which turns out to be just as well, I think. The strangest thing is you coming in from The Falls today. You're right on time to get the news. It saves me from sending a long telegraph to Mrs. Billings on behalf of the youngsters and herself."

The youngsters Avery meant were, incongruous though it seemed, January Billings's aunt and uncle, children of her grandfather's old age. Given her male cousins had expected to inherit the Flowers fortune when Joseph Senior died, the youngsters had not been a welcome addition to the family.

Neither had January. Most definitely not.

Avery wrangled Eli into one of the deep, horsehair-covered chairs in front of his desk and called for his clerk to bring coffee. They got comfortable.

Or as comfortable as Eli could be. "That was Bethany Flowers who just left. Why is she out of prison and walking around free. She tried to kill January. She was convicted."

Avery shrugged. "It seems she's not without influence even while in prison. She found an attorney willing to take on her case and he got her out on appeal."

"Found an attorney," Eli repeated. "You?"

"Certainly not." Avery sounded offended. "Let alone taking her on as a client would be a gross conflict of interest, this is the same woman I helped send to prison in the first place. I know she's guilty. I'm not at my best," he admitted, "when I can't in good conscience form a defense. And she is not only guilty of what is stated in her conviction, but more. It's my hope she'll be sent back to Walla Walla to finish her sentence."

Biting back the questions on the tip of his tongue, Eli had to wonder if Avery protested too much. Years as a bounty hunter had taught him the criminals he brought in did not always receive the punishment they deserved, thanks to clever lawyers who could talk their way around most anything. And by the same token, not every person accused was guilty of the crime but ended up being punished anyway—also due to attorneys who might not have tried hard enough. He was thankful to be out of the bounty hunter business.

Now he was a rancher and a sometime, usually at January Billings's beckoning, seeker of justice when other, more legally approved means failed. He found the association with her more dangerous than when he'd been a lone bounty hunter. In more ways than one. His heart had gotten all tangled up and affected as well.

But he figured he'd better pay attention to the here and now. Delbert Avery had kept right on speaking and all he'd caught was something about a hearing for a mistrial scheduled for two weeks hence. Anger burned.

All this, and he had yet to reveal the reason he'd made the trip from The Falls to Spokane on the morning train. Except now, it all made a foreboding sort of sense.

"Listen to this, Mr. Avery," he cut in when the attorney paused to wet his whistle with a couple sips of heavily creamed coffee, "and tell me what you think."

Avery stared at him over the brim of his cup, maybe, finally, getting a sense of Eli's concern. "What's wrong?" he asked. "Is it Mrs. Billings? One of the kids? The trust?"

Eli's brows drew together. "Yes," he said.

"Which?" Avery looked even more alarmed.

"All of them. Jem is mixed up in a bit of trouble.

That fancy boarding school he's been attending—at court order if you recall—they've expelled him."

"What? Expelled him? They can't do that. Why should they?"

"According to Jem, it started out because of who his mother was. Boys began with slurs, then turned to hazing and teasing, and when he ignored them, they went beyond tolerance." Eli was trying to be diplomatic, although under the circumstances, there wasn't a lot of point to it. "They had plenty to say about January too. Word had gotten out about her scar and how she came by it. That and her taking on the job of a lady lawman doesn't set well with certain people. They know her reputation. And then, the fact she inherited the Flowers fortune instead of her cousins."

"Those people should be proud of an association with Mrs. Billings," Avery grumbled, frowning. "But I don't understand. Why did Jem come to you? Why not Mrs. Billings? He should've told her about the situation and let her deal with the school. She'll *have* to deal with it in the end. She's extremely competent." He said the last as if trying to convince himself.

"She is." Eli couldn't agree more. "But apparently Jem is embarrassed. He got into a fistfight with an upperclassman four days ago and broke the kid's nose. So now, according to the headmaster at the school, he's an unruly savage who doesn't belong in a fine educational facility like the one he runs, and Jem is a danger to the other students. Never mind it was the other guy who started the fight and Jem just finished it."

"Ah, so he's reached the stage where he wants to impress..." Avery broke off what he'd been saying and tapped his front teeth with the nib of his fine Waterman pen. "There's more, isn't there?"

Eli nodded. "There is. If only a fight, I'd let Jem handle it himself. But then this other thing came to light. So I paid Headmaster Bitters a visit this morning."

"What other thing?" Avery spoke as if he dreaded the answer.

"Rumors began circulating."

"Rumors? What about? Is it—"

Eli broke in, his voice hard. "What it is, is the most ridiculous story you've ever heard. And yet, serious."

The attorney's expression froze. "Tell me."

"In a nutshell, they're accusing Jem of theft. Supposedly, an item belonging to the headmaster's wife."

"They're what? Who is? What is he supposed to have stolen? What would be at the academy Jem would even want? I don't believe a word of it." Avery had met Jem and naturally, leaped to his defense right away.

"Nothing. He stole nothing." Eli grimaced. "But the boy Jem fought and the headmaster, the two of them are saying Jem took a necklace."

"A what?" Avery's eyes opened wide.

"A necklace. One belonging to Mrs. Bitters."

The attorney snorted like a disgruntled bull and slapped his hand on the desk. "That's insane! Who'd believe such a thing? A rumor easily rectified, I'm sure."

Eli shook his head. "That's what I thought, at first. Now I don't."

Avery stared at him. "What does Headmaster Bitters say?"

"He's standing by Jem's accuser."

"I can't imagine anybody believing a word of tall tale like that." Avery's face set hard. "Why in God's name would a boy steal a woman's necklace? Especially a boy like Jem Flowers. It doesn't make a lick of sense."

"I know." Shifting his hat to his other knee, Eli stayed quiet while Avery thought things through. He didn't want to set the attorney against Jem. Or January if the situation went so far.

Avery frowned, his mustache tucking inward as his lips tightened. "The story. There's no truth to it is there? Any part of it?"

Eli snorted. "No. That boy is as honest and responsible as the day is long. In the first place, why would he steal a diamond and sapphire necklace? What possible interest could he have in a woman's gewgaw? I doubt he planned on braiding it into his horse's mane—if he was even allowed to have his horse at the school."

"Which he isn't," Avery said. "Is he?"

"No."

"You're right, of course. He's not like those grandsons Joseph got saddled with. I remember Calvin—" Avery eyed Eli for a moment. "Headmasters do frown on fighting and that sort of thing. As I'm sure you know. You strike me as a fellow who may have spent some time in a school much like this one. If so, you'll realize the boy doesn't want to be there."

"No. He doesn't. But he wouldn't steal, not anything, as a way to get expelled."

Eli had to admit Avery wasn't far off the mark when he guessed at Eli's background. He had spent time in a school much like the academy. Except even a western-bred boy like Eli attending a strict eastern boarding school had had advantages over a mixed blood lad like Jem Flowers. And while Eli'd had his battles—literally—he'd never been accused of theft.

At this, the attorney set to pondering again, chewing the end of his meticulously groomed mustache in an uncharacteristic show of agitation. Definitely a sign he was thinking over the ramifications of the accusation.

"What's more," Eli said finally, when the silence had gone on longer than he liked, "there are a great many unanswered questions Bitters refuses to answer. For instance, how would Jem get into the headmaster's house in the first place to do the deed? I understand no student goes there without a specific invitation. The kid Jem whipped has been there. Jem, never, though he says he actually saw the necklace in question. He says it looks too fancy to belong to a headmaster's wife. In fact, he said, it had an uncanny resemblance to a necklace he saw Bethany Flowers wearing a few times, back when he and Hattie lived in Joseph Senior's basement."

"Ah." Avery breathed the word in an enlightened sort of way.

A grin touched Eli's lips at the sound. "Then there's the motive and opportunity aspect. In plain fact, I doubt there was a theft at all. There may have been a pay-off."

Avery tapped the pen on his teeth yet again and made a few more notes. Proof that the pen was not just for signing wills and such. Evidently the tapping helped him think. "Was this alleged theft investigated? Were the police involved?"

"No police," Eli said. "Apparently, the headmaster did his own investigating and, according to him, came to the conclusion Jem stole the necklace. And now the headmaster is not only asking—no—demanding reparation, but he wants payment for further damages. So does the father of the boy Jem beat up. Oh, and the father happens to be the headmaster's brother-in-law, whose wife just happens to be a close relative of Mrs. Bethany Flowers. A cousin, or something. Any of that sound fishy to you?"

"Yes." Much struck, Avery said, "Yes, indeed. It does. The whole thing must be a setup, pitting Jem's trouble to off-set Mrs. Flowers's appeal. A distraction to keep Mrs. Billings and me concentrating on him rather than Bethany. And to think..." He trailed off as he thought some more, then said with a frown, "And Mrs. Billings hasn't been informed of any of this, even though she is Jem's guardian?"

"Not that I've heard. Or not as of today, anyhow. Apparently the plan was just hatched two days ago."

Avery grunted. "Coinciding with Bethany's release."

"I suppose they're hoping to take January by surprise and force the money out of her before she has time to think." Eli couldn't help himself. His anger was about to boil over again, and Avery's note taking gave him some time to cool.

"How did you find out about all this anyhow?" the attorney asked. "Did Jem send a letter? And why you? Why hasn't he notified Mrs. Billings?" He rattled off more questions as fast as a telegraph machine.

Things had just now gotten a little awkward to answer, Eli had to admit. "Jem told me, but not in a letter. He sneaked away from the academy yesterday, hopped the afternoon train, and showed up at my place yesterday evening. He didn't want to go to January as he figured Headmaster Bitters would head straight there."

"And has he? Bitters, I mean?"

"Hadn't yet when I talked to him. Not that I know of."

Avery's mouth twisted, skewing his gray mustache.

"Jem sneaking away might not have been such a good idea. Makes him look guilty."

Eli huffed out a deep sigh. "From what he said, Jem thinks he's already convicted."

"Poor lad." Avery took out a clean sheet of paper. "Our first step is to write Mr. Bitters and the Bakewell Academy a letter. A very strong letter. Let's hope I can put a stop to this without further action."

"Do you think a letter will work?" Eli asked bluntly.

Avery shrugged and, opening his ink well, sucked ink into his Waterman pen. "I guess we'll see, won't we? Tell Jem not to worry."

Easy enough to see the attorney was some worried himself. And January?

Before he caught the train back to The Falls, Eli hiked on over to the police station and paid a visit to his friend Milt Ferguson. Milt, a policeman in the Spokane department—and perhaps the most honest man there —had done favors for Eli and January before. Best, he thought, to let Milt know about the anticipated shake-down. Have him keep an eye out in case Bitters did call in the police. Milt could be trusted to keep quiet unless something happened, and to let him know ahead of time if it did. Eli already had a plan on where to send the boy so he'd be safe if worst came to worst.

But first, he had to face January, and she would not be happy. Not that he blamed her. This being her long anticipated moving day into her new house, she'd been depending on his help. Breaking this news added one more worry to the chain of events since she'd become the Flowers heir. Life had to calm sometime. Didn't it?

# CHAPTER 4

Blue Eyes fluttered around January as they made their way into the house. The girl kept trying to lend January a hand but mostly got in the way. Pen followed on their heels, her toenails pattering on the floor as she paced a circle around them.

The girl hadn't taken time to dress before coming downstairs. She still wore one of Hattie's nightgowns, now stained with January's blood. In all, with her blonde hair straggling every which way around her face, she looked like a model for a gothic novel cover. January had seen such a novel in a Spokane bookstore on her last trip there. Intrigued, she had actually bought the book, but not yet read the opening sentence.

Once inside the kitchen, January collapsed onto a chair. Even so short of a walk had set her head to whirling again. The house had gotten cold, which made her realize the front door stood open from when the dead man had forced it. Summoning her energy, she said, "Close the door, please. Then build up the fire and heat some water on the stove. No need to start the boiler."

"Yes, ma'am." Obediently, Blue Eyes skipped around the body without looking, giving January the impression she already knew him and didn't care about him being dead. Returning in the same vein, she poked the fire into flame, filled a pot with water and at January's direction, hunted up a clean rag.

"Go upstairs to the bathroom," January said. "There's a box in the cupboard. It's marked with an X. There are bandages and powders. Bring them down. Oh, and the hand mirror. I'll need that." She was going to need those headache powders as well. They were good for more than just headaches. Anyway, she never got headaches.

The girl nodded and flew up the stairs where January could hear her rummaging about. Now she thought about it, very likely Blue Eyes didn't know an X from an angel. But she probably knew a bandage when she saw one.

Sitting back, January closed her eyes. The supplies included a needle already threaded with her finest silk, then boiled and packaged to stay clean, although how she was to make use of them might prove to be a problem. One she didn't look forward to solving.

Pen, meanwhile, lay her head in January's lap and watched her with mournful eyes. The dog's nose twitched, smelling the blood, and knowing her mistress's distress.

When Blue Eyes reappeared, she carried the box. The correct box. And she was dressed again in her own clothes, such as they were, that had dried after their wash. She set the supplies on the table with a thump. "What now?"

January struggled out of the heavy sweater she wore. But, with fingers already at the buttons of her shirt, she had a second thought. The girl had been so adamant about her own nakedness not being seen. What kind of a reaction would she have to January without clothing?

She had no recourse. With the sweater, which had sopped up quite a lot of the blood, and then her shirt, equally as saturated, both removed, she didn't see any choice but to strip out of her chemise, as well. But she hesitated.

"Don't look if it makes you sick." She forced a smile. "Go on up to my bedroom. See if you can find me another shirt. And in a dresser drawer, another chemise and sweater. Just plain stuff," she added, thinking she didn't want her best attire spoiled. "It's apt to get bloodied too."

The girl bounded up the stairs again, her legs churning as if glad to get away.

Stifling a groan when she really wanted to yell her head off, January got out of the chemise and discovered by contorting herself she could bring the wound partially into view in the hand mirror if she propped it just so. Enough to see the bullet had grazed rather than penetrated the thickest part under her arm just above the ribs. The furrow was as deep as it could be without actually breaking a rib or two. There must've been a healthy vein there as blood seeped steadily down her side. Stitches were most definitely required to contain the gaping wound.

Footsteps on the stairs heralded the girl's return with clothes. She had, January noted with some surprise, chosen wisely, copying what she'd been wearing before.

"Thank you. Now," she took a deep breath, one that stretched the wound and brought a fresh gush of blood. She hadn't realized she'd been breathing so shallowly. "If you'd bring the basin with hot water and the rags over, I'll clean this up."

Blue Eyes, she noticed, had quit talking again. That's all right, she thought. She quit talking herself as she washed the open wound and the blood kept coming. Her stomach roiled. But at last she dried her hands and picked up the needle.

Behind her, the girl let out a sharp gasp.

January lifted her arm and braced it along the top of a chair, her tight grip turning her knuckles white. Without waiting, she plunged the needle through one side of the slash and out the other, drawing the edges tightly together. She finagled some kind of a knot. First stitch in.

More were needed.

She heard herself breathing with shallow gasps.

"Merciful heavens." Closing her eyes, she let her moan escape, aware of her hand shaking worse than aspen leaves in a windstorm. Did she have it in her to place another stitch? But she must—as soon as she could see again. The room had gone black, with silver sparkles bouncing around the edges of the darkness.

She felt the needle being taken from her fingers. "I'll do it," Blue Eyes said, hardly loud enough to hear. "I can do it. You just keep your arm out of the way."

January managed to nod. She clutched the chair top tighter and tried to think of something but the pain. For instance, being wishful the girl could sew a straight seam. Although, and she gave a hiccupy sort of giggle, what was another crooked scar to add to her collection?

What happened next surprised her even more than when the girl took over the needle. Blue Eyes talked as she worked. As much, January suspected, to keep herself from thinking about what her hands were doing, as to keep the patient still.

"My name is Wren," the girl said, still in that faraway voice. "I ain't got a last name like most people, on account of my mama don't know who my pa is. Says she don't, anyhow. And Mama didn't want to give me hers, 'cuz she don't want anybody to know it in case word ever got back."

"Got back to who?"

"Her folks. She don't want them to know she's a...a dove."

January tried not to be shocked—but she was, even though she'd suspected something like this. "I see," she managed to say. "Hello, Wren. Your mother gave you a lovely first name. Wrens are very smart you know."

Wren paused mid-stitch. "They are?"

"They are. I welcome them in the orchard."

"Oh." The girl went back to work.

January couldn't help herself. She cried out. Not loud. Mostly just a squeak. How many times had she felt the needle go in and out? She couldn't think.

Wren continued to work—and speak. "Them men. They beat my ma something terrible. They said as how I'd be next, so she told me to run." Her hand paused again. "Run like hell. I think they might've killed her. I don't know. But now they're a comin' after me cuz they think her and me both mighta seen who they was meetin' with. And maybe heard 'em talkin' 'bout something that's supposed to be a secret."

"Oh." Some of the blackness receded as January's heartbeat sped up. "And did you? See and hear something secret, I mean?" Did she dare ask what? Maybe not yet.

The needlework paused again and Wren tied off a knot. "Sure. Ma and me both seen those people. And I heard the same things she did. So I reckon they mean to kill me, too, quick as they catch me."

January had to discover the secret. It was too dangerous not to. She hoped the girl would tell on her own.

Wren's voice faded again. "They beat another girl there in the house one time. Gus and the one you killed did. She wasn't ever right in the head after they was done. Scrambled her brains, I guess. Didn't keep the old lady from usin' her, though," she added. "The old bitch."

Once she got started, Wren turned into a fountain of information. None of which settled well with January.

"This old lady..." January hesitated. "Will she take care of your mother? If she..." She couldn't finish the thought.

Wren did it for her. "If she ain't dead, you mean? Or if she is. Maybe. Hope Ma don't end up like Allie, though. Allie bein' the addled girl I told you about." The girl stabbed into the skin again, harder this time, making January gasp and jump away from the pain.

"Ma is a good earner," Wren continued, as if she hadn't noticed January's jump. "Men like her and she's pretty. Or," she added bitterly, "she was pretty, at least.

Unless those men scarred her up too bad. Is that what happened to you?"

January winced. She'd been waiting for the girl to ask about the S carved into her cheek. The mutilation that had left one-half of her face scarred, and the other half pretty. Or she'd been told she was pretty, anyway. Shay, and Eli, too, had said so. And a Deputy US Marshal named Ford Tervo hadn't been repulsed. But she wouldn't think of them now. "Not exactly," she said. "This happened when I was a little girl. My grandfather did it."

"Your grandpa? Why'd he do something like that?"

"He went insane. And he had evil intentions toward me."

"Evil intentions? Huh. Is that what I think it is?" Apparently, Wren had no illusions as to men's intentions.

"Probably."

Wren plied the scissors and cut the last stitch. At least, January hoped it was the last. She lowered her arm and saw it quivered uncontrollably. "Thank you. That's much better."

What a lie. Not only did the wound not feel one iota better, it felt much worse. She just didn't want to say so. In plain fact, her whole side felt as if it were on fire, even as a little blood still seeped. First a bandage, then, struggling, she got the chemise over her head to cover her nakedness.

"We should sleep now," she said. "Both of us. Tomorrow will be a busy day."

The girl stared at her. "What about him?" Her thumb indicated the body sprawled on the front room floor.

She snorted. "He'll keep until morning. Lord knows he isn't going anywhere." For the first time, January was glad she hadn't had time to put any rugs down. She'd have hated for the new one to be fouled with a killer's blood.

Wren's lips trembled. "I reckon he ain't at that. And Gus and Vern?"

Vern, January decided, must be the one she'd been calling Slick. "They're not going anywhere either."

Wren's story had given January a lot to think about after she crawled into bed and, instead of fighting the pain, simply let it wash over her. Impossible to sleep. Every muscle twitch sent spasms coursing along tortured nerves.

Somehow, she knew, she had to get the whole story of Wren's escape. Including what the overheard secret was about. Where had Wren come from? Who were the holders of the secret? Why had Wren come here, to the area around The Falls? It struck January as an odd place to flee only by simple chance. But the only other option made it deliberate.

So many questions, with not a single answer among them.

Yet.

\* \* \*

UPON LEAVING AVERY'S OFFICE, Eli discovered Milt Ferguson, though usually a font of information, had heard nothing of a dust-up at the posh boy's academy located on the north side of the river. In order to please Eli, the policeman had even gotten a peek at the list of complaints reported during the past several days.

Nothing concerning Bakewell Academy or its students appeared.

Eli couldn't decide whether to rejoice or to worry. A supposedly stolen necklace? A fight? Only the fight struck him as possible. Jem Flowers had a stubborn streak. But theft? Never.

Milt turned deep-set blue eyes on Eli. "No report, no problem. Simple. Quit your worrying, Pasco."

They'd chosen to walk along the river, the rushing water as it went over the falls drowning anything they might say. At this time of day, the mills, both grist and saw, were loud. The few pedestrians paid them no mind. Still, Eli felt warning twitches, as if he were being warned of trouble to come.

"I've got to say it would be easier not to worry," he said, Milt's report making him all the more nervous, "if I hadn't just heard Bethany Flowers is out of prison pending an appeal for a mistrial." What did the head-master have in mind? From things Jem had told them, the man would expect to be paid for silence. Pure hokery-pokery.

He noticed Milt staring at him with his mouth open and his eyes bugged.

"What?" Milt spluttered. "That woman is out? You sure? When her and Joseph are guilty of every accusation against them? What does Mrs. Billing say?"

"I saw Bethany with my own eyes. As for Mrs. Billings, she hasn't heard yet, neither about Jem's trouble nor Mrs. Flowers who is apparently swanning from lawyer to lawyer spreading word about a mistrial. I think she's attempting to get public opinion on her side."

"Hope that don't work," Milt said, although he sounded too doubtful for comfort.

"Yeah. Might though." Eli shrugged. "Putting two and two together, I smell a plot."

"Two 'n two?"

"A connection between the headmaster of Jem's school and Bethany Flowers. I suspect it's a good way to prejudice a judge in advance by making the younger Flowers, and January as their guardian, out as lawless hayseeds."

Milt scoffed. "Like the Flowers dame and that damn family of boys ain't some of the worst hooligans this town has ever known."

"But rich hooligans, with a lot of influence. Also determined to become richer, no matter what it takes or who gets hurt." Eli drew out his watch, its gold chain draped from his vest watch pocket. "I've got a train to catch. If you hear anything, send me a telegram. Don't worry. I'll reimburse you."

Seeming a little offended by the offer, Milt's ears went red. "You bet," he said, but didn't explain whether he meant about the telegram or the pay back.

Eli ended up having to run for the train.

\* \* \*

SQUIRT, owner of the livery where Eli had stabled Windswept this morning before he caught the train, had the horse brushed to a shine, saddled, and ready to go when he got there. It was already half-dark as Eli paid the hostler, adding a bit extra for the polish he'd put on Windswept.

Purveyor of all the newest news about town, Squirt

looked puzzled when Eli made a point of asking him if anything he should know about had gone on while he was gone.

"Not that I know of. It ain't like you been gone a week. Or even a full day. Why? You expecting trouble?" Squirt scratched his head with a forefinger under his hat band. "Course, you always do expect trouble, I reckon."

The comment struck Eli as being a little dry, but he couldn't say the man was wrong. He did always expect trouble. And with January back at home after spending part of the winter traveling back and forth to the city and paying long visits there, the chance became more likely. Trouble had a way of following her around. The false accusation against Jem meant he needed to use caution. Then the deal with Bethany Flowers, who'd openly vowed to kill January, made the possibility of violence extra strong. Or more likely, certain.

He tried to pass the question off, but Squirt, after his involvement with a couple of January's more dangerous adventures, was too wily to let the subject go.

"Should I ought to oil up my Winchester and my Colt? Why, it's been a few months since I last had to shoot anybody. I've missed being in the game."

Eli had to admit Squirt's joke, if joke it was, didn't fall far from the mark. On the other hand, he and his helper, Sam, could always be depended on to help out if a situation got tense.

He must've been slow to answer since Squirt's eyes narrowed. "Oh-ho. You got something eating on you, Pasco. What is it?" He winked then. "Is it Mrs. Billings? I see you're all slicked up like a city feller. Got a problem with her being an heiress? Or are them kids causing her trouble? They're both at school for another month though, ain't they?"

The old codger was entirely too sharp. And for some reason that always surprised Eli, the hostler kept track of January, and now her wards, as if he were their grandpa. Swinging aboard Windswept, Eli shook his head. "All is well. But still, you know as well as I do that it's always wise to keep your firearms in good working order. Especially when Mrs. Billings is concerned."

Delighted by the answer, the hostler grinned. "I'll tell Sam to clean his shotgun. Could it be we'll be seeing some action soon?"

Eli shook his head. "I didn't say that."

"You didn't have to."

Eli got out of there before he put his foot any farther into his mouth. But in a way this had been a good warning. Squirt would be on the lookout for anything out of the ordinary going on around town and he'd be sure to let him know.

Jem was waiting for him when he rode into the ranch dooryard, champing at the bit to hear what Eli had learned. Eli knew his preference just by looking at the kid's face. Too bad he had to dash his hopes.

# CHAPTER 5

Morning arrived. January, every muscle aching, crawled out of bed just as dawn rose above the trees covering the hill overlooking the valley. The effort took all of her fortitude to accomplish, although once up, she actually felt better. A little better. As long as she kept her arm still and prevented it from rubbing over the wound in her side, anyway.

A glance showed clouds gathering on the horizon. She hoped they weren't an omen of what was to come. One-handed and as awkward as a seamstress sewing with her toes, she made coffee and went out to the shed to shake feed into a trough for the horses and her cow.

"Sorry, Bossy." She patted the cow's rump. "You'll have to wait until Johnny gets here. You can hold off until then, can't you?" The cow, more used to precise milking times, lowed once. January couldn't decide if that meant yes or no.

Over where the root cellar's door was camouflaged by a wild rose bush with wicked thorns, she heard muffled shouts and thumping. Her upper lip curled. If

Gus and Vern thought to kick the door in, they were out of luck. She'd built that door herself. And made it fit to hold off an army although its metal supports original intention had been to repel bears.

The worst thing of all? Looking into the front room as the daylight grew and seeing the dead man stiffening on the floor. Johnny, although January figured he should be getting used to such goings on around her, was sure to be unhappy when he learned of this new turn of events.

And what about Eli?

Pen, hackles raising along her spine, stared into the room and growled before backing away. January felt like doing the same. Only maybe she'd prefer to go far away and leave the entire situation behind. When building the house, she separated the kitchen area from the front room by bookcase partitions, which left a wide opening in the middle. It had seemed like a good idea at the time. Right at the moment she wished she had a door to close.

Pen's ears flicked as she went on alert. Giving a short bark, she dashed toward the back door as Johnny, right on time, rode past the kitchen window and stopped at the porch. Relieved to see him ride in, January dreaded giving him the news about this turn of events. Still, she knew she could count on his support. Thought she knew, anyway. Things had changed for him since he and Evie got married.

Through the window, she watched Johnny dismount and flip the reins over the porch rail. A frown spread across his face as he ventured a cautious look around. Turning to his horse, he eased his carbine out of the saddle scabbard. Only then did he approach the porch steps, pausing a moment to look down at the bullet hole in the floor. The dried blood on the steps caught his attention.

Her shotgun had peppered the support posts when she fired between the two men last night, while scuffs where the men had kicked at the door showed clearly on the new paint.

Johnny considered the signs a few moments. But he must've heard Pen whining inside. He'd begun to twist the knob when January opened the door. He hadn't knocked. He was too wise to act so carelessly when he sensed trouble. Pen lunged out to greet him.

"Come on in," she said.

"You okay?" He ignored the dog long enough to scan the room. His gaze went past her to fix on the medical box still sitting on the table, then the basin where Wren had dropped the soiled items she'd used while stitching January's wound. The stack of bloodstained clothing January had discarded and been too weak, and Wren too ignorant to dispose of right away, drew his attention. But since no immediate danger seemed pending, he finally settled on her.

One look was enough. "No. You ain't." Johnny answered his own question and asked another. "What happened?"

Pen pawed at his knee, enough to make him look away from January. She stepped back, an invitation to enter.

Her movement put the front room and the dead man's body on full view through the open doorway.

"Holy— Already?" Johnny's mouth gaped open. But then he set his jaw. "Who is that? Anybody I know?"

"I hope not. I wouldn't want you hanging around with men like them."

Johnny, who'd started into the other room, had sharp ears. He stopped. "Them?"

"There are a couple more down in the old root cellar."

She probably should've expanded on that a little, January reflected when Johnny swallowed hard and said, "Dead?"

"No. Just him." She indicated the corpse. "The other two are very much alive. They've been arrested and are being held prisoner until I can see them to town and into jail."

Grunting something unintelligible, he continued moving until he stood over the body. January, though somewhat reluctant, joined him. Using the toe of his boot, he turned the man's face so he had a good view. They stared down. "Nope," he said after a quick study, "don't know him."

This was the first time January had taken a good look at the dead man. Earl, she remembered one of the prisoners calling him. He'd stayed on his horse yesterday, not saying a word. Her attention had been centered on the other two. She saw now that his most outstanding features seemed to be a propensity for all dark clothing, hair so black she thought he might use boot polish on it, and narrow features with a thin, cruel mouth.

"Me either," she said after a moment.

"You don't?" Johnny turned toward her. "Then what is he doing laying dead in your front room? How'd you come to shoot him?"

"Long story."

She tried a weak smile but Johnny wasn't looking for excuses. "What the dickens has been going on, January? You ain't even been in this house a day and you already been attacked and had to kill somebody. Wait a minute." He squinted at her, his eyes half-closed. "You're wobbly yourself. So I reckon it's your blood I see all over the kitchen. Maybe you'd better sit down."

January couldn't agree more. After her morning efforts of nothing other than making coffee and feeding the livestock, she felt more than a little woozy.

"Pour some coffee and take a seat." She sank onto her own chair, relieved to get off her feet. "I've got a lot to tell you."

"You bet you do." For a long moment Johnny stared at the mess on the table again, then at her wan face. "That's a lot of blood." He took another long look and shook his head. "You ain't looking so good, boss lady. First thing we do is get you into town to see Doc LeBret."

She shook her head. "Not necessary. I've already been doctored up just fine." She hoped. "What I need is food. Lots of food. How about you fixing me breakfast, Johnny?"

His thumb pointed at his chest. His mouth opened in astonishment. "Me?"

As though that had been a cue, Wren's tousled blonde head poked around the kitchen partition. "I'll do it. I can cook. A little."

She'd been silent coming down the stairs, footsteps so light neither January nor Johnny had heard them. And if Pen had, the dog had already become used to her and didn't bother to alert on her presence.

Johnny, taken by surprise, nearly dropped the coffee

cup he held. "Who's this?" he demanded. "Another outlaw? She looks like she might be. Sure sneaky enough to be one."

"I am not sneaky." Wren took offense and let him know it. "I'm—"

January smiled at the girl. "You're somebody who's having a lot of new experiences, right, Wren? A doctor. A cook. But can you milk a cow?"

"Is that a hint to say Bossy needs milked?" Johnny grumbled. He scowled. "I repeat, who is this?"

Introductions, never mind explanations, seemed in order. "This is Wren," January said to Johnny. And to Wren, "This is Johnny Johnson. He's my right-hand man and helps me with anything and everything that needs help."

The brevity of Wren's introduction must've struck Johnny because he shot a quick, puzzled glance at January.

Johnny and Wren nodded at each other, making January huff. The nods on either side hadn't appeared real friendly in her observation.

"Have you had breakfast, Johnny?" she asked, just as a way to get them past the moment.

"Sure," he said. "My wife fixes me a good breakfast every morning."

She had to smile. Johnny, though barely twenty years old, had married Evie Langley in February, and the two were cute as fledgling love birds. She intended for them to live in her old house as soon as she got everything cleaned out. Right now they were living with Evie's parents and two brothers. The Langley ranch house was a bit crowded.

"Good." She grinned at him. "Exactly as I expected.

So you can take care of Bossy while Wren fixes breakfast for herself and me. Then we'll all sit down and I'll tell you everything. All right?"

"I got a choice?"

"No."

"I figured." Johnny collected the milk bucket and went out to the shed, Pen accompanying him. Stomped out to the shed, January amended, watching them go. He didn't like being put off. She was relieved to see he took his carbine with him. Smart man. He hadn't forgotten about the two live men she'd locked in the cellar.

Wren, standing beside her, had a question. It consisted of just one sad word. "Everything?"

January winked. She didn't pretend to misunderstand. "Everything he needs to know."

Mollified, Wren got busy in the kitchen where, as January soon discovered, she could've used more practice cooking. Knowing *a little* turned out to be optimistic.

Eli, having made an early start, arrived before Johnny finished the milking. Pen, who liked to get a squirt or two of milk straight from the cow—and Johnny always indulged her—dashed out of the barn to greet him. So did Johnny. If she hadn't been in such rough condition, January believed she might have too.

Standing by the window and waving away the smoke from Wren's burned toast as she waited for her breakfast, January watched the two men confer. Eli spun, staring toward the house. His mouth moved. With a sharp nod at Johnny, he headed off toward the root cellar, no doubt bent on checking the prisoners were still secure.

January, cautious about moving her arm, managed to clear away the detritus from last night before he finished his inspection. She couldn't bear to welcome Eli into a kitchen that looked less like a place for eating than Doctor LeBret's surgery just after the cutting was done.

Waiting, her impatience growing, January polished off the eggs and biscuits—the toast having been abandoned and biscuits of her own making reheated—that Wren served up. The expected tap on the door caused the girl to leap to her feet. "Shall I leave?" She seemed uneasy, more so than when she'd met Johnny. Looking over her shoulder, she was ready to bolt.

"Sit down, Wren," January said as she turned to face the door. "Mr. Pasco won't hurt you. He'll be your best friend. I guarantee." Louder, she called, "Come on in, Eli."

Perhaps, January decided, shaking her head, Wren's nerves were jumpy because Eli appeared all too dangerous with his Broomhandle Mauser worn openly in the holster crossing his chest. But then, it struck her, he was dangerous. In more ways than one.

He hardly glanced at Wren, what with the way his dark, dark eyes fixed immediately on her. Johnny, she thought, had no doubt told him about the girl and that she, herself, had been hurt. But Wren, oddly enough, most certainly stared at him. As if struck dumb, her blue eyes wide and round and as if she believed some kind of wild beast—a wolf perhaps—had entered the house. She hardly seemed to breathe.

A wolf? Maybe. But January liked this particular wolf, though maybe not so sure she liked the way he was looking at her at the moment. Embarrassed by his scrutiny, she tried not to notice the way her insides started vibrating.

All unconscious, she'd gotten to her feet. That made it easy for him to wrap his arms around her. He sort of crushed her face against the gun holster, but she didn't mind. Acting if she were as fragile as a porcelain doll, he didn't squeeze hard at all. Funny, really. He, of all people, knew she was tough as a leather boot strap.

He pushed her back and pinned her with a sharp gaze. "Johnny told me about the shooting. Where are you hit?"

She made an indication, wincing as she lifted her arm without thinking.

Eli noticed. "Looks as if you've lost more blood than is good for you, sweetheart. No roses in your cheeks. Sit down and let me see." Without asking permission, he shifted her loose shirt aside and bent to look under the bandage.

*He called me sweetheart.* January thought, hardly aware of the invasion to her privacy. He mentioned roses in her cheeks as if her scars were invisible.

"Who put in the stitches?" Replacing the dressing, he pulled her shirt down and smoothed the fabric.

"My new friend Wren." January finally had the opportunity to direct his attention to the girl. She had to wonder why Wren appeared gobsmacked by Eli. Granted, in her own eyes—and more than a few other women's that she knew of—Eli was a most attractive man. His dark eyes were enough to make practically any female swoon, but somehow, swooning in admiration wasn't the reaction Wren showed. She still looked, if January had to pick a description, frightened by him.

She'd been immediately prickly with Johnny, and not afraid to say so, but she didn't utter a word to Eli.

Not even when he turned to her and said, "Well done, young miss. Doctor LeBret couldn't have made a better job of it."

January nodded. "Very true." Not but what, she thought dryly, those aforementioned scars were proof Doc's expertise had been somewhat lacking the night her grandfather carved the letter S into her cheek.

Eli, being Eli, noticed right away how Wren shrank from him. He sent January a questioning look, to which she shrugged.

Tried to shrug. The action pulled on the wound hard enough to make her gasp.

He pulled the medical box, still sitting handy on the table, and rummaged through the contents, pulling out a roll of gauze. "This will do. You got a towel. Or maybe a tablecloth? You need to keep your arm in a sling."

She thought. "A towel is too small. A tablecloth too big. I know. A teacloth. Wren?"

The girl, huddling over by the kitchen range, shifted her wary gaze to January.

"In the chest there, please look in the middle drawer and see if you can find something that looks like a small tablecloth." January knew it would probably easier for her to fetch the item, but Wren needed something to do just then. Something to get her moving instead of cowering as if she'd like to disappear.

It worked. The girl edged over to January with a selection of embroidered cloths. January picked one that had a small stain. "This do?" she asked Eli.

He shot a glance at Wren. "Just fine. You, girl, can you fold that into a triangle for me, please?" At her silent nod, he unwound a few yards of gauze and, very gently bound January's upper arm at her side, leaving the forearm free to bend. A loose binding because, he said, "you don't want it so tight as to shut off the air, but also, not so loose you're tempted to lift the arm."

Finished, he rigged the sling to support the forearm. "Better?"

"Yes. Thank you." No lie. His ministrations most certainly did ease the pain. If Wren hadn't been a witness, January would've kissed Eli just then. He was within reach and she really, really wanted to. All she'd have to do is lean forward and...

Deviltry danced in his eyes as he turned his head and faced her. Sure enough, he knew the thoughts running through her mind,

Just as well when Johnny came in with the milk pail clutched in one hand, keeping her from making a fool of herself. "Where are you going to set up the milk separator, January?"

Oh, yes. Definitely better to get back to normal, January thought. If that were even possible.

"Just dump the milk somewhere away from the house this morning," she said. "I'm thinking I ought to get a hog to raise. It could use the leftover milk."

"You do," Johnny said, his eyes narrowing, "you better plan on caring for it yourself. I ain't working with any damn hogs."

She had to grin. "On second thought, I don't guess I want a pig stinking up the yard."

Johnny's immediate relief kept the grin on her face a moment longer. Then the gravity of the situation struck again. "Speaking of stinking up the yard, I've got two men locked in the root cellar I'd just as soon get rid of.

Wren and I, we have a story to tell before I take those men to town, and I don't want to tell it more than once. Right, Wren?"

All eyes shifted to the girl as if for her agreement.

Wren, apparently mute once more, nodded once, not the most enthusiastic agreement January had ever seen.

"What's the matter?" Puzzled by the girl's odd behavior, her brows drew together.

Wren, lifting her hand as if it weighed more than she did, pointed at Eli. "It's him." Her voice thickened. "They're going to kill him. Eli Pasco. That's what the man said. And then they're going to kill me." She looked head on at January. "And you. Especially you." Her eyes moved to Johnny. "And probably even him."

# CHAPTER 6

As a conversation stopper, Wren's announcement worked a treat.

Until Eli snorted and broke the sudden silence. "Who's going to kill me? I believe I might have something to say about that."

Wren must've used up all her words because she simply shook her head.

He showed no particular alarm. "Whoever 'they' are, they won't find the murder of three people easy, Wren, thanks to your warning. But can you be a little more clear about the whys and wherefores?"

Eli sounded so calm it made January's thumping heart and twisted gut feel a bit overwrought. But then, she was the one who already had taken a bullet to prove this was not a product of a young runaway's imagination.

"Yes, Wren, who? Do you mean those men in the cellar?" January made the most logical connection. "Offhand, I'd say they won't get the chance."

"Yes. Them men in the cellar. They're the ones that

beat my ma. The ones who want to hurt me."

No wonder she'd been so terrified. No wonder she distrusted everyone. January patted the empty chair beside her. "Sit here, Wren. Tell us everything."

Johnny found a convenient wall and leaned against it. "Not again. Might've known. Boss, how do you always manage to get mixed up with folks like this? More grown men—"

He left the rest unsaid, but January knew he was thinking of his own pretty young wife and wondering if their association would put her in danger. Having been aware from the start that the three men had potentially lethal intentions, Wren's warning came as no big surprise—at first. But when she said their intention had always been to kill Eli and her, well, that stretched her imagination. Why? What did Eli have to do with Wren? What did she?

"But there's others besides the ones you caught," Wren went on to say, and January's heart seemed to sink like a stone. *Others?*

"Some I don't know," Wren said. "They wasn't the kind of people who come to Mrs. Gerson's house for... you know. They wore fancy clothes and talked fine. 'Specially the woman."

"The woman?" January said.

Eli turned his head to stare at Wren, his attention sharpening.

January's eyes narrowed as she glanced at him. What had that meant to him?

"Start from the beginning," she told Wren. "And don't leave out the reason they aim to kill Mr. Pasco. And me. Did they say why him in particular? Or why me? How did you know to come here? And why didn't you say something before?"

"Cuz I...I figured you'd throw me out. That's after I knew you was her." Tears started and drizzled all the way to Wren's chin. Pen, in her kindness, padded over to nuzzle against the girl's knee.

January frowned.

"I came on account of Ma. She was listening to them talking when I come to ask her something so I only heard part of it. Then they spotted us and came at Ma. That man—the dead man—" Her eyes swiveled toward the body in the front room, a look quickly averted. "Him and Gus beat her up bad, but when ole Mrs. Gerson was tryin' to shoo them off, she told me...she screamed at me to run. Ma did." Horror seemed to shake the girl. "Lordy, but she was in awful shape. They even ripped out some of her hair, and choked her so's she couldn't hardly talk. And her ear..."

January had an idea that preventing her from talking had been their intent. Evidently Wren's mother had a strong will to get past the pain.

Wren looked up at her. "We both seen'em, but it wasn't just them three. There was another man there. And the woman. I saw them, too, cause I snooped when I first spotted the woman. She was wearing the prettiest pink dress. It rustled real nice when she walked. But she held the skirt way up off the floor and put a hanky over her nose and mouth like she was afraid she'd get lice. Or fleas." Her eyes seemed to smolder. "Well, maybe she would. I hope she did." Eyeing January again, she nodded. "She's the one said she wanted you dead. I heard her plain as day. And she's the one gave directions to Earl about a ranch somewheres hereabouts. And Ma said I should run away and tell you if I could. Only I didn't know it was you when I got here so I hid from both them and you." Her face puckered in thought. "Seemed as if you lived somewheres else."

"I did, until yesterday." Nothing made sense to January. She didn't have anything to do with a fancy-dressed woman talking to men in a bordello, did she? Not with Ruby Pasco, Eli's father's ex-wife in prison. But that was another story. "What did this woman look like?" she asked Wren. "What did the man?"

Oddly enough, when January glanced at Eli, she knew from his expression he had some idea of who this might be. "Eli? What do you know? You're holding back, I'll be bound." If she sounded angry, well, she was.

"Let the girl talk," he said. "My news will wait until she's done."

Naturally, that only served to make her curiosity grow. And her temper. But she nodded at Wren. Johnny straightened from his stance against the wall, pulled up a chair and sat with a thump. Evidently, he felt the same as she did.

Wren cast an accusatory glare at Johnny. "I only just figured out you must be her when he called you January. That's what the woman said. January Billings. I never heard of anybody else by that name."

"I see." She couldn't remember. Hadn't she told the girl her name?

"And him." Wren nodded toward Eli. "Eli Pasco. So I got to the right place after all."

Tired, and convinced this was all taking too long, January snapped out, "The woman, Wren. Did you hear *her* name?"

Wren jerked. "No. I didn't hear their names. Neither

one. They wasn't real friendly, see. The man just handed Earl some money and told him to go get'em. He said he'd pay the rest when it was done. That's when he seen Ma standin' in the hall and he said, 'The whore. Take care of her. Make sure she don't talk, first. Not to anybody.' But they saw me hiding behind Ma and knew I'd heard and seen'em too. That's when Ma quick told me to run. So I did. I ran and hid until they got tired of looking for me and left. And that's what happened." Her lips clamped shut as though to stop their trembling.

January sighed and looked at Eli. "Now what?"

"Might ring a bell if we hear these thugs looked like," he said. "Starting with the man passing out the money."

She turned to Wren. "What did he look like?"

Wren shrank down in her chair as three sets of eyes focused on her. She nodded toward Eli. "The man, he's taller than him, and skinnier. Skinny like he ain't got any muscles, I mean. And he moves kind of jerky like. Got a bald patch. I seen it when he took off his hat. Oh, and he wears spectacles. Good thing too."

"Yeah? Why's that?" Johnny asked.

"Cuz he's got squinty, mean eyes."

"Oh." January found it hard to believe eyeglasses were able to do a thing to cover up mean eyes. She didn't think it precisely described anyone she knew.

"And the woman?" Eli got the question in before January finished absorbing the description.

Wren's face got that puckered look again, taking on an expression as though smelling something bad. January wondered if the girl was unconsciously mimicking the woman. "Brown hair, but not dark brown. Blue eyes, red cheeks. Wearing too much paint, I'd say," she added critically. "Oh. And a little mouth like this." Wren's mouth pursed, also causing her nose to wrinkle.

January gave a little gasp. No. Couldn't be. It sounded a lot like Bethany Flowers, but that was impossible. She shook the thought off as Wren continued. "Kind of hefty. Got big tits."

This time it was Johnny who gasped. A grin twitched Eli's lips before quickly fading.

"She's the one said to report to her as soon as it's done. Whatever that means, but I think it means as soon as everybody is dead." Wren spoke matter of factly, as though such things were part of her everyday life.

And maybe they were, January reflected. She didn't know much about the lives of women who worked in a brothel. Or their children. She didn't think they were supposed to have children, although...

"Good work," Eli said. "You've been a big help. We owe you, Wren. There'll be a reward."

Wren's eyes went big. "There will?"

January forced a smile. "There will. But first, we need to see you stay safe." She looked over at Eli and Johnny. "We need to get those two in the cellar into town and secured in the jail. I'll send a telegram to the sheriff over at the county seat and maybe he can send someone to pick them up." The Falls had no sheriff as a local, steady presence anymore. Only a town marshal, a lackadaisical sheriff's deputy who only appeared if he felt like it, and January.

Eli nodded. "Are you able to ride, January? Or do you want me and Johnny to take care of their transport?"

"We'll all go. And Wren, you'll come with us. I

wouldn't feel right, leaving you here by herself. It's hard to tell who else might decide to drop in unexpectedly."

Wren opened her mouth, then shut it again. She nodded.

\* \* \*

WITH THE TWO of them working, it didn't take Eli and Johnny long to saddle the horses and tie the dead man onto the horse he'd ridden in on. Johnny tossed a nervous-looking Wren up on Mollie, and helped January, whose left arm was useless in the sling, onto Hoot. Eli went to collect the prisoners from the root cellar by himself.

The two emerged from the dark, squinting in the bright light. Sunshine glinted off the stream running nearby, the sparkles leaving imprints even on January's retinas. Gus, she might've known it would be him, began cursing and complaining, only to choke when his eyes adjusted and he spotted the third man's body.

"You're gonna be sorry," he said. "When she—"

Vern stopped him. "Shut your mouth. Always spoutin' off when you oughta keep quiet. I don't know why she keeps you on."

Gus glared. "She owes me."

"Yeah?" The other man jeered. "What's she gonna do about this? Nothing, I'll be bound. She can't."

"She will," Gus insisted.

While January found their back and forth interesting, she didn't have the patience to listen to them for long. But Eli seemed to find the crosstalk illuminating. She suspected he already knew the woman's identity. And January, though an idea had crossed her mind, didn't think it possible. But the description Wren had given raised doubts.

Eli, meanwhile, left the two prisoner's hands tied and boosted them onto their horses. Wary of the tricks men like them, meaning stupid ones, might try, he was ready when Gus lunged against him, attempting to knock him down. A quick cuff on the back of the head stopped anything further.

Stupid, indeed. Even if he'd succeeded in taking Eli down, Johnny and January were ready for any other stunts. While one arm might be in a sling, there wasn't a thing wrong with her shooting hand and her holstered .38 hung from the saddle only inches away.

They set off for town, Pen following just to the left of Hoot. Johnny led the way, the prisoner's horses on lead shanks. Eli followed them. Wren and January rode last in line. Though Wren proved a beginner horsewoman, she clung to the saddle horn and stuck like a barnacle to a ship's bottom. They made good time.

After a while, Eli dropped back and encouraged Wren to go on ahead. "Doing all right?" he asked January.

"Sure," she said, lying only a little. She didn't figure to faint and fall off her horse. On the other hand, she couldn't say this was any kind of pleasure jaunt.

He smiled crookedly. "Liar."

But January had her question ready. "Who is she? I know who it sounds like."

He didn't mistake who she meant. He also didn't answer directly. "I know you wonder why I didn't show up to help you move your things yesterday. My apologies. Something came up. Something important enough for me to make a trip into Spokane."

She looked over at him. His heart-stopping dark eyes were fixed on her. "What?"

"Jem showed up at the ranch day before yesterday."

"Jem did?" Her brows drew together. She hadn't expected this. "How? Why?"

"He hitched a ride on the train and walked from the depot. That's how. As to why..." Obviously unconscious of the motion, his right hand went to the butt of the Broomhandle Mauser lying against his chest. "He's been accused of stealing."

Shock had January sitting straighter in the saddle. She drew Hoot to a stop. "Stealing? Jem? What did he supposedly steal?"

Eli sucked in air through his nose. "A diamond and sapphire necklace."

"A what?" It came out explosive. "That's ridiculous. Why on earth... Jem has about as much use for a diamond and sapphire necklace as...as..." She couldn't think of a single thing that fit. "Says who? Who is accusing him?" she added belligerently. "And why didn't he come to me?"

"Embarrassed, I think. Afraid you might believe it. You know, the stolen item being a necklace and you being a female." Seeing her reaction, Eli smiled slightly. "Plus, he looks up to you and doesn't want you to think less of him."

January spluttered. After a moment, she got the most important question repeated. "Who is accusing him? And why hasn't the headmaster, Mr. Bitters contacted me? Why did he contact you?"

"He didn't. But I had a talk with him yesterday." Eli was riding Henry, his steady saddle horse today, and he edged the gelding over closer to Hoot. Speaking quietly, he said, "There's more news, not much of it good. I also had a visit with Delbert Avery yesterday."

"You did? Because of Jem? Where is Jem, anyway?" Worry suffused her. Why hadn't she asked before?

Eli reached out and squeezed her hand. "He's at my place under orders to stay out of sight. He's not to come out for anybody except me or you."

She gasped a little. "Is his predicament so bad he needs an attorney? Needs to hide?"

"Maybe. Unless we can get this cleared up right away. Oh, I'd suggest bringing Hattie home as well. Get her here before you find out she's in trouble over something. Or maybe has had an accident."

January's face, already pale from blood loss, went ashen. Unconsciously lifting her bad arm as if to push his advice away, she winced. "You're saying Jem's trouble is because he's a Flowers. And that Hattie is next. Or maybe parallel and we just don't know it yet." She fell silent a moment, then nodded. "But who is the instigator? Can Joe III arrange anything so underhanded from prison? Because I don't believe John B would do something like that even if he could." She put names to her cousins, the men who'd expected to inherit everything from their grandfather. But Joseph Senior, disgusted with their behavior, had left the whole kit and caboodle to January instead, with his hopes she'd share with Jem and Hattie, the children of his old age, when they grew up.

Eli's lips tightened. "Hold on a minute, January. You haven't heard the next part. The important part."

"More important than that?" And yet, she noticed he turned away to survey the countryside before he spoke. Definitely, she believed, a bad sign. He was trying to decide what to say. Which meant more bad news. She was sure of it. "Tell me," she said, and tried to set herself.

Even so, she couldn't stop a rush of fury when he said, "I know Wren's talk of the woman in a pink dress struck a chord with you. Well, it did with me, too, because Bethany Flowers is out of prison." He held up a hand. "For now, while she makes a case for a mistrial."

"How did she manage that?" January heard what almost turned into a screech coming out of her mouth and put up her free hand over her lips to stop. "But—" Yes, Wren's description of the woman had given her the thought. She just hadn't believed it.

He nodded. "Yeah. Kind of disturbing. She was in Avery's office when I got there. He said she'd come to tell him she has an attorney to represent her. He also said she seemed confident she'd soon be released."

"Why would she tell him?" January, thinking out loud, found it all hard to fathom. "He's the main reason she's in prison now. Or should be."

"Gloating, he called it. Throwing her accomplishment of working a release in his face. But he wasn't buying it." Eli shrugged. "She didn't see me, but I saw her. You want to know what she was wearing?"

She didn't have to think. "A pink dress."

"Yep. And do you remember what the headmaster of Bakewell School looks like?"

This answer didn't come quite as rapidly. "Skinny, like he has no muscles. Bald patch. Wears spectacles."

He nodded.

"So this is all a conspiracy? Bethany and this man, Headmaster Bitters, are in cahoots and out to get rid of Jem and Hattie—and me."

"Well, you can probably count on Joseph III being in on it too."

January seethed the rest of the way to town, even past the spot in the road where her husband had been murdered. A mix of fir and pine trees overhung the exact place where his body had been discovered. She always got shivers as she went by. Today she didn't much notice. Nor did she notice the wary glances kept Wren sending her way.

As for town marshal Adam Southbrook, it turned out he'd been looking out the window and spotted them coming. Stepping outside the jail, he took one long look and, chest heaving, uttered a loud sigh. Wordless at first, he took in the dead man and the two men with hands cuffed behind their backs. Then he shook his head. "Who you got here, Deputy Billings?" he asked.

Behind her, January heard a funny little "whoof." Wren, who hadn't quite believed when January said she was a real deputy.

"Would-be assassins who picked the wrong victim," January said.

Southbrook opened his mouth, closed it, studied her a few seconds, then said, "Appears as if they might've got in a lick."

"As you see." Nothing wrong with his eyesight, she decided. But then, the sling did make it sort of obvious.

# CHAPTER 7

Nothing in the town of The Falls escaped Squirt, owner/operator of the livery stable, whether the sighting of a new face, a birth—although the hostler might blush at the mention—a death, or a shoot-out. Three out of the four was plenty to have him following hot on the trail of their little cavalcade as they rode up to the sheriff's office.

In this case, since the street to the local hoosegow went right past the livery, Squirt arrived before Eli and Johnny had time to get the prisoners off their horses and into a cell. He trod over to lend a hand. A short tussle with the prisoners ensued and January, not even trying to suppress a smile, figured Squirt to be in a high state of enthusiasm about the situation and hoping for a full-on brawl. The dead body flopped loosely over the horse didn't deter him at all.

First though, he stopped beside Hoot and squinted up at January, who sat back and let the men handle the transfer. She always had the impression townsfolk sort of disapproved when she personally jailed someone—

although it never stopped them from calling on her when things went wrong. But this time, she had a good excuse. She plain didn't feel up to it.

"What happened to you, Mrs. Billings? What's that sling for? You ain't been shot, have you? Now you mention it, you're looking kind of poorly. Who are these yahoos?" He stopped for breath and stared at Wren until her cheeks went rosy. "And who's this little gal? She another cousin or something? Thought at first you had little Miss Hattie with you until I seen this'un don't ride for beans and Miss Hattie does."

As a matter of record, Hattie rode almost as well as January. Give her a few years and she'd probably ride better. Wren? Not so much.

January couldn't help smiling at the hostler. He'd always been a good friend to her. "Where shall I start? Yes, I've been shot. Not, as you can tell, enough to put me out of commission, although I'll admit it hurts plenty. The three men Eli and Johnny are handling, the living and the dead, are the ones who did it. More specifically, the dead one. Umm, what else did you want to know?"

Typical of a man with unending curiosity, Squirt demanded more details. "I want to know how the shootin' match came about, that's what. Didn't know you was on the trail of any owlhoots this week. And this here young lady. Is she a relative?"

"It's a long story. I'll tell you later. But let me make introductions. Squirt, this is Wren. Wren, this is Squirt. Neither of you, as far as I know, have last names. Maybe you're related, but Wren and I are not."

Squirt appeared to ponder. "Nope. Us neither. Not I know of."

Wren may have looked a little horrified as Squirt, when in a certain mood, was something of a steamroller in the way he questioned people. Still wordless in the face of meeting another new person, she shook her head hard enough to set her hair flying.

January couldn't exactly blame her. The old codger was unshaven, crumbs sprinkled his mustache, no doubt from an apple fritter—his favorite, she knew—cadged from the bakery located a short way up the street. Right now he smelled strongly of the barn cleaning in which he'd been engaged. At his best, Squirt wasn't exactly a paragon of respectability. Or cleanliness. But then, when January thought about it, Wren, as she'd appeared yesterday, had little room to talk.

The prisoners safely locked up under loud protest, the marshal volunteered to take the dead man to the funeral parlor. "Sooner this feller is off the street, the better. You gonna put this on the county bill?" he asked January as he took charge of the body. The county, notorious for penny pinching when it came to the outlying towns, had been known to try to leave financing such problems to the city.

"No. Go through his pockets. I'm told the three of them had money in hand. He can pay for his own burying."

Cheered, Southbrook headed off, saying he'd meet them all at the livery. They'd long since learned to meet somewhere other than the wide-open jail where prisoners might overhear any discussions.

Meanwhile, on orders not to take no for an answer if Eldridge down at the telegraph/post office tried to deny him, Johnny set off to collect any mail or telegrams having arrived for either January or Eli.

"There should be something from Delbert Avery, by this time," Eli said.

At the livery, Eli came to help first January, then Wren from their saddles and usher them inside. A stall in the big barn had been converted to an office-cum-living quarters for Squirt who resided there. It had also become their meeting place of choice.

January sank onto a beat-up old straight chair Squirt had probably found at the city dump and sighed relief. Wren echoed the sound, which made January smile.

"Bottom sore?" she asked.

Wren, with a shy glance at the men, who pretended not to hear, nodded.

They waited then, for Southbrook and Johnny to return. Squirt's idea of hospitality being a choice of either coffee or water, Eli said, "Coffee," and January opted for water. Not that she intended to drink it. The communal dipper in a bucket sitting on a dusty shelf put her off. But Squirt's coffee, as she'd mentioned more than once, could cause heart failure in the unwary.

Quietly, she shook her head at Wren. "I'll buy you a soda from the drug store when we leave here. All right?"

Wren's eyes lit up as she nodded again. Still not talking. January let her get by with going mute—for the moment. But she'd have to tell her story soon. The men would have to know.

Marshal Southbrook arrived back first. Johnny, shortly thereafter. He shrugged aside the argument he admitted to having with Eldridge over releasing January's mail and tossed a letter and two telegram flimsies into her lap.

Eli had also received a telegram. He glanced at the

signature and scowled. "This ought to be interesting," he said. "It's from Bitters."

"One of mine is, as well," January said. "Go ahead. What does yours say?"

He read quickly. "Says: BOY RUNNING OFF PROVES GUILT SURRENDER CHILD INTO SCHOOL CUSTODY BEFORE FRIDAY OR HE WILL FACE CONSEQUENCES HEADMASTER PHILIP BITTERS" He looked up. "Since Bitters knows Jem is with me, I think I'd best get him collected and placed somewhere safe."

January's innards curled into a hard knot. "Yes. Where do you have in mind?"

Clearing his throat, Squirt twitched. "Guess that feller don't know you very well, Eli, if he figgered a letter like that would have you running scared."

"He doesn't know me at all. But he will. Count on it."

January, aware of Wren trembling beside her, felt her anger come to the blazing point. "He may not, but Bethany and Joseph do know you. And so do some of those underlings they had working in their interests. They know me too. I'd say this is meant to give you—and all of us—pause. And give them time to catch up with Jem."

Southbrook turned his attention to her. "Sure enough sounds like a threat to me. What are you thinking, Mrs. Billings? I don't know the whole story yet, but do you have it in mind they'd actually harm the boy?"

"I think they intend to kill him." She knew she sounded stone cold. Didn't feel that way, however.

Wren gasped. "Him too?" she squeaked.

Southbrook glared at her. "What do you mean, *him too?* Who else?"

The girl went mute again.

"She means herself. Herself and her mother." January took over for her. "That's why she's here. That's why there's already a dead man waiting in the funeral parlor. She came to warn me about a plot she and her mother overheard being discussed between those men in your jail and the prime instigator."

Wren nudged her.

"And Headmaster Bitters was in on the meeting as well. He's the one who paid the men to beat her mother and then her." Time to drop the bombshell, she decided. "Bethany Flowers oversaw it all."

"What? Can't be. She's in prison." Southbrook stuck a finger in his ear and waggled it around, acting as if he couldn't believe what he'd heard.

"Not at the moment, I'm afraid." January went on with the story. "When Wren escaped, they came after her and tried to kill her." She grimaced. "They found me instead."

The following silence carried its own tale.

"Where should Jem go?" she asked Eli after a few seconds.

He shrugged. "I don't know yet."

"He can stay at Langley's place," Johnny suggested. "Evie and I will move into your old house right away, January. Don't worry about fixing anything up for us. Art and Jem are friends. Bent and Pinkie'll look out for him. You know they will."

He and his young wife had been staying with her parents until they could get their own place. Now January had finished her new house and made the move, they were going to live in the old one. But the

Langleys were good friends. Good enough she didn't want to put them in any danger.

"Let me think on it," she said, and saw Eli nodding.

"Well, dang," Squirt said. "These fellers are playing rough. The kid can stay here if he wants. The Langleys are good folk, but Bent ain't no hand with a gun. Me and Sam, we can keep Jem safe, long as he slips in quiet-like so nobody sees him and doesn't give hisself away."

January's lips twitched. "He'd probably like that. Thanks for the offer, Squirt."

"What do your telegrams have to say, January?" Eli moved restlessly. January could tell he wanted to get back to his ranch and make sure Jem had stayed put.

She flipped open the telegram from Bitters. Her face set as she read. "Huh. Jim—" she looked up, scoffing as she did so. "He misspelled Jem's name. Unless he didn't care enough to learn it in the first place."

Eli clamped his mouth shut and made a hurry-up gesture.

"JIM FLOWERS HAS RUNAWAY. DUE TO THEFT SCHOOL WILL PROSECUTE UNLESS SAID CHILD RETURNED TO SCHOOL BEFORE FRIDAY UNDER THREAT OF PRISON NO EXCUSES ACCEPTED. HEADMASTER PHILIP BITTERS." She looked up. "I wonder at the way this is worded. He seems adamant Jem be there on Friday in order *not* to prosecute. It doesn't make sense."

Eli barked out a laugh. "Only he'll be on the receiving end of prosecution, what with a witness on our side. With Avery already on the job in Spokane, Mrs. Flowers and Headmaster Bitters are due for a surprise."

January wished she could be so sure. She glanced at

Wren and cleared her throat. "If we can keep the witness safe."

Beside her, Wren nodded. Tears gushed into her cornflower blue eyes. "If they didn't kill my ma."

January had been talking about Wren herself. Somehow, she doubted the mother had survived the beating.

Eli pulled no punches. "If they haven't, we'll get her out of where she is and see they don't."

"Promise?" Wren's voice caught.

"I promise," Eli said.

"So do I." Solemn, January nodded.

All of which meant there were more plans to make. Over the gaggle of argumentative crosstalk, January opened her second telegraph. This one was from Delbert Avery. His message was cagey and mentioned no names. "GIRL IS WARNED. PINKERTON ON WAY TO TAKE HER IN HAND. DON'T WORRY. AVERY."

January wasn't sure whether this terse message helped or not. The knot in her belly continued to wind tighter as she opened the third communication. Glancing at the letter heading, she saw it bore the name of another attorney. The same one who'd worked for the banker who'd tried to quash her grandfather's will and put the Flowers fortune into her male cousins' hands. For a fee, of course.

She thought he'd been disbarred.

Apparently not, as here he, a certain W.P. Ingerson, Esquire by name, was attempting yet another unethical stunt meant to hoodwink her into signing papers giving control to his clients. The letter informed her that Bethany was free while they worked on grounds to declare the previous trial invalid. It said funds would be held off limits while the attorneys worked through the case. She, so the letter said, was under investigation for undue influencing of the minor children, whom had yet to be proven were the youngsters mentioned in Joseph Flowers's will. And all of that meant, according to Mr. Ingerson, she must surrender her claim while the case was decided. The children, known as Jeremy Flowers and his sister, Harriet Flowers, if legitimate would become wards of the court under a court appointed guardian of the bank's choosing until such time as a new guardian could be named.

January pushed back at the panic rising in her. "Can this be true?" she asked the room at large. "Can he do that?"

Marshal Southbrook shook his head. "Some of it maybe; unless this Avery feller can stop him. If he can't, those kids might be in big trouble."

"That's why they're not putting their hands on either Jem or Hattie." An unconscious gesture took Eli's hand to the big pistol holstered across his chest. "And that means we've got to get moving on this. Squirt, I'm heading out to collect Jem and bringing him to stay with you. I'll explain what's going on to him. He's a level-headed kid. He'll cooperate. I hope," he added more softly.

Squirt nodded. "I'll be here. Me 'n Sam."

"You know Jem will want to play a part. He'll be hard to control." Uneasy with the premise, January shifted in her hard chair. Across from her, Johnny, having become well-acquainted with Jem these last few months, nodded his agreement. "We've got three—no—four people to care for," she continued, "and these crooks having a head start on us, we don't have time to waste.

Wren and I will take the morning train, pick up Hattie, and settle with Mr. Avery to get him started. I'll talk to Milt again, as well. Maybe he can take a hand in this."

The men nodded.

Finally, Wren found her voice. "What about my ma? Please? Can anyone help her?"

A silence met the question. Until Eli gritted his teeth and said, "I'll head on over to the..." he hesitated to mention the house where Wren had said her mother worked, "to where Wren's mother may be staying. I'll find some place where Bitters or Bethany or their hired guns can't get at her."

Her young face set, Wren's lips trembled. "If she ain't already dead."

Eli nodded. "I'll go as soon as Jem is safe here at the livery. I'm going under the assumption she's fine," Eli said. "Johnny, might be best if you go with January."

Johnny nodded, even as January began a protest, though not, perhaps, one as vigorous as usual.

Eli overrode her. "You're not running at one hundred percent. Johnson will escort you."

The marshal was also forming a plan. "I'll be walking the town, watching for strangers. The minute I see somebody I don't like, I'll have them in the hoosegow no matter what charges I have to invent."

His determination brought a half-smile to January's lips.

"C'mon with me, Wren," she said as she rose. "We've got things to do."

"Train's not due for another hour," Squirt said.

"I know." January nodded. "First off, I'll ask Ollie if he can stay at the house and take care of my animals while I'm gone." Ollie was an old-timer who took odd jobs around the area and he'd served as a caretaker for her before.

"Plus..." She smiled down at Wren and if anyone noticed the smile was forced, they didn't react. "I promised Wren a soda, and I need to put some cash money in my pocket for the train." And maybe bribes, she thought. Whoever was bankrolling Bethany—she supposed it must be Headmaster Bitters—had a bevy of toughs to choose from. Could be her own tactics wouldn't be much different.

\* \* \*

TWO HOURS LATER, ignoring Jem's protests that he could take care of himself, Eli put the boy under Squirt's orders.

Squirt, far from catering to a Flowers, immediately put Jem to work. Credit where credit was due, the boy calmed at working with the horses, and Eli was able to set off for the small settlement outside of Spokane that Wren had mentioned.

A stop-over near the border between Washington and Idaho, it had once been a hell-on-wheels town. Now, it was nothing more than a wide spot in the road consisting of a pair of saloons, a store, a blacksmith shop, and a double-dose of competing brothels. A dusty road bisected the cluster of buildings into two parts, each side as shoddy as the other. Locals called the place, The Junction, and it was notable for the character of its residents. Outlaws, real and those who wanted to be, had made the place their own.

Eli had to admit the location was good if you were running a whorehouse or a saloon. After all, most business got done at night, conducted by people whose commodity didn't depend on genteel surroundings. Plus, the location was convenient to a major city and a couple other decent-sized towns. Not to mention being close to the railroad tracks and a route down from Canada.

Riding across country, Eli reached the place in late afternoon and stopped at the first of the brothels. The moment he saw Vera's House of Women, the sign making the business's nature clear, with a closed notice tacked to the door, he knew he'd hit paydirt. He figured the closure meant Wren's mother had died. Without wasting time at the front, he rode around to the back and found a kitchen door hanging open. Dismounting, he tethered Windswept to a hitch rail and walked inside.

His boot heels quiet on linoleum worn down to the canvas backing, he passed a pot of something simmering on the stove as he moved farther into the house. Whatever they were cooking smelled good. Funeral fare?

The next room he entered had once been a dining room. Now it appeared to be a sort of reception area. Through a door off to the side was a small room that sported a desk and matching chair, a filing cabinet, a safe, and a matched set of comfortable chairs set before a fireplace with a cold hearth. He figured this for the madame's personal room, possibly opened by special request to her most important customers. Or people like Bethany Flowers and the headmaster of a prestigious school when they required a very private meeting.

Beyond that, a larger parlor had been turned into a common room where the doves must meet their clients.

In there, a pair of mismatched red velvet settees faced each other. A large armchair sat between the couches at each end, one blue, one brown. The brown one had a long, badly repaired rip. The blue bore a stain that looked suspiciously like blood. It also looked fresh.

From here, he heard voices. They came from upstairs, where Eli figured the real business was done.

Clamping his jaw, he went up. Keeping to the strip of faded carpet laid down the middle of a lengthy hall, he followed the voices to the end room, pausing to listen a moment before poking his head around the corner.

A small knot of women stood around a narrow bed, looking sort of lost. A slight body barely lifted the blanket tucked around it. Blonde hair spread across a pillow. Hair matching that of the child January had taken in. Even from the doorway he could see the woman had been beaten unmercifully. A broken eye socket and cheekbone, along with a bashed nose. Lips split. An ear almost torn off.

Rage blinded him for a moment. One mercy. At least the little girl hadn't had to see all of this damage.

Most of the women, Eli saw, were weeping—or acting as if they were. A couple copiously and loud, the other two not so much. The latter pair included the woman he figured must be the boss as she was well past middle-age and so scrawny as to emphasize a maze of impressively deep wrinkles set in an expression of fury. Not the kind of female most men would pay for service.

From habit, Eli took off his hat, holding it awkwardly in his hand. "Miss Vera?" His soft query didn't go unheard, even in the midst of sobbing.

The older woman lifted her head. "Place is closed.

Get out." She had a voice like gravel crunching under the wheels of wagons.

He ignored the demand. "Is this Wren's mother? Is she dead?"

The woman's glance darted to the younger women who were now staring at him. "What does she look like to you?" She ignored the part about Wren.

"Dead."

"Well then, you'd be right. If you ain't the under-taker, and you ain't, get out. We're gettin' ready to plant her. A pauper," she added, full of bitterness. "Madeline wasn't a gal for savin' her money. Guess she figured she had forever. Well, I ain't payin' for any big to-do."

Wren hadn't mentioned her mother's name, or not that he'd heard. So he asked again, "Is this Wren's mother?"

"What's it to you?"

He sighed. An admission of sorts, he supposed. "Wren was discovered hiding in a chicken coop owned by a friend of mine. This friend took her in, which included defending the girl's life. A man was killed. Wren asked—no, begged—my friend to please help her mother. If her mother was still alive." Eli took another look at the body and shook his head.

"Where is she? Where is Wren?" the madame, Vera, demanded.

Eli hesitated before answering. "I don't think I'll tell you that. We can all see what those men did to her." He nodded toward Madeline. "Looks to me like it's best for everyone if you can plead ignorance."

Vera's lips tightened. Maybe, Eli thought, she'd been hoping for payment if she gave the information to

Bethany. In fact, he was sure she had. But that wasn't
going to happen.

"That girl belongs to me." Vera's mouth set in a hard
line. "She'd better get back here or I'll have the law after
her."

The two weepers stared at her, hate, if he knew
anything about hate, showing plainly on their faces. But
only for a few seconds, until they hid the reaction
before she could see.

Hiding his outrage best he was able, Eli made his
chuckle light. "I don't think so." He waited, but she
didn't say anything more. Just then, the sound of a
wagon drawing up outside the building announced
another visitor.

One of the women went to the window. "Undertaker
is here," she announced, a timely intervention.

Pity for Wren softened Eli into seeing Madeline's
body taken over by the mortician. He made payment for
a wooden coffin and a graveyard plot. He figured it was
what Wren would want. What January would want.

Only when he was a couple miles into the ride home
with night drawing on did it occur to him he should've
gone back into the brothel and tried to get more information from Vera. For instance, did Bethany and Bitters
intend on meeting there again? Had she—or any of her
girls—seen more men than the four that showed up at
The Falls?

But, distracted by dealing with the undertaker, he
hadn't, and by the time he was done with the burial
aspects, Vera had locked the brothel door against him.
He didn't plan on forcing his way back inside. The place
and the scrawny woman disgusted him beyond tolerat-

ing. Still, the idea that the omission might be a dangerous oversight nagged at him.

Worse, with both himself and Windswept weary from the long ride, he got back to the livery only to find Jem had escaped Squirt's eye and headed for the ranch.

"Chores to do," the boy had told Sam when Squirt's back was turned.

"Which ranch? Mine or Mrs. Billings's?" Eli tried not to show too much annoyance.

"Why, I don't reckon I know," Sam said. "The kid didn't say."

# CHAPTER 8

THE DAY HAD DAWNED BRIGHT, CLEAR, AND COLD, AND looked to remain that way. Eli, on the way back to the ranch, held Windswept to a lope as the trail permitted. He lived on the other side of The Falls from January, but actually closer to town, so while the ride was only around two miles, the land rose toward the mountains. Nevertheless, he felt driven to hurry. One of those feelings that had been right too often to ignore prodded at him.

He slowed as he neared the ranch gates, a new addition to the place. Letters spelling out his name had been carved into the tall arch over the gate, then painted black to contrast with the wood. Right now, he was thinking erecting the arch might have been a mistake. He'd made it easy for anyone looking for him to know they'd found the right place. The trouble is, in hindsight, too many of those people were likely to have a grudge.

While still within the line of timber shading the ranch yard, he drew Windswept to a stop and sat listening. He heard nothing, where there should've been something. The horses should've come to meet him, a habit a couple had picked up when they'd grown accustomed to being treated to apples or carrots. Even the cat that lived in the barn, though she spent most of her days sitting in the middle of the doorway and blinking into the sun, was missing.

Windswept blew and stepped forward. The sudden movement is what saved Eli from the bullet passing mere inches from his head, and thudding into a tree trunk instead. Eli didn't see where the shot came from, and he didn't stop to gaze around. Dropping from the saddle, he lay prone on the ground under cover of bushes beginning to show signs of leafing out. Aware of the bulky Broomhandle Mauser digging painfully into his chest, he didn't move when Windswept, spooked by the gunfire and Eli's quick exit from the saddle, trotted off toward the barn.

Eli waited, unmoving. As much as five minutes passed before, raising his head a scant inch, he saw movement stirring in the barn's hay loft. A figure appeared in the opening. Two figures. One was Jem. Though Eli didn't have much of a view, he didn't recognize the other.

The figure standing behind Jem jerked the kid forward. His voice reached Eli, loud and clear. "See there, you little twit. Told you I got the bastard. One shot." He was laughing, bragging. "One shot and he dropped like a rock. Guess he warn't so much after all. C'mon. I wanta see where I got him."

As far as Eli could tell, Jem didn't say anything. Maybe he couldn't.

Motionless, Eli stayed where he'd fallen a few

seconds longer. Then, knowing he had a little time while they climbed down from the hay mow, he grabbed the Broomhandle out of the holster and put it under some leaves, his outstretched hand covering it. Resuming the first position, he lay still.

Soon Jem and the man appeared in the barn's doorway and headed toward him. A rope noose was tied around Jem's neck, his head cocked at an awkward angle. The shooter dragged the boy along like a uncooperative dog. Every once in a while he'd yanked on the rope and laugh at the sight as Jem gagged and coughed.

Hot blood surged through Eli's veins and he felt himself shaking with anger. Soon as the desperado got close enough, he'd be changing his tune.

Eli managed to still the shaking, but not his anger.

Their footsteps shuffled right up to his head. They'd hurried and the man was breathing hard. So was Jem, Eli realized, but his breaths gave a little distressed whistle as the rope pulled tight and shut off his wind.

Eli allowed his eyes to open a slit. Holding the tail end of the rope in one hand, the outlaw stretched toward what he thought was a corpse, grinning like a Halloween pumpkin.

The instant Jem's captor bent down, arm reaching to roll him over, Eli lunged upright. He rammed head-first straight into the outlaw's gut with all his weight behind it.

The outlaw screamed a single short note. The rope dropped. His diaphragm spasming from the force of Eli's plunge to his belly, he gasped for air. His fingers twitched as he tried to reach his gun.

That wasn't all. Jem, with only enough wind for a

heavy grunt, swept the man's legs out from under him, and gave him a resounding kick in the kidney with the toe of his sturdy boots.

Finished off, the outlaw flopped on the ground like a dying fish.

Jem's face was dusky red as he finagled the noose and tore it over his head. "I knew he missed you." His voice sounded raw. "I knew it." Spinning around, he kicked the man again.

Eli bent down and retrieved his Mauser from the leaves.

"Better take his gun before he hurts someone." Eli knew the shot had come a whole lot closer than was comfortable. He kept his voice even. Far from what he was feeling, but he didn't want Jem going further off the rails. Or maybe only a little. A very little. "Is he alone?" he thought to ask.

"Yeah." Jem seemed embarrassed by the fact. "He sneaked up on me while I was brushing Henry and Badger. He thought I was you at first." Eli had assigned Badger to him to use.

"Where's his horse?"

"He put him in a stall. Didn't want you to see a strange horse when you rode up. Guess he figured on waiting all day if that's what it took."

Eli huffed out a sound of disgust.

Showing some of the good sense Eli had seen in the boy before, Jem, plenty cautious now, circled around the fellow still writhing through the leaves. At first chance, Jem stepped on the hand reaching for the gun, which he snatched away and tossed in the bushes. "He's got a knife in his boot." He fished a bowie knife honed sharp enough to cut fine silk from a sheath sewn into his boot top. To finish, he stamped down hard on the leg to avoid a kick, causing the outlaw to howl anew.

Eli, brushing himself off, studied their prisoner, who, going by his noise, had recovered his wind. Now his face had come untwisted and resumed a more natural color, Eli noticed he bore an uncanny resemblance to Gus. A brother, perhaps. One slightly older and wearing a larger paunch. But part of the same gang. That much was clear.

Jem, in a single triumphant gesture, gathered up the noose he'd been forced to wear and flipped it over their prisoner's head. He jerked it tight. But not tight enough to strangle. "Was there any word from Mr.—" He stopped and glanced at the outlaw. "From you-know-who?"

Eli grinned at Jem's careful question. The moment faded all too fast. "Yes. But that's not all the news." He gave the outlaw a meaningful glance. "Later."

Always a quick study, Jem nodded his understanding, leaving Eli to ponder the situation. Jem was more than ten years younger than January, and his sister Hattie a couple years even younger. Joseph Flowers, wealthy beyond most folks' dreams, had been their father and her grandfather. Due to the kids' ages, he'd left the Flowers fortune to January, but in a letter had asked her to take these two in hand and, first off, make certain the grandsons didn't kill them. He'd asked her to make provision for them. January, who never knew she had relatives at all until her grandfather's death, hadn't wanted any part of the estate and planned to turn it all over to the young ones after following certain qualifications in the will. Meanwhile, though inexperienced with children, she was doing her best.

And Eli, while trying to remain unobtrusive, did his best to help her.

Also, as he admitted to himself, he liked the kids. Jem had been smart and resourceful last fall when January had been kidnapped and nearly killed by her cousins. Eli had a lot of respect for the kid, no more than fourteen, who'd showed extraordinary toughness. And the girl, Hattie, matched her brother in every way.

He jerked the outlaw to his feet, ignoring the man's protests about the kid breaking his leg. He didn't believe it. "Move. There's a jail cell in town with your name on it."

"We've got to watch out, Eli," Jem said. He gave the rope around the man's neck a yank to get him moving. "He said his brother and a couple other men are gonna meet him here any minute. He thought at first you were one of them."

Eli shook his head and clicked his tongue with a "tsk, tsk" sound. "Then he'll have to wait until he gets to town to meet with them. See..." He turned to the outlaw, knowing he'd guessed right about two of them being relatives. "Gus and Vern will be right in the cell next to yours. It'll be a real family get-together."

The fellow's jaw dropped. "What...no. Wait. You got Gus and Vern? Where's—" He stopped.

"Where's Earl? Is that what you want to know?" Eli stopped and studied him. "He's at the undertaker's parlor. Dead."

The outlaw glared. "Nah," he said. "That can't be. Not any of it. You're lyin'. I'll bet Earl got away. Yeah. He got away. He'll show you. You and this damn kid, both. And the girl too. Same as her ma, nosing around where they didn't belong."

"Dead as a Sunday dinner chicken," Eli said, seeming to ignore the thug's tirade. What had him puzzled was why this had started off with accusing Jem of theft. It didn't make any sense. He caught Jem looking at him as if asking a question and shook his head.

"Liar," the outlaw shouted. "You ain't going to trick me. The boys'll take care of you. Both you and this little jackass." He meant Jem. "You can't get all of us. We got you outnumbered, bounty hunter."

Eli frowned. Were there more men in the gang than the four they knew about? Apparently, Joe III had enough money squirreled away out of the lawyers' hands to pay for a small army. Disturbing.

"Move. Head for the barn." The thing is, Eli thought as a boot to the rear got the outlaw moving, the kids being of a mixed Indian heritage made everything tougher for them. He had a notion this deal with the school might never have come about otherwise. Not that Jem—or Hattie—showed much Indian. They had the same distinctive mix of greenish brown eye color of every one of the grandchildren. Their hair was only a little darker than January's mahogany-colored topknot, and their skin no darker than Eli's own Mediterranean complexion.

It seemed clear Bethany and Joe Flowers had begun their objective to obtain the Flowers estate with their appeal for a mistrial. Even from prison, Joe had probably hired some of the thugs he'd met during his incarceration. They'd picked Jem and Hattie as the easiest targets, that's all. Smart, Eli supposed, to make use of

Headmaster Bitters's prejudice against Jem's mixed blood to begin the vendetta. Most White people were all too willing to accept as fact when people of Indian or mixed blood were accused of theft.

Yes. The kids were chosen as easy targets.

Especially since they'd found January a whole lot harder to deal with than they'd expected.

Why now? Apparently, because Bethany had somehow gotten released from prison pending a mistrial, while her husband's case against the estate was on appeal. Eli had to wonder if she'd been the driving force all along. Even above her husband and his cousins, John B, and Calvin.

Windswept, recovered from being startled by his rider's fall, had ambled over to the corral to make use of the watering trough when Eli and Jem prodded their prisoner into the yard. The outlaw had left his horse saddled in the barn. Jem needed only moments to throw a rig on Badger. Mounting, the three started back to town.

Eli sensed Jem was bursting at the seams to learn what had happened with January. Even so, he gave only short, low-voiced answers to Jem's many questions. He didn't want the outlaw overhearing. Not at this point. Marshal Southbrook, though working outside of his jurisdiction, would know what to ask as they pried answers from the man. Gus and Vern had been close-mouthed about their employers. This fellow, whatever his name might be, ran his mouth almost without ceasing. The only thing he didn't say was who'd hired him.

"We know who hired him," Jem said, surprised when Eli mentioned this.

"We think we do, but he needs to admit it."

"Well then, we'll make sure he does."

Eli quirked a grin. "We will." Unwarranted confidence. Could be the man didn't know himself.

# CHAPTER 9

NOT BEING ONE TO RENEGE ON A PROMISE, JANUARY escorted Wren into the drug store where they settled onto stools at a short counter. Mirrors behind the counter reflected the gleaming glassware, as well as any patrons in the store. Everything was meticulously clean.

Wren, spinning on the stool, gazed around the store with wide blue eyes and whispered her awe. "I ain't never been in a store like this before." She seemed fascinated by the sparkling glasses and shiny spoons, a row of flavored syrups, and frost-covered bins surrounded by ice cut from their very own river in winter that kept the ice cream frozen.

January wasn't about to admit that after her grandfather had scarred her face so badly, she hadn't gone in any drugstores, either. Or much of anyplace else. Only now, after her husband Shay proved he loved her, scars and all, and convinced her not to hide, had she quit avoiding people. Not that she flaunted those scars.

Mrs. Brady, the druggist's wife, hurried toward them. She wore a white cap over her graying brown hair, and a voluminous bib apron over her dress. "Mrs. Billings, you haven't been here in ever so long! Only once since you shot that awful man out back of the store. What can I get for you? A nice ice cream sundae?"

January, aware of her face growing hot, caught the way Wren opened her eyes wide and mouthed the word *shot,* and figured there'd soon be questions forthcoming.

"Two root beer floats, please," she said. "My friend here has never had one."

Mrs. Brady smiled at Wren. "Well then, dearie, you're in for a lovely surprise." She set about opening one of the bins and measuring a scoop of ice cream into each glass, talking as she worked. "May I ask what has happened to your arm, Mrs. Billings? Has Dr. LeBret had a look at it? Will you be laid up long?"

Wren opened her mouth as if to say something, but January cut her off with a nudge of her foot and a slight shake of the head. "A small accident, Mrs. Brady. It'll be fine in a day or two."

Wren's face puckered at the lie. But when, efficient from long practice, Mrs. Brady set the glasses on the counter before them, the girl's smile was blinding.

January handed over coins, which Mrs. Brady tried to refuse, saying, "No, no. No charge to the woman who saved our lives that day."

This time, January knew for certain her face was glowing red. Yes, she'd shot the man who'd been holding the Bradys and their customers hostage, but since he'd been shooting at her at the time, she'd also been aiming to save her own life.

When she and Wren had finished their treats, they went on to the bank. She left the money on the counter.

If thrilled by the drugstore, the quiet formality of

the bank intimidated the girl. She shrank against January. "The old biddy used to keep her money in a bank," she murmured, "but she wouldn't let my mama or the other girls leave their money there."

January had to stop a moment and think who the old biddy was. *Ah, yes. Mrs. Ger...*

Wren continued her explanation. "She said it was on account of she didn't want anybody to know how much her girls made a night, but Ma said it was so's she could steal it when the girls were busy. Ma caught her doing that once."

"That's not the bank's fault."

"It kind of was. The girls was scared to go there because they knew the men, so then the men treated them rude so's the womenfolk could see how righteous they was. Otherwise, the girls might've put their money there to keep it safe in spite of the bitch."

January could visualize this.

Wren fell silent as they stepped up to the teller's cage. The better, January believed, to study on how business was conducted.

Then they were off to the train depot, where they found Johnny waiting for them. They boarded the train, Wren fidgeting and acting alternately enthralled and terrified. She jumped straight into the air when a giant puff of steam rolled over them.

Johnny laughed—a nervous laugh, January noted.

"What if it goes off the rails," Wren said, sounding almost faint in the noise of the car. "I heard about that. Maisie Sue, she came up from somewhere on the coast, and she said a train did that right in front of them. Said they had to wait two days without food or water while men cleared the mess. Lots of folks was bleeding all over the place."

January doubted most of the story, while Johnny, himself looking uncomfortable since train travel was new to him as well, openly questioned the girl's facts. By the time she'd made peace between them, they were underway. The pair of them leaned their faces against the dirty windows and watched the countryside flow past. Meanwhile, January closed her eyes and, if she didn't sleep, at least she rested.

Arriving at the Spokane depot, although they both protested, she had Johnny and Wren wait until most of the passengers had dispersed, leaving the platform open.

"If anyone is waiting for us, I prefer to see them first," she told Johnny. "Watch for anybody who shows too much interest."

Johnny became impatient and began fingering the revolver January had insisted he hide beneath his coat. "Let'em come." He scowled, an unfamiliar face for him to wear. "That's why I'm here, ain't it? At least, we'd know who they are, then."

"You have a point," January admitted, "but I'd rather not have a fight here at the station. We'd be tied up here for hours, trying to make explain things to the Spokane police." She peered around. "Not all of them are my friend."

In fact, she spotted a familiar face edging around the corner of the station as if hoping not to be seen. It belonged to a cop who'd been a pal of a man named Lynch, and he'd been one of Joseph III's hangers-on.

As for Wren, she kept saying, "I've never seen so many people all in one place. What are they all doing?"

Or, "There's an awful lot of big buildings. Will we get lost?"

The depot platform finally emptied, except for themselves and a bewildered appearing family confused on where to go. A new crowd had not yet gathered for the boarding.

The only thing January feared losing was her patience as they, apparently safe enough for the moment, made their way to Delbert Avery's office. His clerk showed her, but not Johnny or Wren, immediately into Avery's office. Johnny, ignoring Wren's scowl, didn't appear pleased at what he called a baby-tending job. And Wren didn't seem any happier at having him boss her around.

Avery came forward to shake her hand and show her to a seat. "I've been waiting for you," he said.

One would've thought—and January smiled inwardly—she was a great lady dressed in an elegant gown instead of a common rancher woman wearing work clothes consisting of her usual split skirt, boots, and a plain white shirt under her coat.

"Were you expecting me?" she asked, worried by this aspect of the greeting.

He took his seat across from her. "Yes. Mr. Pasco sent a telegram. In it, he said to tell you Jem is fine and safe."

"Thank God." Relieved, January became aware that she'd been holding her breath, and let it out slowly.

He was looking askance at the sling holding her arm, but January put him off for the moment. She disliked the thought of telling him the whole sordid story of last night's incident. "Is Hattie all right? Have you heard?" She leaned forward in the chair. "Have you been able to clear up the lies about Jem stealing from the headmaster at the Bakewell Academy?"

"There's a police detective looking into it." Avery didn't seem happy. "He hasn't been able to question Mr. Bitters, as yet. It seems the headmaster is out of town and out of reach."

January jerked. "And Bethany Flowers?"

"Apparently, against the terms of her release while on appeal, she, too, is out of town and out of reach." Avery sounded dry as desert dirt.

"And nobody knows where they've gone?"

"No."

"Is anybody looking for her?"

Avery shrugged. "She still has connections. Friends." In other words, no.

They both were silent a moment, until January asked again, "What about Hattie?"

"She, I am relieved to say, is on her way to town with the understanding she will be brought directly to my office. We can decide what is best to do when she gets here." He stilled the question forming on January's lips with an admonishing finger. "No reason to get upset," he said. "I hired a private detective, one of Pinkerton's best, to escort her. Don't worry, Mrs. Billings. They will be arriving in town within the hour, and in this office shortly after that."

But they weren't. And when Mr. Avery sent his clerk to notify the police and set an inquiry into motion, there was no trace of her arriving in Spokane. It appeared she, and Marche, had somehow disappeared after boarding.

Hattie and the Pinkerton man, a certain David Marche, had been passengers on a train coming up from Pullman, where she was enrolled in a school for young ladies. That much they knew. People had seen them take their seats. The conductor had taken their tickets. There'd been two stops along the way, in Rosalia and in Cheney. Nobody saw them get off at either stop. Nevertheless, they didn't make it to Spokane, even though some of Hattie's luggage had been left on the platform. Officials from the train said they'd have it delivered to Avery's office.

"Pinkerton's best." Johnny unimpressed, growled his scorn as they waited.

Tension grew. Johnny went in and out of the office, walking around the block surrounding Mr. Avery's office building.

January paced around the waiting room when Avery had to meet with clients. Then she paced the hall, only to come back inside and perch like a flighty bird on one of the waiting room chairs.

Wren looked on, wide-eyed and worried. She knew she faced threats. "Am I gonna disappear?" She'd elbowed January—unfortunately in her sore side—and asked in an almost whisper.

January didn't know how to answer. "Not if I can help it," she finally said.

Benjamin Carlton, Avery's assistant, had handled the hiring of the Pinkerton. "They told me Mr. Marche was the best," he insisted, flapping his hands in dismay. "He is the best. His record—I demanded to see it—said he has the finest record of any man in Pinkerton's Spokane office."

"Who is investigating?" January asked. "Are they from Pullman or Spokane? Or in-between?"

Avery, who'd just had a private telephone conversation with the sheriff, clamped his lips together, which

January didn't think boded well for Hattie or the Pinkerton. "They're discussing jurisdiction. I suggested they each work from their end. The sheriff seemed amiable to that, but who knows what the Whitman County sheriff will say."

While January agreed to both working, she had her own opinion. "Better yet, we get an investigator of our own. Every minute that passes lets whoever did this get farther away."

Avery tried again to soothe her. "We don't know what has happened. Harriet may be perfectly fine. Perhaps she got off at the wrong stop and Marche went to find her. He's bound to take care of her no matter the circumstances. I'm sure we'll hear from him any minute now."

But they didn't.

January, constrained by the waiting, began making plans to form her own search. Wrapped up in worry for Hattie, she had almost forgotten Johnny and Wren. Until Wren, fighting tears, burst out, "They'll kill her, dammit. Beat her to mush just like they did my ma. Like they planned to do with me."

"Be more likely to shoot her, I expect," Johnny said. "I'll do it, January. I'll go look for her. This woman, Bethany Flowers, she don't know me from Adam. Nor does that other feller. Hattie will trust me if she sees me coming."

Grateful beyond words, January smiled at her young ranch hand. "I'm grateful, Johnny, but I'm not putting you in danger. You're a newly married man. I will not make Evie a widow." She was nothing if not blunt.

Johnny flushed, although January knew he was grateful.

However, he didn't care for her opinion of his abilities and blustered a bit. "What makes you think I'm gonna get killed? I can handle myself. Mr. Pasco trusted me to watch over you here in town, so I guess I can watch over you on the trail just as well. We'll go together."

"Me too," Wren said.

He certainly knew her well enough to know January would be in the thick of the search. And it was true, January reflected. He could handle himself. Up to a point, but not if, as she feared, Bethany, Joe, and this Bitters fellow, had hired a gang of practiced thugs.

"Wait a minute," Avery appeared seriously alarmed now, what with his best client stepping out her preferred place. "You aren't thinking of going yourself, are you, Mrs. Billings? No, no. That wouldn't be wise. Not wise at all."

But Johnny answered for her. "'Course, she's going. Why do you think they made her a deputy over at The Falls? She knows what to do." He grinned at her.

She grinned back. Still, she thought, it would've been more convincing if she hadn't already been shot.

\* \* \*

THE LUGGAGE ARRIVED AT LAST, brought to Avery's office by a messenger from the railroad. There wasn't much as Hattie had been used to doing without for most of her life. As Joseph C. Flowers' unacknowledged daughter, she'd been kept a secret right up until he died, as had Jem. As an attendee of the young lady's school, she'd been required to wear exactly the same attire as every other girl. January was amused, if she could actually feel amusement at the moment, to see she'd left the uniforms behind at school. The delivery consisted of one medium-sized satchel.

January had thought there might've been a note tucked away inside the satchel, but there wasn't. She ceased her one-handed search in disgust.

"Nothing?" Avery said.

She shook her head. "Nothing."

The attorney, noticing Johnny and Wren were wrangling again, spoke quietly. "Do you think this means they killed her? Dumped her body off the train?"

Her breath caught. She'd been thinking the same thing, but she said, "Why would they do that? Alive, she's an incentive for me to sign whatever they put in front of me. Dead, there isn't." She hesitated. "But I'm willing to bet they'll find the Pinkerton's body somewhere along the tracks. Provided he isn't one of them, that is."

He nodded. "I hope you're right about the girl. Unfortunately, I'm sure you're right about the detective."

January swallowed hard. She'd hoped he'd disagree. "The sooner they find the detective, the sooner we'll have an idea on where to start looking for Hattie."

*  *  *

THE AFTERNOON WORE INTO EVENING. Avery closed his office and went home. January, Johnny, and Wren took a hack to the Spokane apartment where Joseph Flowers Senior had lived. January stayed there when she came to Spokane to attend to business concerning the huge Flowers estate. Though she supposed the apartment was technically elegant, she felt uncomfortable there, and much preferred her home at The Falls. Both the old one, and now the new one. They were hers. Not a part of some unasked for inheritance and the attached strings that had come with it.

Earlier, during the slow afternoon, January had placed a telephone call to the police department. She'd asked to speak with Milt Ferguson, Eli's old friend who worked on the force

"He's on night shift," the person who answered the call said, and promised to deliver a message to Ferguson from her. She'd begun to think he'd neglected to deliver on the promise when at last the telephone, located in the foyer, jangled.

"It's me," he said.

Fortunately, she recognized his voice. "Officer Ferguson. I was beginning..." She stopped herself. Best not get too pushy.

But Ferguson was no soft-centered daisy. "Yeah. Guy at the desk forgot until just now. That's all good. I know what you're calling about. I've got news. Now, I only got a minute, so don't interrupt. First, deputies down around Cheney found a body. It's the Pinkerton that Avery said was missing. He'd been shot. Body is kinda beat-up, like they either just threw him off the train while it was moving or beat him up. He fell behind some rocks, which is why it took so long to find him. A bunch of birds gathering around the body pointed the way."

January shuddered. "What about—"

Ferguson interrupted. "No sign of the girl. A feller, well, call him the town drunk, hangs around the Cheney depot along about train time every day. Deputies talked to him. He told 'em he saw a man manhandling a young girl to get her off the train an instant before it started back up. He didn't pay much attention until the girl starting cussing the feller out and trying to kick him in the..." He stopped and cleared his throat. "Says he was shocked—that's what he said, shocked—because of the language. He described her, but not the man. They're pretty sure it's the Flowers girl."

Finally getting a word in edgewise, January demanded, "Did he see which way they went?"

"Not exactly. Says another feller had a buggy sitting in the trees back of the station, and that he saw some dust being raised off toward the west a little later, but don't get your hopes up. That could've been anybody."

It could have, but January figured they'd better check. What's more, she knew that if Hattie had been able to set foot to ground, she had found some way to leave sign. They just had to find it.

"Are you on the job?" she asked.

Ferguson sighed. "Not me. I'm still black-balled from anything to do with the Flowers case. Got a pal, though, who said he'd let me know what's going on. I'll do what I can. Meanwhile, you'd best tell Pasco to get hisself over to Cheney before our yahoos screw up any sign there might be. And you, you stay out of it. Trouble follows you."

"Trouble not of my making," she said sharply. But then she crossed her fingers and lied. "I'll tell Eli. Thanks, Officer Ferguson. You've been most helpful."

He broke the connection.

Good advice, she knew. But she couldn't draw Eli off from seeing to Jem and tracking Headmaster Bitters.

That was equally important. She would have to go herself.

She looked up at Johnny who'd followed her into the foyer to listen. "We've got a lead to follow. The Flowers Trust has some horses boarded at the Model Stable on Main Street. The hostler will know which ones they are. Rig them out, and bring them here, please. We're catching the next train out to Cheney and we'll load them in a stock car."

Johnny's eyes brightened. "Finally. Wait. Why Cheney? What's happening there?"

"Just bring the horses. I'll tell you on the way."

"I'm coming, ain't I?" Wren demanded gruffly. Gruff, but shaky.

"You are. I prefer not to leave you alone and unprotected."

But in the end, she had to do just that.

# CHAPTER 10

THE FLOWERS APARTMENT ENCOMPASSED ALL OF THE third floor of the Flowers Office Building, and was reached by a wide, elegant staircase to the second floor, then a narrower one to the third. Both the first and second floors were leased out to the likes of attorneys, stockbrokers, and a couple import/exporters. January had wondered how honest the second-floor stockbroker was when she first met him, but so far, he hadn't been arrested. Besides, he paid his rent on time.

All of which meant the building, except for one old man who'd taken over janitorial duties when the young Flowers' maternal uncle had been murdered, stood empty on nights the apartment was unoccupied. And that was most of the time. January preferred her ranch at The Falls.

January had been thinking, not sure she liked where her thoughts were going. Mainly, because while she and Wren waited for Johnny to get back from the livery with the horses, Wren went sound asleep on the couch.

The girl, although January had noticed her fine,

porcelain skin before and wondered if she ever got out into the sun, had become even paler as the hours drew on. January believed Wren to be undernourished, for one thing, and exhausted, for another. She didn't like to force a long ride on horseback onto an inexperienced rider already suffering from the effects of her escape from men out to kill her. And though Wren denied any effects, January knew better.

Johnny was soon back from saddling the horses, and if he'd looked worried before, he looked worse now. January, who'd stuffed a saddle bag with things she thought they—and she—might need, had put it in the foyer and was waiting for him, ready to go.

He had a sort of uneasy look on his face. "Uh...." he said, "I only got two horses."

"Two?"

"Yeah, one of yours got kicked in the leg by some yahoo's half-wild critter and lamed it. The hostler says to give you his apologies and he'll knock some off the boarding fee this month. He wants you to tell him what to about renting one for a girl."

Impatience made January want to scream. Or start chewing her fingernails. But then, she had another thought. Wren had admitted she didn't know if she was up to a long, hard ride, especially since they were in a hurry.

In the living room, she reached down and shook Wren awake.

"We leaving?" the girl asked, sitting up and trying to open her eyes.

January glanced at Johnny, who quirked his eyebrows. He'd certainly noticed Wren's fatigue. "Johnny and I are. What would you say to staying here by yourself, Wren? I can see how tired you are. And scared. You don't much like horses, do you?"

The girl, her blue eyes big now, shook her head.

"There's food in the ice box to tide you over until we get back. If you'll leave the lights off until daylight, even if anyone thinks to look here, they won't suspect the place is occupied. We shouldn't be longer than a day or so. Hattie has things in the second bedroom. I'm sure she won't mind if you choose some clothes or read..." She stopped, having temporarily forgotten she didn't think Wren *could* read. "I know there are some puzzles in boxes. Or some art things if you'd like to draw." January did her best to sound persuasive. "So. Would you rather stay here?"

This time, Wren, although she looked nervous, nodded. January thought she was used to being isolated.

"I'd slow you down," Wren said. "I'm not good on a horse."

As if January hadn't noticed.

*Smart girl.* "I showed you how to bolt the door, right? I want you to it the second we go outside."

"You'll come back for me?"

"Absolutely."

Johnny nodded agreement.

Wren swallowed and took a shaky breath. "All right."

Also a brave girl.

Waiting only to hear the bolt—added since January had inherited the building—slide into place, Johnny and January clattered down the stairs to the horses and mounted. She was aware of the girl watching from the window as they rode away. Guilt and fear filled her. But she couldn't stop. Finding Hattie was the important job right now.

Without speaking, they threaded through the dark and empty back ways to catch the first train to Cheney, a freight hauler with a stock car for the horses.

Afraid she'd done the wrong thing in leaving Wren to fend for herself, January fretted all the way to Cheney. Right to the point where Johnny got up and moved two seats away. He told her he was tired of being poked in the ribs every time some new worry occurred to her.

Marriage had changed her ranch hand. Johnny had become bolder. Franker with his opinions. Different from the shy boy she'd hired those two years ago after Shay was murdered.

\* \* \*

IN CHENEY, they unloaded their horses from the stock car in a hurry, the train halting only briefly for the unscheduled stop. From there, they made their way to the sheriff's office, passing through streets quiet and dark enough to make the town seem deserted. Not even a dog barked.

They found the sheriff's office after a short search per the directions Milt Ferguson had given January. Inside, a rather corpulent man with a huge brown mustache was busy dozing in a chair. He wore a tarnished-looking star pinned to his vest. A name card displayed on the front of the desk said, Deputy Lipinsky. He startled awake when Johnny forcefully cleared his throat, an unnecessarily loud process. What's more, Lipinsky didn't appear pleased to see them. He rubbed his eyes and viewed his visitors with suspicion, focusing on January and her scarred face. He didn't bother to rise.

The blatant stare almost made her wish for one of the concealing bonnets she used to wear. Then she changed her mind. Lipinsky's opinion didn't matter.

Johnny whispered that Lipinsky's ma must never have taught him any manners. However, he wasn't too careful whether the deputy overheard or not, which January felt sure had been his intention. After all, he was correct. But it took only a second for Lipinsky's gaze to return to January, evidently sensing her to be the one in charge.

The deputy regarded her, absorbing the fact her arm was in a sling. She'd taken care to wear her badge where he could see it as a way to show her bonafides right up front. That's not to say he saw it right off. Or pretended, anyhow. Generally, she kept the star hidden on the underside of her coat's lapel. In the northern end of the county, where most folks knew her, she didn't see any reason to show the badge off. Here, apparently, he'd never heard of her. Or else he'd decided to put on a show.

He peered at her emblem of office and shook his head. "Say, lady, I can run you in for impersonating an officer. That's against the law. Hand over that there fake badge."

Johnny, though not hot-tempered as a general rule, spoke before January could open her mouth. He scowled fiercely, his face burning with anger. He leaned right in on the deputy.

"You don't know what you're talking about, buster. Certain sure, if you paid attention to your own position, you'd know Mrs. Billings is the only duly elected female deputy in the state. And she's the Flowers—"

January stopped him with a hand on his shoulder. "Easy, Mr. Johnson," she said, quelling her own urge to scream at the man. She met Lipinsky's eyes. "I am Deputy January Billings from The Falls. Young Miss Harriet Flowers, one of our residents, has been kidnapped off the train somewhere between Pullman and Spokane. Mr. Johnson and I are here to help with the investigation as she was headed into town at our request. Now," she overrode whatever the deputy, who lowered his gaze first, opened his mouth to say, "the last the Spokane police told me, is that the Pinkerton agent assigned to protect Miss Flowers while enroute has been found murdered a few miles from here. Also, that a witness spotted an event that might possibly place the girl here at the Cheney depot. Have you caught up with whoever was driving the buggy?"

She could see the deputy thinking over what she'd said. She had too much information not to be legitimate. A real deputy. And yes, she rather thought he *had* heard of her, a fact just now sinking into his brain. His slow brain.

"It wasn't her," he muttered, low enough to be almost imperceptible.

"Pardon me?"

"At the depot. It wasn't her, the Flowers girl. Ole Bart Mellon. He seen something, but when deputies Nixon and Prentice followed the tracks, they found out it was just Mr. and Mrs. Red Linnerwood who'd been having a little set-to. They ain't been married long and when the missus got back from a week-long visit with her ma over in Colfax, they ran at each other and went to hugging and kissing and her to crying real loud." Lipinsky's face puckered. "Got a little overly enthusiastic, I reckon. Anyways, Mellon already had filled his tank and was drunk as a Lord. Couldn't tell the difference between a fight and whatever it was them two was doing."

January frowned. "When was this?"

"When? You mean what time? Along about four—five—o'clock, I guess."

"You guess? Did it never occur to anyone to let the Spokane police, or The Falls sheriff's office know?" January seethed. "Time wasted."

"Now hold on," Lipinsky said, homing in on her anger, "you folks ain't running this investigation."

"Is anybody? Anybody competent, that is. And don't you forget we all work in the same general territory. We need to work together."

"Do we?" He heaved his body out of the chair. "Listen here, missus, Deputy Nixon is a fine officer of the law, and him and Prentice have been busy. They brought in the body of the Pinkerton. Then they had to go right out and follow-up on the buggy sighting. They're having their rest, now."

"Their rest? You mean—"

"I mean they've gone home and gone to bed, a'course. They's tired, what with all the riding they did today. You wouldn't know, being female and all, but it ain't easy, dealing with a dead body."

January, whose day had started with the dealing of a dead body—one she'd killed herself—snorted like a sneezing filly. But Lipinsky had apparently said all he intended to say as he puckered his mouth shut. She turned to Johnny. "Like I said, incompetent."

Certain she'd get no more cooperation out of this

man, January knew she'd have to wait for daylight to make her own investigation. She'd talk to these two deputies then and start looking where they'd found the bodies. Meanwhile, she had to give in to exhaustion. Besides getting shot, this was the second night in a row she'd gone mostly sleepless. It seemed logical that she'd be better, more efficient after a nap. Maybe Nixon and Prentice weren't neglecting their duty, after all. She'd see in the morning.

Besides, her side where the bullet had grazed a furrow hurt plenty bad enough to make anyone cranky.

* * *

JANUARY OPENED her eyes to a ray of sunshine, though grateful for the clean white sheets, she rued the fact she hadn't slept well. Not even her weariness had kept her anger from seething throughout the night. But now she awakened late, a cause for alarm.

A small mirror hung above an old-fashioned wash-stand. After a look into the wavy glass, she sighed and washed her face with cold water. Having forgotten a comb, she ran her fingers through her hair hoping to straighten the tangles. Success was no more than so-so. Tilting the mirror for a better look, she moved the dressing under her arm aside, and peeked at the still raw wound. A scab had formed. Wren's stitches were holding. The wound still hurt like crazy when she moved her arm, but all seemed well enough to forgo the sling.

Johnny had been assigned a room a couple doors down the hall. Doublechecking for the correct number, she rapped on the door. After a few seconds without an answer, she rapped again, harder this time, and waited.

Again, no answer.

Her fist was raised when a woman stepped from the room between them. "If you're looking for that nice looking young man in the room next to me, he isn't there," she said. "I saw him leave about fifteen minutes ago."

"He left?" January blinked. Was she so late he'd taken matters into his own hands?

"Yes. I noticed him when I was coming back from breakfast. If you're with him, I can tell you he started to knock on your door, then seemed to think again, and went on downstairs." The woman, maybe thirty years old, was fashionably dressed and wore a perky, dark blue hat set atop a Gibson girl hairdo.

To January, she appeared the type to have a sharp eye for men. Even men ten years younger than herself. And especially if they were as fine looking as Johnny Johnson.

But, considering what appeared to be yet another cranky mood, January took herself in hand, thanked the woman, and went on downstairs. The smell of coffee and frying bacon wafted up from the dining room on the ground floor, and she was hungry. She figured to find Johnny there, filling his stomach.

Johnny wasn't the only one she found. Two men sat at a table with him, both with bags under their eyes, and badges displayed on their chests. The two deputies, Nixon and Prentice, she assumed. And they all seemed to be getting on well with each other.

Johnny jumped to his feet when he spotted her coming. A faint smile lifted her lips.

"Morning." She nodded first to Johnny, then the deputies. "Sorry to be late."

Instead of saying good morning back, Johnny frowned. "Where's your sling? You all right? Dang it, Mrs. Billings..." He was being very formal in front of the strangers. "I knew you were doing too much too soon, what with you just being shot and all."

She took notice of the look the deputies shared and used the opportunity to play on Johnny's opening. "I know my duty, Mr. Johnson, and that is to catch the men who committed a murder while snatching Miss Flowers from the train. I need both arms."

And that, she decided, comprised as much as the deputies needed to know.

As it turned out, and a bit to her surprise, they apparently agreed with her.

The deputies, meanwhile, had taken a cue from Johnny and risen to their feet. The taller of the two pulled out a chair and invited her to sit. The other waved at a passing waiter and demanded more coffee and a breakfast special for the lady deputy.

January couldn't help being impressed. How could these two be so different from Deputy Lipinsky at the jail last night? So, she asked. And they weren't shy about answering.

"Ah, Lipinsky," the tall one, Nixon, said. "He's related to the mayor, who pulled some strings with the sheriff. He tries to let on like he's the boss. Lipinsky, he don't ever get out of the office. Mostly, that's fine with us."

Prentice nodded agreement. "The one time he did, he got in the way and the rest of us damn near...excuse me...come near to getting shot. His fault, barging in and acting important. Nixon here, he's pretty fair with a gun, had managed to get the drop on a drunk feller shootin' off his six-gun before he done more than shoot a hole in The Cheney Free Press'—that's the local newspaper— front window. When Lipinsky got involved and fouled up the arrest the drunk feller took to shootin' again."

Nixon took over the story. "Norm Alexander, he's the editor of The Press, just missed gettin' his rear end shot off," Nixon said. "He was bent over doin' somethin' with the type at the time. Alexander was a leetle upset. Made sure Lipinsky didn't get the chance again."

They were still laughing when January's food arrived, eggs, ham, and a stack of fluffy hotcakes. She ate every bite and sopped up all the syrup.

Outside, the streets had yet to awaken from their overnight quiet. Johnny had already been to the livery and retrieved their horses. Nixon and Prentice were prepared, as well.

"Let's get goin'." Nixon pushed back his chair and got to his feet. "I expect you want to see where this Pinkerton feller got murdered."

She did.

Before long, they left the town behind, following the tracks backward in a southeasterly direction.

In a couple hours, they reached a particular area of channeled scablands. Boulders emerged out of the earth in erratic formations, and it was behind one of these that the deputies had found David Marche's body.

January took a while, noting the distance of the outcropping from the railroad tracks. The blood pooled behind the rocks, but where none had left a trail from the train.

She frowned. "How fast was the train going when it came through here?"

Prentice shrugged. "Dunno, exactly. A pretty good clip, seeing as how it's flat ground and straight."

"Then how did they get off. Did you find any spot where they might have chanced jumping?" She was thinking of Hattie. Yes, the girl was deceptively tough, but she was no Oriental acrobat.

"First off, we looked both sides of the tracks. Examined a mile both ways. Didn't find anything. So when we got back to town, we checked with a half-dozen folks who came in on that train. They all agreed. The train stopped for a couple minutes along here. Just long enough for the stoker to walk on ahead and clear about a foot of sand off the tracks. They all figured the wind done it. Blows pretty hard around here sometimes. Then they hurried so's to make up time and keep to the schedule. So then we came back out and found him."

"But not the girl," Nixon added unnecessarily.

She sighed. "Well. That explains a couple things, doesn't it."

"Means they didn't kill Marche until the train was gone, don't it, January?"

Johnny, she was happy to see, caught on fast. And he was back to calling her by her first name.

"I'm afraid so. Which is probably why nobody heard the shot. Or shots?" She looked a question at Nixon.

"One bullet to the back of his head. He was on his knees at the time."

"Execution style." Her mouth drew into a straight line. "And I expect it means Hattie was right there to see it happen." She took a breath, aware of her stitches pulling, and pain arcing along her nerves. "Dammit," she burst out, and didn't apologize for her language.

Though over the next hour they searched for sign in

every direction, whoever the killer, or killers, were, they had been meticulous in covering their tracks.

Disgruntled, the trio headed back toward town. January, though constantly watchful, pondered hard on Hattie's disappearance. They hadn't found Hattie's body, which gave cause for hope. And though it made her heart pound and her stomach twist into knots, one overwhelming question beat at her. If Hattie was still alive, where had they taken her? An answer to this question seemed impossible to guess. To start with—but then she did. Take a guess, that is.

Of course. Bethany and Joseph—and probably this Headmaster Bitters—needed Hattie as a bargaining chip. Threats against her would work to force January into relinquishing the inheritance, no matter what the will said. There were sure to be ways around the stated requirements. If Hattie—and Jem—were held under threat, they figured January would have no choice but to give into their demands.

And they were right. Except she didn't plan on giving them the chance to demand anything.

As to the question of where they'd taken her young relative, the conclusion that struck January seemed obvious.

She pulled the black mare, the one Jem said was his favorite of the three mounts January generally kept ready for the Flowers' use in town, to a halt. "I've got an idea where they've taken her."

Her exclamation startled the men.

"What?" Johnny asked. He pulled a big roan up beside her. "Where?"

Nixon and Prentice looked back at them. "What's the fuss?" Nixon wanted to know.

"I've got an idea where they may have taken Miss Harriet Flowers."

Nixon pushed back his hat and wiped at his forehead. "Yeah? Where's that?"

They didn't like the answer she gave them.

# CHAPTER 11

ON THE OUTSKIRTS OF TOWN, ELI STEERED JEM AND THE outlaw toward the back of the jail, where it backed onto the woods. They met no one on the way. Once, a young girl came out of a ramshackle house and stared after them, but it struck Eli that she squinted, as if her eyes were too weak to make out who they were.

He waved. She didn't wave back.

A relief, as an idea had taken form.

They stopped before reaching the edge of the trees, and Eli dismounted. "Stay here and guard him, Jem. I want to discuss a thought with Marshal Southbrook before we take him inside."

Jem sent the outlaw a sideways glare. "What if he tries to run. Can I shoot him?"

Eli chuckled. "What do you say to putting that noose back over his head. If he tries anything, you've got my permission to yank him right off the back of his horse. Go ahead and drag him around a bit if you want."

"Hey," the outlaw began, but Eli told him to shut up, and Jem seemed a bit disgruntled.

"I'd just as soon shoot him," the boy insisted.

Shooting someone, as Eli knew from experience, changed a person forever. Especially the first person put down under your own gun. His first shooting had turned real messy. A disaster, in fact. He had never forgotten it and probably never would. It wasn't something he wished for Jem at this young age. Or any age, for that matter. "Last resort," he said.

Slipping around the side of the log building, he scanned the street and waited for a rider to go past before entering the sheriff's office. He found Southbrook seated at his desk with the parts of his Colt strewn across the desktop. The smell of gun oil hung in the air, pungent and fresh.

Southbrook jerked his head up as the door opened only far enough for Eli to slip inside. "Good. You're back. I was starting to get worried. The Flowers boy all right?"

"He is," Eli said. "But he just about wasn't." Soft-voiced, he went on to report what had happened.

When Eli finished, the marshal stared at him. "That gang works fast; I'll say that for them. What do you want to do?"

Eli spared a moment to wonder why the marshal was asking him. After all, wasn't Adam Southbrook the closest thing to law they had in The Falls, even if technically he had no authority beyond the town limits?

So he asked a question of his own. "Has anybody asked about or seen your prisoners?"

Southbrook shook his head. "Not a soul. Weren't many out and about yet this morning when you brought them in. Well, Squirt and Sam at the livery, but as far as I know, that's all."

"Good. I suppose Squirt still owns the old building we used to hold prisoners back when Nelson Peel tried to take over the town. Let's get together with him and see if he's game to conceal these for a while."

The marshal's eyes bugged a little. "What for?"

With a patience he didn't feel, Eli said, "To keep the fact we've caught them in the act of attempted murder from getting about. If the people who hired them learn they're here, there's apt to be bloodshed. Innocent bystanders could be caught in-between."

Southbrook finished putting his cleaned Colt together, fitting the barrel into place. He nodded, got up, and belted on the gun. "I'll meander over to the livery, have a talk with Squirt." He grinned. "You know as well as I do he likes a little excitement in his life. Sam, too, though you'd never think it to look at him."

Relief loosened some of Eli's tension. "We'll have to move those men's horses out of Squirt's corral. Maybe take them out to Mrs. Billings's place. Or mine. It's closer."

"I'll tell Squirt," Southbrook said. "Keeping his livery safe is likely to have him cooperating real quick."

Eli went out to check on Jem and his prisoner. He found the boy with a firm hand on the rope around the outlaw's neck. As for the outlaw, his face was red, just short of choking.

"You might want to give him a little slack," he said. "Everything all right, otherwise?"

"Fine and dandy," Jem said. "Except I'm hungry."

Eli laughed.

As it turned out, Squirt not only approved the use of his sturdy old makeshift jail, which consisted of a deep foundation once intended to support a house. The house never got built, but the dug basement acquired a roof and became a fortress, perfect for holding outlaws prisoner as long as they weren't too tall. Sam agreed to stand guard over the place.

Squirt, always a handy fellow to have around, even had a suggestion on how to keep Jem safe. "Send him out to Bo Cobb's place. He can take over Johnson's chores while Johnson is helping Mrs. Billings."

"I don't think Jem has worked with cattle before," Eli said doubtfully. "Have you?"

Jem shook his head. "Just the horses."

"And he's good with them." As Eli well knew as Jem had spent some time with him.

The hostler just shrugged. "He can learn, can't he? Cobb took Johnson in at about that age and turned him into a fine man."

Jem protested, so informed, protested the idea. "I can handle myself. I want to help January. And Hattie. She's *my* little sister and *my* responsibility. Mr. Flower told me so, though I already knew it. Besides, I want to take care of her." He frowned. "When she'll let me."

Eli took of notice the fact Jem never called Joseph Flowers Senior "dad," or even the more formal "father." Maybe because it had been a closely held secret. One only publicly revealed when January took the young-sters in care.

"Ordinarily, I'd agree. But look what we've got here, Jem. Four men came after a girl just because she knows more than she ought. We don't know how many thugs Joe has got working for him. One came after you with the intended purpose of seeing you and me dead. January is on her way to collect Hattie. You know you wouldn't have been able to withdraw her from school."

"Hattie," Jem said, "could've got herself away from school. You know she could. All I'd have had to do is bring her a horse."

Eli sighed. "I do know." The little female imp was probably better at taking care of herself than her brother.

It was a thought belied when not fifteen minutes later, Eldridge from the telegraph office sent a boy to the livery with an important yellow flimsy clutched in his hand. Seeing him coming, Eli and Jem removed themselves from sight.

"You're supposed take this telegram out to Mr. Eli Pasco." Eli heard the boy tell Squirt. "Right away, quick as you can."

Right then, Eli figured more trouble was on its way. Beside him, Jem drew in a breath.

"I am?" Squirt repeated. "To Pasco? Why me? Who's it from?"

The delivery boy sassed. "I dunno. That's for him to find out, ain't it?"

Squirt snatched the flimsy from the boy. "All right. You scoot. I'll take care of this."

Telegram in hand, Eli had it open by the time the boy, paid a couple pennies for his service, reached the door.

Squirt watched him, concern shadowing his eyes. "What's it say? If I may be so bold as to ask."

Eli didn't think of telling him no. Raising his eyes, he stood silent for a full minute, drawing a worried look from Jem. Finally, he answered. "It's from January. It says..." His hesitation and the way his glance slid away from Jem gave warning. "...it says we were too late. Hattie has disappeared from the train. The Pinkerton

Delbert Avery hired to escort her has been murdered. January and Johnny are in Cheney, closest place to where the body was found. She says they've been trying to find her. January says she thinks they've left the area. She has an idea where to look and they're heading back this way now."

All expression fled from Jem's face, along with all color. It left him curiously white and blank. He didn't speak.

"What do you figure?" Squirt asked, then waved his hand as if to negate the question.

But Eli had an answer. "I figure to meet up with January and Johnson. Whatever has happened, whatever she plans to do, I don't intend to let her take on a shooting match with any desperados Joe and Bethany have hired."

Squirt looked eager. "Need a hand?"

Eli forced a grin. "Stand by."

Far off, they all heard the afternoon freight coming. Eli glanced at Jem. "Stay here. I'm going to catch the train and go meet up with January. We'll find Hattie. Try not to worry."

Jem's jaw set. "I'm going with you."

Eli started to shake his head, then, seeing the boy's determined expression, he changed his mind. Better, maybe, for him to keep an eye on the kid, he figured. A close eye. "All right. Let's go."

He hoped he was doing the right thing.

# CHAPTER 12

BY THE TIME THEY ALL GOT BACK TO CHENEY, NIXON AND Prentice had begun wrangling over something or another, their faces turning red and their arms waving. Whatever it was, the argument threatened to continue for a while. Disgusted, January sent Johnny off to pay their livery bill, while she counted out money for the hotel. After half an hour, they returned to the sheriff's office to find the pair of deputies still at it.

Taking care not to get in the way of a flailing arm, she stepped between them. "Enough. The train will be here any minute. What is going on with you two?"

They glared at each other, but finally, Nixon spoke up. The argument concerned which of the deputies should accompany January and Johnny to where she suspected Hattie might have been taken. One or the other of them should stay in Cheney to keep an eye on things. Or so Nixon insisted.

"Flip a coin," she advised. "Or both of you stay. But make up your mind." She took a step toward the depot. "Come on, Johnny. We're not missing the train."

"We don't even know how many attacked the Pinkerton man." Nixon pressed his point that someone had to go, and someone had to stay. He turned and pointed at her. "Just like you, Deputy Billings, don't know for sure where they went with that girl. If anywhere. They might still be around town and laying low."

January couldn't deny that, but it didn't stop a growing impatience from putting a snap in her voice. "Then neither of you has to come with us. Johnson and I can take care of the situation by ourselves. I have another man I depend on in matters like this. We can handle it." She didn't find it necessary to mention the fact neither Johnny nor Eli were actual deputies.

But Nixon insisted one of them had to follow through since the Pinkerton's death had taken place in their area. Moreover, since he had more time on the job than Prentice, Nixon said he should be the one to decide. "And I'm the one stayin' to home."

Prentice scoffed, but quietly and not hard enough to change Nixon's mind.

Finally, after a delay that went on much too long, January got Johnny, Prentice, and their horses on the next train headed east. There was a siding she knew of a few miles out of Spokane. Using her official capacity, she'd demand the train stop there long enough to let them off. From there, only a short ride would get them to their destination.

Without Nixon to do the talking for the both of them, the laconic Prentice spoke only when spoken to. His silence made for a quiet train ride.

The sun was just going down when the men lowered

the ramp for the horses and January's little posse departed the train.

Concerned at the two normally argumentative sheriff's offices working together—there'd been that dust-up between moving the county seat several years back—and naturally curious about the unplanned stop, the conductor demanded to know what the fuss was about.

Prentice answered him. "Got a missing girl. We been searching high and low for her."

The conductor's eyes bugged. "You think she might've run off to join the—" He left the last part unsaid, but from the way the menfolk's glances avoided January's, it seemed obvious he knew all about the nearby border settlement.

She took a guess at what he had in mind, but Prentice shook his head. "No. Gal has been taken hostage. We're gonna nail their hides to the table and serve 'em up raw."

"Hostage! What—"

But no more time remained. The ramp back in place, wheels clattering on the rails, the train moved on down the line, the conductor swinging aboard at the last second.

Johnny had an opinion too. "I ain't saying you're wrong, January. I don't think you are. But why would they take Hattie to a place like this. They must know Wren has told you where this all started."

She had been worrying over this same thing and had an argument. "Exactly for that reason. They may believe we wouldn't think of them using the place twice.

"Plus," she added, "I doubt either Bitters or Bethany Flowers is exactly familiar with criminal hangouts. Now they know about this one, they'll be reluctant to give it up. It's unlikely any passing acquaintance would catch sight of them at a disreputable joint like this one." She snorted. "Nor believe their eyes if they did."

Prentice reasoned through the explanation. He nodded. "Ain't fancy, for sure." His eyes flicked away from hers. "So I hear."

They picked their way through the half-dark toward the little settlement. Once, when January started to the right at a fork in the road, Prentice sort of cleared his throat and mumbled something about thinking they should go left.

Hiding her grin, January complied. Johnny, riding beside her, winked. "Bet he's been here before."

She figured so too.

A half-hour later, when lights from several buildings up ahead showed they were near their destination, they pulled their horses to a stop while January studied the place. She pointed. At her direction, Prentice led them off into the trees, a mixture of cottonwoods and spindly pines, that lined the riverbank behind the scattering of roughly-sided structures. Signs, such as grass chewed down to the roots by bored horses, along with a couple randomly placed hitch racks, suggested they weren't the first to use the area for secretive purposes. They dismounted, claimed one of the hitch racks for their horses, and went forward on foot.

January removed her sling, having resumed it during the ride, and tried to ignore the burn as her freed arm rubbed against the bandage covering her wound.

As they got closer, she glimpsed motion off to the right, and stopped. The way the men, there were two of them, were moving through the dark, she believed their intent was to keep their identities unknown.

"Does this joint have a name?" She spoke softly to Prentice.

His reply barely reached her ears. "Vera something or another. So I hear."

He added the qualification again, but for some reason, it annoyed her this time. "I know you've been here before, Deputy Prentice. No need to pretend. I'm grateful you have some experience with the layout of the place."

But something else occurred to her. "I think there are two of these...ah...businesses here. Are you familiar with the other one, as well?"

He grunted.

January thought it indicated yes. "I don't judge," she said, but if she were being truthful, she did. How could she not? Johnny showed no signs he knew anything about the place. And since he wasn't all that good in concealing his facial reactions, she was glad. For his young wife Evie's sake, if nothing else. Disease ran rampant in most houses like this one. The brothel in The Falls had proved something of an exception.

Her thoughts suddenly fixed on Wren.

"Is this the most likely of the two places for a meeting?" she asked Prentice.

He nodded. "Cleaner. Prettier women." He seemed to realize whether the women were pretty or not didn't matter in this case. "The old sow who runs the place has a private room. When I worked this end of the county, we had occasion to see inside."

She'd had no idea he'd worked this end of the county before. He could've hidden his other knowledge of the place from her by bringing up the work aspect. Not that it mattered, but that he hadn't seemed to prove his honesty.

"Move up. Let's go see what we can see." She led off again, her footsteps quiet. Johnny stuck close to her. Prentice shuffled off to the side. He headed right toward the back door, until January grabbed him by the arm and stopped him.

"What? Ain't we going in?"

"That's my intention. But it's wise, Deputy, to see what is going to be behind you first. There's a woodshed over there. I'm going to see if wood is all that's in there. Johnny, you go around to the right and check out the front. Deputy, you do the same on the left. We'll meet back here when you're done. As long as it's clear, we'll go inside then."

Johnny, used to taking orders from her, simply nodded. In a moment, he'd melded into the night.

Prentice looked like he thought he should be the one giving orders, but only for a moment. Then he nodded as well and strode away, his steps surprisingly quiet.

A tinkling piano and laughter, loud and decidedly unmelodious, burst out as the door suddenly opened and a man peered out. January, who'd started to move toward the shed, froze where she stood.

The man looked back over his shoulder. "All clear," he yelled to someone inside. "You're seein' shadows." The door closed again.

Only slightly disturbed by the few words he'd spoken—and who they were meant for—January hastened to the shed. The door, some wider than an ordinary door, ran on a track, allowing easier access when packing armloads of wood into the house. There was no lock, although it was latched with a heavy hook.

She had a moment to think anyone caught inside would be there to stay until someone let them out. Shrugging, she forced the hook upward and slid the door open.

The scent of newly-cut stove wood was the first thing she noticed. Then she stumbled over the chopping block in the dark and pain arced through her knee.

She gasped. "Ouch. *Hijo de Perra!*" She couldn't help herself. It was the same knee Bethany Flowers had shot with an arrow.

As the pain ebbed, she realized another smell overlaid the fresh scent and she was holding her breath to avoid it. This one was less pleasant, old, musty, and rotten. No wonder the chopping block was right in front of the door. Who would want to work in such a fetid atmosphere?

Wishing for one of those newfangled electric hand torches, she stepped back and pushed the door a little wider. More light helped see the way. Enough to catch sight of a small person sitting hunched against the outer wall. At least the person didn't seem to be the source of the smell. The repellant odor came from the other side of the building, where the only thing January saw to account for it was an abandoned canvas tarp in the far corner. As if, she thought, a dead body had been stored there at some time in the past. Her heart lurched. Was this brothel a regular stop on the outlaw trail?

At least the hunched over person was alive and moving.

And moaning, in a young girl voice. A voice January knew.

Forgetting her knee, she rushed forward, even as the door began closing. That wouldn't do. She didn't want caught in here. A thin piece of wood jammed under the door so it couldn't fully close solved the problem.

She continued over to the girl. "Hattie?" She knelt on her good knee, reaching out to touch the girl's face. "Hattie, it's me, January. Wake up, now. You need to wake up."

There wasn't enough light for January to see what had so pained Hattie as to make her moan. The girl had been sick, as well, adding to the smell. She'd have to get her outside where there was enough light to judge. Worry clutched at her. Why didn't the girl answer? As soon as she tried to put her good arm under Hattie's in order to lift her, she discovered ropes bound the girl's hands behind her. Apparently her captors had simply tossed her inside the shed to fall where she may.

"Hattie, come on, honey. You've got to wake up." For the first time, it struck January that Hattie had been drugged. Drugged thoroughly, because when she felt for a pulse, it seemed very slow and weak.

She jiggled the girl and pulled her around. A ranch woman always carried a jackknife, a sharp one, handy to cut twine or whatever else needed doing. This time it sliced through the rope, dropping Hattie's hands forward. Hattie moaned again, but this time, January thought she caught a gleam as the girl's eyes flickered. Her lips moved.

"January?"

January's breath gushed out. "Yes. It's me. I've got you. Can you move?"

"Yes," Hattie said. But she couldn't. All she could do, for the moment was cry, silently though sobs racked her whole body. But not for long. No more than a minute passed before she managed to stretch her cramped limbs and, with January's help, struggled to her feet.

The shed door had slid mostly closed, but not locked, thanks to the shim January had shoved under it. An excellent bit of foresight on her part, as it turned out, although they were surrounded in inky darkness.

"Be careful." January spoke very low. She was leading Hattie, steering her toward the entrance. "There's a chopping block in front of the door." They shuffled forward.

She had her hand on the leather pull ready to yank the door open when she heard people speaking from the house porch. A man, probably the same one from before, called out, "You see? It's good. The door is shut. She ain't goin' anywheres. Still out, most probably."

"She had better be," a woman said. "I have no desire to deal with the little freak. Come inside. Harold will pay your fee. Just get rid of her where nobody will ever find her."

"Consider it done."

Beside her, Hattie stiffened.

But then, so did January. She knew the woman's voice. Carefully modulated when out in public, but all too ready to become harsh, like right now. It gave her a proper chill.

Hattie stood up close to January, and almost as tall. "It's Bethany."

"Yes. How many men does she have here?"

"I don't know." Hattie's voice faded, making it easy to hear the door to the house close.

Presumably, the two had gone back inside. Time to move. January started forward, promptly striking against the chopping block yet again. This time, she didn't even try to muffle the response.

Hattie giggled. Maybe it was wrong of her, but January felt encouraged. Her young relative might've been held hostage, drugged, and witnessed a murder, but her spunk remained.

They stepped out into the night. January spun at a movement on her right, hand going to the .38 on her hip.

"It's all right." The whisper came to her; a man's shadow loomed. "It's me." Over it all, Hattie had begun panting in an odd kind of way.

"Johnny?"

"Well, yeah. Who else was you expecting?" He sounded put out.

"Have you seen Deputy Prentice? Let's get out of here. Hattie is done in and only half-conscious. She's been drugged; God only knows with what."

"We aren't going in to get these guys?" Johnny sounded astounded.

Prentice loomed out of the dark. "Too late. The woman and a tall, skinny man just left together. Their driver was whipping the horse like they wanted to get away fast." It wasn't hard to tell Prentice disapproved.

"What about the fellers they have working for them?" Johnny asked. "There's one—"

"I heard him. We can wait until he comes for the girl, but if there's two or three of them instead of just the one, it could get chancy, working in the dark like this." Prentice pointed out the obvious problems, and January added to them.

"I'm working at half-speed," she said. "And Hattie is bad-off. She needs a doctor." She had another reason she didn't mention. Johnny, never lacking nerve, had a wife depending on him. January had almost gotten him killed once before. She wasn't going to put him in a situation like that again. Not if she could help it.

If she knew him—which she did—he was game to the end and he'd argue. But not if she used Hattie for an excuse. Not that it wasn't already a primary consideration.

In fact, Hattie was leaning right up against her now, trembling uncontrollably. Some kind of reaction to the drug, January suspected. God only knows what else they'd done to her.

She longed to dash into the house and round everyone in there up and haul them off to jail. Including the doves and the woman who'd kept Wren in order to use her. She wanted to force them to tell her what had happened to Wren's mother and admit their crimes. If the forcing opened up a blood vessel or two, she'd count it a win. They deserved to bleed.

Bethany's hired thugs had earned special punishment for what they intended to do to Hattie and to Jem. They'd already murdered two people that she knew of, which made Bethany just as guilty as the man with the gun. Or the one with the fists.

Like it or not—and she didn't—Bethany and the headmaster had gotten away. For now. But their time was coming. Neither the kids nor January would be safe until Bethany and Joseph III were either dead or incarcerated for life.

January knew which she'd prefer. The only sure way.

# CHAPTER 13

JANUARY AND HER POSSE MET UP WITH ELI AND JEM, WHO were heading at speed toward them, not far from the railroad siding.

Neither party recognized the other until they were almost face-to-face, what with the half moon slipping behind a cloud at just the wrong time. The darkness no doubt accounted for the number of guns drawn and ready for when the moon came out again.

January said, "Eli," at the exact same time Eli said, "January." So their identities were established.

Then they both said, "What..."

Jem spoke over them both. "Have you got Hattie?"

Johnny, who had Hattie bundled on the saddle in front of him, answered. "Yes. Right here. She's safe. She's been knocked around, tied up, and drugged, so she ain't feeling exactly cricket, but we've got her."

A slight girl, Hattie, being mostly covered with John-ny's coat, was practically invisible in the dark. Her face gone ghost-pale, she moved a hand to wave.

At Johnny's first word, Jem swung from Badger's

back and strode toward them. Reaching their side, he peered up into his sister's face. Her eyes opened briefly. They touched hands.

"I'll take her," Jem said, and Hattie reached her arms toward him.

Seeing them together did January's heart good. Especially as the relief flooding through her veins right now made her go weak to the point of feeling boneless. Both the kids were safe. Now to keep them that way. She didn't imagine Bethany would give up easily. Oh no. Not her. She wanted the Flowers money too much to quit now. Not when she'd already resorted to murder.

Deputy Prentice cast a stink-eye on Eli, noting the Broomhandle Mauser strapped across his chest with a jaundiced eye. "Who's this?" The question seemed aimed at January. Or maybe Johnny.

Eli answered for himself. "I'm Eli Pasco. And you are?"

"Eli Pasco, eh?" Prentice repeated slowly. "I've heard of you. You're that bounty hunter who got famous for bringing in the murderer, Wade Lauten. I'm Deputy Harry Prentice. I work out of the Cheney office and come along with Mrs. Billings to see she didn't get in more trouble than she could handle."

The half-moon broke from the cloud cover to show the pair of them staring at each other.

"And did she?" Eli said.

Prentice hesitated. "Did she what?"

"Get in more trouble than she could handle."

"No."

"Didn't figure so."

January was sure she saw his lips quirk in a grin before a cloud turned the night sky dark again.

They went on to Spokane together, an uneasy peace. Once there, all of them weary enough to find so simple a matter as stabling the horses a task best left to the livery's hostlers, they headed for the Flowers apartment above the office building. The men walked in a tight group around Hattie and January. They were taking no chances.

Inside the Flowers Building, they found one man still at work, a bit of a surprise. A fairly recent tenant, or so January understood. She, on the rare occasions she'd passed him on the stairs—he occupied an office on the second floor, the one right under the apartment as it happened—built a picture of him in her mind. Midthirties, she believed, looked prosperous, had a sign painted on his window glass announcing his business as an investment broker, whatever that was. Unfortunately for him, his closely set eyes always seemed to deliberately avoid hers. A short beard only partially concealed a weak mouth. His twitchy fingers and a pasty complexion made her leery of him.

If she'd been doing the vetting of potential renters, his looks alone might have made him undesirable. And then probably induced a feeling of guilt because she knew nothing bad about him. On the other hand, she didn't know anything good, either.

Johnny led the way up the stairs, Hattie and Jem close behind, then Prentice, which left Eli and January bringing up the rear.

Peering out from his office as they trooped up to the second-floor landing, the tenant focused on Johnny, alarm showing on his face. "What's this?" he snapped out. "This building is closed."

The gaze he settled first on Hattie, then on Jem,

struck January as hard, cold, and... something else. It came to her. He looked surprised. His expression changed as belatedly, he recognized her behind the others.

"Sorry. Please do excuse me, Mrs. Billings. I didn't recognize you at first. You look..." He must have rethought what he'd meant to say, and changed it to: "I thought someone had broken in, since it is after hours. I've been hearing noises."

"Probably the janitor." She took another step.

"Yes, well, I see the youngsters are out of school," he said, his gaze resting on Hattie. "Is anything wrong? Will you all be staying long?"

Just behind her, January heard Eli's intake of breath. A warning. "Do you have a problem with that?"

"No, no. Of course not. I just wondered. In case I need to switch some of my appointments around."

She frowned. "I can't imagine why you would. There are people coming and going from this building during every work day. I'm sure neither my presence, nor that of my family, will make any difference to you." The hint was strong that it had better not.

"No. No reason to disturb me. I—"

His name finally came to January and she broke in. "Excuse us, Mr. Granger, if I say *I'm* surprised to find you here so late. According to your lease, tenants are required to vacate the building at six o'clock. Assuming this is a work emergency and not habitual, we don't want to keep you any longer."

Waving the others on, she felt his eyes boring into her back until they reaching the landing into the apartment.

Hattie slanted a look behind her and whispered, "I don't like that man," as January tapped on the door.

"Has he said anything to you? Anything he shouldn't have?"

"Not exactly. But he always stares at me. And he always tries to get close to me. Too close."

Anger flashing through her, January kept her face expressionless and nodded. "We won't renew his lease. I don't like him either."

About to open the door, January hesitated. Eli had told her of his afternoon visit to *Vera's House of Women*. Wren was in the apartment—or she'd better be—and bad news awaited the girl. January didn't want to scare her beforehand. Telling of her mother's death would be bad enough.

Fingers clumsy as she unlocked the door, January was aware of renewed pain even though she'd bound her arm to her side again. Inside, she heard sounds of the bolt being drawn back, but it was still on the chain when Wren's frightened face appeared in the crack. Her eyes got big when she saw so many people.

"You're back. I was afraid—" Wren stopped. She seemed to be searching for another face. One she didn't find.

"Let us in, please," January said when the girl stood frozen.

The door closed and they heard the chain slide out of the track. "Where's my mother?" Wren said as soon as she flung it open.

"Let us get inside." January moved past the girl. "There's things I don't want to go beyond this room."

Wren's blue eyes got even bigger, if such a thing were possible. "The man downstairs?" she whispered. "I seen him through that little hole in the door. He'd tried the knob and trying to look through the keyhole. I hung a coat on the knob."

"Well done, Wren. Very smart." January shot a quick look at Eli and knew he'd heard. She turned back to the others. "Come in, everyone."

At her invitation, they crowded through the foyer leaving Jem to close and lock the door behind them. She didn't miss the open wonder Deputy Prentice's face revealed as he took in the apartment's size and elegance.

He must've been expecting rooming house quality from her after all, January thought, even though he'd surely heard how she'd come by all this grandeur. Lord knows it had filled the newspapers last fall and during the trials of her cousins.

"Find a seat," she invited, but to Wren, "Come with me. I need to...to...tell you..."

"About ma," Wren said. She'd gone stiff.

"Yes."

"I'll come with you." Eli touched Wren's shoulder, pointing the way to the kitchen.

A single light bulb burned over the sink. By its light, January could see the room was spotless. Whatever else Wren had been taught, apparently the need to leave no trace of her presence must've been one of them.

"Did you eat?" she asked the girl.

Shyly, Wren nodded. "You said I should." She dropped onto a chair at the big table in the center of the room. Her shoulders slumped. "Ma?"

January clenched the fingers of her good hand, and Eli set his jaw.

"She's dead, ain't she?" Wren's gulp sounded audibly.

The sound of voices came from the front room where Johnny was telling them about his and January's search for Hattie and the kidnappers. From what January could hear, Hattie barely spoke.

Once Prentice's baritone rose over hers, asking a question, but it was Johnny who answered.

"Ain't she?" Wren asked again.

"Yes," Eli said. He closed the door to the kitchen. "I'm sorry, Wren. She died from the beating. I had an undertaker collect her for burial. I'll take you to the cemetery and show you her grave one of these days. But not yet. Not until this is all over."

Tears welled in Wren's eyes, although she didn't sob aloud. Her voice was thick when she said, "Does this mean I have to stay cooped up in here? Or do I have to go back there. To Old Mrs. Gerson?"

January answered before Eli got his mouth open. "Certainly not there. And we won't be staying here. This apartment isn't safe."

"Is any place?" For a twelve-year-old, Wren sounded world-weary and wise.

"Maybe not," she said, "but there are locations where we can defend ourselves better. You're not the only one they're after, you see."

"I know. They wanta kill you. And him." She pointed at Eli.

"Yes. And Jem and Hattie."

"Will we go to your house?" Wren looked hopeful.

"That's what I was thinking," she said.

Eli cocked his head. "Or my ranch. They won't be expecting that. Not after taking Gus's brother out."

"Wherever we go, it won't take them long to find us,"

January said. "But my place has a few unexpected surprises for unwanted visitors."

"Like them bricks above the door?" Wren asked. "Made me laugh." She wasn't laughing now, though. The tears were drying in her eyes. "I like your house. It smelled good."

January forced a smile at the girl. "I like my house too. And there are some better surprises than the bricks."

Surprises more likely to be lethal, for one. She'd never told Eli about some of the things that had happened at the bridge, back when she was not only fighting to help Shay, but to keep herself alive. About the series of booby traps she'd rigged for their protection. Most of the outside traps were still in place. The others had burned when some very bad men set fire to the barn with her inside.

Eli studied her for a moment, then smiled. "Your place," he agreed.

Which meant the next problem to solve was getting there safely.

"Without," as Wren said, "tipping off that sneaky old fart below us."

And that opened up a whole new approach to a problem.

\* \* \*

Sometimes lately, January wondered if her skill at building things was a combination inherited not only from her master carpenter father, but her maternal grandfather. Joseph Flowers had had a penchant for things like cavities hidden within the bricks of his fireplace, for one, and a secret stairway to the outside in this three-story structure for another. Building those things to his specifications had been assigned to the builder, who, as she'd discovered, had been her father and was how her mother and father met.

She planned for them to escape the building without Granger knowing by opening the stair's entrance. She suspected him of being an informer for her cousin and his wife, and probably not a businessman at all. Eli agreed. She didn't like letting so many other people in on the secret of stairway, however. That not only meant Wren and Deputy Prentice, but even Johnny, though she trusted him with her life. Jem and Hattie had known of the hidden stairway before she learned of it and told Eli.

She preferred not to trust anyone else with the trick of opening the cleverly hidden door. Either coming or going. When closed, no one would ever guess the escape route existed.

At midnight, January awakened with a sense of the house listening. She sat up, the bed springs squeaking as her weight shifted. Hattie and Wren, who were crowded in the bed with her, didn't stir.

Hattie still hadn't talked about her ordeal, or of the murder of the Pinkerton man. After those first terrible sobs when she'd realized January had come to get her, she'd been quiet. Unnaturally so. January didn't think she'd told Jem everything, either. The shock, and maybe the drugs, had taken a serious toll on the girl.

Another thing Bethany needed to pay for, in January's eyes. Rage filled her anew. But first she wanted to get them all away from the city and back on familiar ground. It was too easy for them to be trapped here. She preferred space around her.

As for Wren, January doubted she'd slept more than a few hours at a time since she left the brothel. Until now. Even so, she'd borne up well to the news of her mother's murder. Probably, because she'd expected nothing different for one thing, and for another, Madeline hadn't been the most loving of mothers. The kid had had a rough start. January knew all about rough starts.

She found Eli awake when she dressed and got out to the kitchen. He'd been sitting in the dark, keeping watch.

"We going now?" he asked.

"Yes." She yawned. "I didn't expect to find you up."

"Didn't you?"

Well, yes. She sort of had. "Have you heard him sneaking around?"

She meant Granger. People weren't allowed to make their offices into living quarters, so he shouldn't have been in the building. A clause in the lease stated so. His presence would've put up warning signs even if she hadn't already suspected him, or if Wren hadn't said anything.

"Once or twice, earlier. But I haven't heard or seen him for a while. But I know he hasn't left."

The kitchen window overlooked the street. If the man had left, Eli would've known. She sighed. "We have to go now."

"We can't go out the front, so it'll mean revealing the way out to everyone here."

"I know."

There was an iron fire escape attached to the side of

the building for the use of the tenants—or their clients, should the need evolve. Obvious, for anyone who didn't know about the other. The special one that came in through the back, disguised by the coal shed. The staircase let them out into an alley overshadowed by bushes in need of pruning—which they weren't going to get—and a few trees.

"I wish I could make everyone wear blindfolds," she said.

"Open the door beforehand. We'll leave it dark in here. Prentice and Wren wouldn't be able to find it on their own if they came looking later. It's doubtful they'll ever be back, you know." He tried to reassure her, but she didn't know if she agreed.

"I'll get the girls up" she said, tacit agreement.

"And I'll fetch the men." Eli rose, and ten minutes later, efficient and more silent than mice in a wall, they were ready to leave.

Without any unwelcome interruptions, which came a little to her surprise,.

January hoped Granger had spent a sleepless night. And that he'd been as oblivious as she believed. Bound to silence, they made their way down the alley, joining the street at the corner. Then on to the livery where they collected their horses from sleepy hostlers who made short work of saddling up. They didn't speak until they were safely beyond the city limits.

Along about daybreak, with the sun just hitting the hill overlooking the ranch, they reached the ranch at the bridge by coming in the back way instead of through The Falls. All seemed peaceful, birds woke up singing a sleepy song. The air was still, smelling of dew-dampened new growth. The day promised fair.

January had the others wait while she and Eli rode in alone, making a circle around the yard and watching for any untoward visitors. The place proved deserted, but, they found, there'd been a visitor. Someone, January knew, who Bethany Flowers—or her attorneys—had paid handsomely. Or perhaps only promised to pay.

Disgusted at the damage to her new door, January ripped an envelope from a nail hammered into it and stood staring at the hole. She made a sound remarkably like Pen when the dog spotted a coyote.

Eli eyed her and the paper crushed in her hand. "You going to open that, or rip it to shreds?"

"I know what I'd like to do with it." Extracting a single sheet of paper, she waved the others, who were watching closely and still waiting to approach, to ride on in.

Johnny reached them first. He rubbed sleep from his eyes and, anxious to get back to his wife, said, "What's it say?"

January read the message aloud, her lip curled. "It says, *Give this up and sign the paperwork over to Joseph. Be in W. P. Ingerson's office tomorrow afternoon at three p.m. Otherwise, prepare to die. You and those brats.*"

She huffed out an explosive gust of air. "What a poisonous woman." The note was unsigned, not that it mattered. She knew who'd written it. Another thought occurred. Did Bethany actually believe she could make a threat like this without repercussions? The woman was insane.

Johnny scoffed. "Big talk."

She glanced at Eli and found him grinning. She scowled. "What's so funny?"

He shrugged. "Sounds like Bethany thinks she's a Roman empress, that's all. Prepare to die!"

"More than likely, she's just deranged. Doesn't matter. Either way, I'm the gladiator who is going to take her down. Once and for all." January's words were fierce as any of those old Romans.

# CHAPTER 14

ELI AND JOHNNY MADE ANOTHER SEARCH OF THE SHED, the chicken coop, and even rode out to the copse of trees where the animals liked to take shelter beneath the branches. Meanwhile, January, with the girls trotting behind her, strode through the house with her .38 in hand. She felt a little foolish when nothing turned up to disturb the silence.

Eli stood in the doorway to tell her what he and Johnny had found. Like the girls, exactly nothing.

"Nothing inside and nothing outside. Apparently, the lock held and discouraged them from breaking in. Anyway, we'll be all right." January squinted at Eli, the early morning light showing her a man tired to the bone. She had a suspicion the same exhaustion showed on herself. She knew it dragged at her body and also her mind. "Whoever nailed the note to my door is long gone." She knew Eli and Johnny both were anxious to get home.

Eli scrubbed his hands over his face and yawned, saying he had one last stop to make in town. "I still have to check in with Marshal Southbrook and Squirt, and make sure Gus and those other two men are still penned up." He rolled his shoulders as if to relieve the strain.

Meeting his dark eyes, she could see the weariness there. He'd been on the move with no real rest for the last three days. On the other hand, so had she. And she had a bullet hole besides.

A sudden impulse to lean, just for an instant, into his strength swept every other thought away. And maybe she even made a move to do so. From the quickening of his regard as he gazed at her, she believed he sensed her desire. A faint smile touched his lips.

Heat rose in her cheeks and from the tingle, she knew the scar had begun glowing. It struck her to wonder if he would've recognized the feeling if just maybe he hadn't felt the same himself.

"Walk me out," Eli said and, leaving the young ones to help Johnny finish the chores, she went with him outside.

The sun shone in a cloudless morning sky. Not a breath of wind stirred the trees down by the creek, allowing the rumble of tumbling water to carry clearly to the house. January saw that Johnny had already finished the milking and turned the cow into the pasture, greened up and smelling of spring.

Looking down at her, Eli leaned against his horse. "I'll be back this afternoon, and bring your dog with me. Without her to nose out trouble, you'd best keep a sharp watch. And warn the kids to do the same. Best if they don't go anywhere by themselves. Even Jem. He's had a rough time the last few days. More than you know about."

"More than you've already said?"

He nodded. "Enough, I think, to make him cautious. I hope."

She opened her mouth, questions ready to pour forth, but Eli shook his head. "Have him talk to you if he will. Meanwhile, mind what I said about keeping your eyes open."

"I will. We all will, But the note, it gives three o'clock tomorrow as some kind of deadline. We should be all right until then."

"Or the note might be a trick to make you careless."

Inwardly, she agreed. It struck her as something Bethany would do. She'd laugh her brassy head off if any of them fell for the ruse and left themselves open.

Eli mounted and reined his horse toward the road. Then he wheeled back, facing her. "I shouldn't leave. You shouldn't be alone with these kids."

Although she'd be glad if he didn't, January tilted her face up to him and forced a smile. "Go. Take care of your place. We'll be here when you get back. I promise."

He hesitated, bent down to her in one quick motion, and kissed her full on the mouth. The kiss lasted only a moment before his horse moved away and he sat up again. His eyes smoldered as he looked at her.

"See that you are." He clucked to his horse.

Fuzzled, she couldn't even remember what she'd said that related to what he'd said.

She watched him ride away until he grew small with distance. He didn't look back.

\* \* \*

IN THE HOUSE, Hattie, though far from her old self this morning, had taken charge. Bustling around the kitchen with a big white apron wrapped around her middle, she stirred up flapjacks for breakfast, and insisted on treating Wren as a guest. From Wren's expression, the girl didn't know what to make of it.

January left Hattie to work on her own in hopes putting together the meal might take some of the anxiety from the girl's face. Tired to the bone, January sank down on the chair beside Wren who looked at her with worried eyes.

"Would you like me to see to your wound?" Her eyebrows drew together. "I guess I could put a clean bandage on you if you need one."

January glanced at Hattie. She wasn't sure the girl even knew she'd been shot, and considering all else that had happened, didn't think she wanted to talk about it. "Later." She smiled at Wren. "After we eat. I'd appreciate your help with a clean bandage."

A kind of relief passed over Wren's face so that January realized she had been worried about being left adrift somewhere, with no one to turn to. A reply indicating she was needed must've been profound reassurance.

A little shudder passed over January. What had she let herself in for? Another waif to take under her wing? Was there anyone else who would take Wren in and give her a decent home?

Sitting quietly, January closed her eyes and dropped off into a doze until Hattie startled her with a cry of, "Soups on. Let's eat." Only six minutes, she found in glancing at the clock hanging on the kitchen wall, had passed since the last time she looked.

Jem had come in while she rested, and blinking away sleep, she saw the table was set and food placed handy for everyone. No soup, but bacon and eggs, and the flapjacks with plum syrup. They scrambled for chairs and piled their plates high, the first real meal any of them had had for...well, she couldn't think how long.

They were her family, January realized. A family such as she'd never known before when there'd just been her and her dad. If Eli had been there, it would've been complete.

Eli? What was she thinking? He blew hot, then he blew cold. Sometimes she thought he cared for her like a man cares for a woman. Other times? She just didn't know.

* * *

ELI'S HEAD bobbed in time with his horse's stride. Not exactly asleep; not exactly awake, he passed where January's husband had been murdered. A place that always made her go quiet. He knew she dreaded the place. He often wondered why she hadn't gone ahead and stayed in Shay Billings's old house. Redone the half-log cabin there as it had become too small with Jem and Hattie living with her. She could've built another bridge closer to town on the other side of Kindred Creek where she'd never have to pass Shay Billings's death site.

Or perhaps move to the other side of town, and all the way into his house. If he ever worked up the nerve to ask if she'd marry him. Last fall he'd thought there might be some chance of her saying yes, right up until the Flowers fortune had fallen into her lap. The fortune and Joseph Flowers Senior's young children. Not grand-children, but children. Now he didn't know what to think.

All these hazy thoughts drifted away as he entered the outskirts of The Falls and sat up straight in the saddle. T.T. Thurston's Mercantile was doing a fine business for a weekday. Main street had plenty of traffic. Wagons and horses passed folks on foot. And there were dogs. Plenty of dogs, getting in the way, and even causing his horse to shy once when a brown mutt tumbled under the gelding's feet.

The smell of coffee wafted from the café located cater-corner to Squirt's livery, and it occurred to him he was not only in need of coffee but was hungry as one of the Belgian draft horses January raised.

Sam, Squirt's helper, spotted him from where he was cleaning the front of the livery and waved before disappearing into the barn.

Eli had barely time to hitch his horse to the rail in front of the restaurant before Squirt came barreling out of the barn and headed across the street toward him. Eli waved him inside.

The old gal who ruled the restaurant with an iron hand bustled toward them almost before they had a chance to find a stool at the counter.

"Coffee?" She waved a blue enamel pot at them and they nodded.

"You're here," Squirt said. "And you ain't all woebe-gone, so I reckon that means Deputy Billings and the youngsters have all survived."

Eli nodded. "Touch and go a few times, but yes."

Whirling on his stool, Squirt took a closer glance around the room—almost empty after the early morning and late morning rushes of business—and leaned in. "I checked on them outlaws this morning. They're doing just fine there in the dark. As fine as they deserve, anyhoo." He snickered. "Bitchin' like a street full of New York City housewives."

Eli's sleepy eyes opened wider. How on earth would Squirt know anything about New York housewives, bitching or not?

"That so?" he said.

"That's so. We is going to have to do something with them soon though. Don't know how much longer we can keep them fellers penned up there. Depends on if we get Judge Flute or Judge Parker. Parker, he's a stickler for rules. He finds out we been keepin' them in my old basement, he's apt to toss the case."

The judge had been a little upset the last time they did that. Unauthorized incarceration location, or some such thing, he'd said. And he'd said, "Don't ever do it again." But now they'd gone and done it again anyway.

Nodding, Eli cut into the hotcakes Maggie set in front of him and began eating before it occurred to him he hadn't even placed an order.

"January got another threatening note nailed to her door," he said to Squirt, softly, so there'd be no chance of his voice carrying. "Looks like the situation will come to a head soon."

Squirt took a drink of scalding coffee. "Where at?"

Eli wasn't sure whether he meant where the note was placed, or where the situation would end. He decided to answer both questions. And more.

"The note was at her new house. They want a meeting tomorrow in Spokane. I doubt Bethany Flowers has very much longer to get this settled. Her time out of jail is apt to wind down, plus, I don't know if she can keep paying this the gang of outlaws she's got working for her. I doubt they're doing it for free. Joe must've recruited them while they were still in prison, but they won't toe the line he wants toed for long. Not without plenty of money lining their pockets. They're smart enough to know this might not pan out."

"Drag it out longst as you can," Squirt advised. "The more of them quit, the better off you'll be. In fact, some of them must be wondering where these men we got as prisoners hied off to. Where and why. Or if they're dead or alive." He paused. "How's she holdin' up. Miz Billings, I mean. She's been doing a lot of traipsin' hither and yon from what I gather. That wound bothering her much?"

Eli had to grin. "You know her. Tough as they come."

But Squirt's wrinkled face held a pensive expression. "I dunno, Pasco. She hides it real good, but I've seen'er... well, I'd say inside she's just as soft as any other woman. Softer than most when you come right down to it. She wouldn't be helpin' out all these strays otherwise."

Much struck, Eli slowly nodded. He hadn't thought of that, but now he did.

What else was she hiding?

He got up from the stool and dropped some money onto the counter. "I've got to check my place and get some sleep, Squirt. I'll be back this afternoon and pick up Mrs. Billings's dog before heading back to her house. Send a messenger if there's anything I should know right away."

"You gonna talk to Southbrook?"

"Not now. Later." Southbrook could wait, he decided. After finding Walt Beeson had made his way to the ranch and held Jem hostage, he was leery of leaving the place undefended. He'd sure hate to find the place burned down around his ears or his horses stolen—or worse—slaughtered.

* * *

JEM AND WREN went off to their beds for some badly needed sleep as soon as they'd eaten. Hattie, on the other hand, came to her, her hazel eyes watering just a little, and saying, "I need to tell you something, January. I didn't want to, but I have to."

Inwardly, January sighed. "Now, Hattie? We need to rest. We're apt to have company tonight and I want to be ready for them."

"I know you're tired and you've been shot and everything. Please, though. I feel like I'm about to bust wide open. I can't sleep until I tell you what happened."

What else could she do? With an inward sigh, January gestured Hattie into a chair beside her and settled in to listen. She leaned against the kitchen work table—a lovely piece of maple perfect for cutting or rolling or kneading dough and set on rolling wheels—and tried to situate her arm in a more comfortable position. Somehow, she worked up a smile. "You look worried. Am I going to be mad?"

Hattie nodded. "I expect so."

"At you?"

The girl nodded again. "I'm sorry," she blurted.

Trying to keep the frown from her face, January said, "Sorry for what?"

"He told me... He seemed sincere... I didn't know..."

January held up her hand. "Try a complete sentence, please. He, and just who is *he*, told you what?"

Hattie swallowed hard. "First, about Mr. Marche. He was the Pinkerton Agency man who had gotten me out of school and we were on the train."

January nodded. She knew this.

"We were already halfway to Spokane when all the sudden he jumped up and said he had to go find the necessary." Hattie's expression changed. "His face turned red, January. Real red. I thought it was kind of strange. A man like him, kind of hard, if you know what I mean, acting as if I didn't know people have to, well, anyway— He told me to stay in my seat and not to talk to anybody, then he dashed away into the next car. The door between cars was still swinging shut when this other man sat down beside me."

January stood up straighter and felt her pulse increase. It seemed she finally might get some answers as to what happened.

Hattie flicked her a glance. "First off, he leans into me and says, 'You know he plans on killing you, don't you? That woman, your guardian, she hired him. He's going to push you off the train when we get to the rocks.'

"January, I didn't know anything about any rocks but I could see right away he was a bad man and a big liar. I said, 'Mister, go away and leave me be. I don't know what you're talking about.' And he said, 'I know you don't, but I'm gonna tell you.' And he started in lying to me about how you—" She broke off. Her hands knotted together and twisted.

Anger so hot she couldn't think flared in her brain. January stared at her. Seconds ticked by without Hattie finishing what she'd started. At last, January said, "How I what?"

Hattie swallowed. "How you planned to have us— me and Jem—murdered, and how Mr. Marche had not come from Mr. Avery, but that he, himself had, and had boarded the train to bring me to safety. He told me Jem was already in a safe place and that he'd take me there too."

Fighting to control her not only her voice, but her face, January said, "Did you believe him?"

"No, never. But at the same time, I couldn't figure out how he knew about Mr. Avery sending a Pinkerton for me unless—" Hattie's eyes filled with tears. "He scared me, January. Of course I knew you wouldn't hurt me or Jem. And this man, he had mean eyes. He didn't smell good, either. He was wearing a suit, but it didn't fit him very well, and it had some dark stains on it that looked like blood." Hattie's brow puckered. "Mr. Avery wouldn't hire a man like that. I know he wouldn't. I thought maybe it meant Jem was dead. Or you."

January breathed easier. For a moment she'd thought Hattie had doubted her, an idea that stabbed as if the girl had taken a knife to her.

"What did you do?" she asked.

Hattie's mouth drew into a straight line. "Nothing. I didn't do anything." Her eyes flashed. "Right then and there I should have jumped up and screamed so loud the whole train could hear that this man was accosting me and talking nasty. But then I didn't know if anyone would believe me. Or if they'd care. So I just told him to go away before I called the conductor. I said I didn't believe him and that Mr. Marche would be back in a few minutes and I guessed I'd find out who was lying then.

Oh, January. His face turned so ugly you wouldn't believe it."

"What did he do?"

"First, he laughed. Then he told me Mr. Marche wouldn't be coming back." Hattie's lips trembled. "He drew his finger across his throat as if using a knife and I knew exactly what he meant. I've never been so scared. Not even when Joe and Calvin and John B took me."

January reached for the girl with her good hand, but Hattie drew back. "What happened next was my own fault. There were other men in the railroad car. And women. I should've screamed or fought or cried...or something, right away. But I'd just worked up my nerve to run when he shoved a gun in my ribs and told me to shut up and do as I was told. He said he'd shoot the woman in the next seat if I didn't. And she was holding a baby."

At last she raised her eyes to meet January's. "And like some kind of silly fainting fool, I did. I didn't want to tell you. I knew you'd be so ashamed of me. I'm a terrible coward."

At this, January's eyes opened wide. "Ashamed of you? Hattie, I'm not...how can you even think...I'm not ashamed of you. I'm proud of you."

"Proud of me?" Hattie stared at January. "I did everything wrong. I put you and Jem and Eli in danger. Even Johnny. Him too. I'm not brave like you."

"Brave like me?" January couldn't help thinking of a time when she'd let herself be coerced into taking the coward's way out. It hadn't worked out well for her, either. "Hattie, the important thing is that you lived. That you can testify against these people in a way to send them all to jail for a very long time. You couldn't have stopped them."

"I should have tried." Hattie's regret was echoed in her wail of grief. "When I went with that man and found one of his...his *friends* had Mr. Marche prisoner. January, he...Mr. Marche...looked so surprised to see me. That's when I sort of figured he'd been in on it. They must've paid him to leave me alone."

January's head whirled. How had they gotten to Marche? How had they known him to be somehow vulnerable? Why did they kill him then? Or did it even matter now? "He had a gun on you. Going with him probably saved the woman's life and that of her child."

Hattie shook her head. "I wasn't even thinking of them by that time. And then, when the train slowed, and we all jumped off, they shot Mr. Marche. In the head. While he was on his knees. He was crying and yelling. He said something like, *You promised you wouldn't hurt her.* But I don't think he was talking about me. And he was scared."

"Handwriting on the wall," January murmured, horrified by the picture Hattie painted. With what the girl had had to witness.

Sweat had gathered on Hattie's face, and January could see she was seeing all this again in her mind's eye. She tried to put her arm around the girl, but Hattie resisted the comfort.

"I should've done something to stop them," she wailed.

After what seemed like a very long time, after a great many times of being told there was nothing she could've done, January finally persuaded the girl to go to her room and rest. Hattie steadfastly refused to be consoled.

Half the girl's problem and skewed thinking, or so January suspected, stemmed from the unrelenting terror of her kidnapping. She was another who hadn't really slept in days, having been kept in a drugged stupor.

January could only guess at the thoughts tumbling through Hattie's mind. But she could relate. She'd been in hopeless situations herself, a time or two. And speaking of sleep—

But Hattie hadn't quite finished. Lips trembling, she paused on her way out of the room and looked up a January. "After the guy shot Mr. Marche, I heard them talking. They'd already forced a couple pills down my throat. My head felt like it might float away and for a while I thought there were four men, not two. I guess they didn't care if I heard then or not. Or maybe they thought they'd knocked me out. Anyway—" She paused and shook her head.

"Anyway?" January said.

"I expect you've been wondering why they didn't kill me right along with Mr. Marche. I wondered. I figured they would, right up until they fed me those pills. Anyway, that's what they were talking about. One of them, the one who shot Mr. Marche, wanted to use me, then kill me. But the man in the suit said, 'No, no. We can't kill her. Not yet.' It turned out Bethany wanted to see me and for one thing, make sure they had the right girl, and second, ask me a question. Then he laughed and said, 'after that, we can do what we want with her.' Oh! And they were after another girl and the queen bee didn't want to get us mixed up."

"The queen bee being Bethany?"

"Yes." Hattie paused. "Is that other girl Wren?"

Slowly, January nodded. "Yes."

She didn't think mixing the girls up played any part in Bethany's real motivation. She figured it was simply one more cruel act so Hattie knew exactly what was happening and who was doing it to her.

# CHAPTER 15

JANUARY SLEPT HARD FOR THREE HOURS. NOT LONG enough, to be for sure, for she awakened groggy and blurry-eyed. But even asleep her mind had dashed hither and yon like a rat trying to escape a fire, busily figuring a multitude of problems all at once. She'd promised Wren more tricks and traps and she felt bound to deliver on that promise.

Throwing aside the blanket covering her, she swung her legs over the edge of the mattress and got to her feet, surprised to find herself shaking at the effort. Getting dressed proved a painful process. Supporting herself with her good hand on the wall, she made her way downstairs to the kitchen and got the fire rekindled in the kitchen range.

One of the tricks she'd used to good effect in the old barn before it burned, had been an apparatus that, when set in motion, caused sharp reports that sounded like gunfire. It had certainly fooled her attacker at the time, causing him to run for safety. She figured to set something like it up again, even though some of those old traps had been more suitable to the rundown spaces of the barn than to her house. Another trap remained in place down by the creek, where she had a pump and a water reservoir that went beyond what most would expect. If worst came to worst, she could pull that same stunt again. Seeming to retreat and then be caught in the open.

By the time the young ones awakened, she had most everything arranged. The wound in her side burned like fire and she had trouble lifting her arm. The overhead nets had been taxing, to say the least.

"Come on in here," she told the sleepy-eyed kids, and stuck her arm back in the sling. It helped, a little. A very little. "I've got things to show you. It's important. Pay attention."

Wren was the first to catch on. "Tricks?" Her blue eyes brightened. Any remaining signs of the sleepiness showing in those eyes disappeared.

"Tricks—and traps. Look here. Some of these have contrivances you'll need to look out for. We don't want to set anything off prematurely. You all need to be aware. You really wouldn't want to get in their way yourselves." The explanation went on.

Hattie turned out to have a preference for the noise-maker. Wren preferred the drop-down nets January had attached to the ceiling. The girls' approval made her pain worthwhile.

Meanwhile, Jem was enthralled with a modified ball bearing apparatus that not only shot the balls out with a great deal of force but could be aimed. That one, January thought ruefully, would probably wreak havoc on her walls. She hoped its use could be avoided. Nevertheless, Jem spent the half-hour before dark with the

back door open trying to hit a target he'd placed outside. He was, she discovered, remarkably accurate with the thing.

As for herself, she preferred the weight of her dad's old .38 in her hand, or the scattergun she kept beside the door.

They all spent an hour covering the downstairs windows with some spare lumber leftover from building the house, leaving peepholes so they could see out. She didn't want anyone spying on them from the outside.

Just at dark, January heard a welcome sound coming from her porch. Vigorous scratching and a low whine. Her heart gave a lurch. Pen had arrived, which meant, she knew, Eli must be out there somewhere also. Even so, she took care in opening the door for her dog. Pen's tail wagged like a metronome as she burrowed against January's legs and received pats and praise.

The stir between Hattie and Jem as they greeted the old dog served to break some of January's tension. And when Pen, in making her circuit, went right to Wren, her action seemed to make the youngsters easier with each other.

Not many minutes passed before Jem's anxious glance strayed to the door. "Where's Eli?" he burst out. "He's had plenty of time to turn his horse into the pasture. Do you think he's been attacked, January? What if he got bushwhacked and is laying out there on the road hurt? What if Pen found her own way home? I'd better go out and see."

January, who'd been thinking along the same lines herself, drew her skittering thoughts together and shook her head. "He's fine. Eli is a careful man. He knows what he's doing."

But did he? They were going against a gang of hardened gunmen. Convicts, to whom murder may have been an ordinary affair. Eli was good, but also outnumbered. She didn't like his odds. Not at all.

Not many minutes later a tap on the door drew a tiny gasp of relief. Eli, at last. Unless...

She motioned the kids away from the door and without turning the lock, shouted, "Name yourself."

"It's Eli. Open up."

The reply, though muffled by the sturdy door, convinced her. She flipped the lock and, revolver in hand, backed away. "Come in," she said.

Eli stepped through, eyed her cocked revolver with approval and winked. "All set here?"

"As set as we'll ever be." She imagined her relief at seeing him showed in her eyes. Windows to the soul, or so she'd read. He looked rested now, hard and ready for action.

"Has there been any sign of Bethany, or Bitters, or any rough looking strangers in town?" January knew Squirt and Sam would be on the lookout. Becoming aware of how anxious she sounded, she did her best to quell any emotion. Carefully, she released the hammer on her weapon and put it back in the holster.

"Not that I know of." Eli greeted the kids before setting his rifle and a saddle bag carrying what January suspected was extra ammunition out of the way. "But that doesn't mean they're not coming. I'd expect them either to ride from Spokane and stay out of sight or get off the train at the water tank. Most likely they won't pass through town at all."

more, until they figured everyone was asleep. Then they'd attack.

She smiled grimly to herself. Whoever was in charge of this outfit must be supremely confident. And stupid along with it.

Marking where she knew at least one adversary had settled in, January tugged lightly on Pen's ear and they went on, two black shadows moving in the dark. Right to the chicken coop that loomed up in front of them.

It didn't take Pen standing tight again and pointing with her nose. No great ability was required to understand as her chickens were highly disturbed. The rustle and cluck of hens that should be perched on their roosts comfortably asleep told January as much.

So. She and Pen had spotted another one. Ready to move on, she'd taken a step away from the coop when she heard a murmur from inside, just on the other side of the wall. Then a commotion, and the flutter of wings. Birdish protests. A terrific, and loud, squawk.

And a man, liberal with muttered curses. "Stinking...bird crap on me....wring your...neck."

January stopped. So did Pen.

Inside, a great flapping of wings indicated the man was attempting to follow through on his threat. And the noise of the hen fighting back.

"Peck at my eye you..." The man's voice rose above the whisper, this time.

Fearing her chickens were in danger, anger coursed through her. She wasn't about to allow some ruffian to kill them. They were all good layers.

It struck January that the hen had thoroughly distracted him from his job. She patted Pen and made a "stay" motion with her hand. Creeping to the half-open door, she edged inside. Though very dark, she knew her way around. One side of the coop held barrels of chicken mash and a keg of water, a short-handled, heavy wooden implement used to scrape soiled straw from the nests, and a rake and shovel propped against the wall. The door side held shelves with egg gathering baskets and a candling apparatus. Two sides held nests and perches.

She picked up both the scraper and the shovel and slipped forward to where the man, his back to her, was struggling to contain three or four hens and a rooster. They flew about, the rooster hopping up and beating at the man with its strong wings.

The thug, busy fighting off the angry chickens, didn't notice her. Smiling to herself, January stayed behind him and waited until the rooster tried an especially violent attack. Not unexpectedly, the man jumped backward. The shovel, now dropped beneath his feet, sent him stumbling sideways, flailing his arms at the hen flying up to beat at his head.

Synchronizing with the chicken's attack, January slung the nest scraper as if wielding a baseball bat. The heavy wood met his head with a resounding thump. He dropped to his knees, the chickens swarming over him.

And he let them.

She clubbed him again for good measure.

As silently as she'd come, January left him to the birds. She didn't think he'd cottoned to her being there at all. Just him and the birds.

She smiled as she melded with the night, allowing Pen to lead her down to the river, and from there to the bridge.

# CHAPTER 16

JANUARY TAPPED ON THE DOOR IN THE PATTERN SHE'D shown the kids, then stood back and waited. They'd be taking time to extinguish the light before opening up. Or they would if they followed orders. But then, she figured Eli would see to that.

From the other side of the door she heard Jem say, "Name yourself."

She almost laughed, thinking how he copied her caution-filled inquiry when she'd opened to Eli. He was a quick learner.

"It's me," she said. "January. Quick now."

A scraping sound indicated the bolt being drawn, and even as the door began to open, she sensed motion behind her. She spun. *Pen didn't alert.* The thought flashed through her mind, before she recognized Eli standing there. She hadn't heard a thing. Neither, evidently, had Pen.

Eli pushed into the house behind her, closed and bolted the door. "You didn't think I'd let you go alone, did you?"

The gaze she settled on him wasn't entirely admiring. "Sneaky. And Pen didn't react. You're very good at trailing someone." Although, come to think of it, the dog had stared off to the side a time or two. And, since Pen probably considered Eli part of her pack, his presence wouldn't have caused her any alarm.

"You're not so bad yourself. I stayed far enough away that if anyone had spotted you, we'd be able to corner them between us. Though for a minute, I thought...well you can tell us about that in a minute." He glanced around at Wren who stood holding a spoon aloft. "Supper ready?"

"Almost," Wren said. The girl was looking at January.

January wiped the scowl off her face. Eli had to be talking about the man in the chicken house and she hadn't intended to tell anyone about that. Not all of it, anyhow. Thinking back, the whole incident struck her as comical and clown-like—although the fellow she'd clunked in the head might not agree. But also dangerous.

Taking a seat near the stove, Jem propped his carbine beside the chair. "Tell us what, January? What's Eli talking about. What happened out there?" His young face anxious, he wasn't letting go of his worry.

"It's them, isn't it?" Hattie, who'd been laying out plates and utensils, stood frozen. "They're here, aren't they?"

An astute question. January didn't see any sense in hedging the facts. "Yes. I spotted three. There may be more, but I know there's one in the shed, one in the bushes at the bridge, and one in the chicken coop. Those are for sure." She flashed Hattie a smile. "The fellow in the chicken coop may be out of commission."

"Not enough of them for us to worry about," Eli assured Hattie.

January knew he'd seen Hattie's reaction and drawn the same conclusion she had. From Hattie witnessing the Pinkerton detective's murder, to being drugged and held hostage herself—for the second time in her young life, no less—her confidence had been shattered. For now. But she was resilient. Strong. She'd be all right given time.

Hoping to ease the tension, she launched into a telling of the chicken coop fiasco. The story provided entertainment until Wren removed the lid over the frying pan and called them to eat.

They didn't gather around the table. Instead, each filled a plate at the stove, then found a chair separate from anyone else to sit and eat. Eli suggested the strategy, saying it would be best if they didn't all ball together around a table. They be too easy to hit if those men outside commenced shooting at random.

His suggestion sort of ruined January's appetite.

But not Hattie's. "I've been thinking," she announced, scooping up the last of some potatoes fried in bacon fat with onions and some minced meat. The girls had made a large panful for the five of them and done a good job seasoning the mix.

Hattie's doing, January suspected.

Struggling a bit with balancing the plate on her lap in consideration of her sore side, January finished her meal and took the plate to the sink. "Thinking about what?"

The girl went at the question in what struck January as

a guarded manner. "Well, I doubt Wren is their main target. Not anymore. Those men you've already got penned up in town are the ones who...you know." She swallowed hard, as if a lump clogged her throat. "The men here right now probably aren't worrying as much about her. It's really Jem and me. We're the ones they want dead."

January's lips tightened as Eli grimaced. "Much as I hate to say so, I agree," he said. "I expect I'm high up on their list. They know they need to get rid of me to make it easier to get to you."

Jem and Hattie passed a glance between them. Both nodded.

"Which leaves January." Hattie discovered a last bit of spud and chased it around on her plate. "They'll come for her last."

Startled, January stared at the girl. "They will?"

Hattie nodded, and January was surprised to see both Eli and Jem nodding agreement.

"Why would they spare me?" she asked.

"They won't forever. But if Jem and I are dead, that only leaves you and them. I mean Joe and Bethany— well, and John B, I guess, but I don't think he's in on this. So there's just them and you."

"John B is probably in the clear," January agreed. "But—"

Hattie had a thoughtful look on her face as she interrupted. "But they don't want you dead."

"They don't?" January arched an eyebrow. She was pretty sure they did. It all depended on the timing.

"Not right off, anyway." Hattie accompanied the amendment with a shrug. "They'll want you to sign papers first. Papers bequeathing—that's the right word, isn't it—bequeathing everything to them. You know, so it looks all legal and passes through probate with no questions asked."

January's lips didn't even twitch. These two kids were entirely too smart for their own good. The paperwork Hattie described was much like that she'd signed when Mr. Avery settled the legalities of the inheritance left to her by Joseph Senior. She had then bequeathed the Flowers Trust to Hattie and Jem at her passing. Actually, she intended them to have it just as soon as they became of age. They knew all this. She'd explained it to them.

She'd bet Bethany had been spending her time out of prison finding, and coercing, an attorney to concoct paperwork in legalese almost identical to those same papers, while changing only the names of the beneficiaries. Effective immediately.

Wren stared at each of them in turn, her blue eyes wide. "Are you very rich?" she asked into the quiet.

Jem turned to her. "Yes. Or at least, January is, for right now. Then it'll be Hattie and me." He didn't speak with any pride. To the contrary. January heard dread in his simple declaration.

"But not for the next several years," Hattie finished. "We hope."

"Oh," Wren said in a hushed kind of way. "I'd like to be rich."

"Not if it means people are gunning for you," Jem said. "Look at the mess we're all in now because of it. Even you, and you're not even a Flowers."

They were silent again until Eli said, his voice sounding choked. "So. We'll just have to see none of us winds up bleeding on the floor. I'd hate to ruin all the work January has put in building this house."

January sucked in a breath. "See that you don't. I intend to work in the garden this spring, not spend the nice weather redoing what I've already done. And I need to get that set of Belgiums ready for sale. I'm expecting a decent price out of them."

An assumption there'd be a future. It was just too bad nobody in the room seemed to be counting on that happening.

Not being one to sanction her house being left in a mess, January asked the girls to clean the kitchen. The job quickly accomplished, there was nothing to do but blow out the lights and wait for the expected hammer to fall.

Jem, hunkered by the kitchen window where a gap between boards allowed him to keep an eye on the shed and chicken coop, soon grew impatient. "What are they waiting for?"

Eli answered, calm and cool. "Reinforcements, I expect. From the looks of things, your ex-headmaster has funds enough to hire as many men as he can find."

Jem's lips blew a rude sound. "Then what?" he demanded. "They gonna shoot this house full of holes until they kill us all?" He glanced at January. "Except you."

"I suspect that is their plan." Eli chuckled as if undisturbed by the idea.

Wren, sitting by herself in a corner, uttered a smothered little moan.

"Then why are we sitting here waiting for them?" Hattie inched over to sit beside her brother. "Why don't we go out and get them first? Why didn't you shoot that man in the chicken house when you had the chance, January? You could have, I bet."

It was true. She could have. And in the process, not only killed another man, but drawn the other two—or more, but two for sure—watchers right down on her. Chances were, had Eli joined her, they could've made it back to the house unscathed. An equal chance said they both might've died there in the open, leaving the kids unprotected. It hadn't been a probability she wanted to bet against.

She opened her mouth, prepared to set out the strategy—again—when Pen sat up and let out a soft "ruff." Laboring a little, the dog got to her feet and padded toward the door.

Before January could more than blink, Eli's Mauser Broomhandle was out of the holster and in his hand.

"January, take hold of your dog," he said, his voice quick and sharp as a blade. But it was Jem who hurried to grasp Pen's collar. The boy's expression as he stared at Eli seemed awed. Probably at the speed of the draw.

"I've got her." Jem urged the dog away from the door.

"Are they coming?" Hattie whispered the question, as if afraid whoever was outside might hear her.

Eli answered her. "Sounds as if. Everybody take up their assigned position. Now."

January tried for a calming smile, feeling the scar on her cheek stretch with the effort. "Girls, why don't you scurry on upstairs. When the shooting starts—if it starts —I want you to climb in the bathtub and hunker down in there."

Wren stared at her. "In the bathtub?"

"Yes. It's cast iron. It'll protect you from any stray bullets."

The girls, not even Hattie, moved. "I want to help," Hattie said. "This is my fight too, just as much as yours. Or Jem's. Or—"

"Just do as I say, Hattie. Take Wren. Please. And hurry."

Hattie, her reluctance all too clear, finally nodded. "All right, but I want a gun. Just in case."

January hesitated.

"I can shoot," Hattie said. "You know I can. I'll protect Wren."

She told the truth. The girl did know how to handle a revolver—or a rifle. An advantage of having an older brother. But what if she got distracted? Or scared? Or panicked?

"Don't need protectin'." Wren clamped her lips shut as if offended. "Maybe I oughta have a gun and protect you." She glared at Hattie.

Under other circumstances, January might've found the stand-off amusing. Now she was just impatient. But she handed her ankle gun to Hattie, who promptly broke it open and inspected the cylinder for loads before snapping it back together.

"C'mon." Grabbing Wren by the hand, she tugged on the other girl. "Let's get out of here."

Sighing relief as their footsteps pounded up the stairs, January checked both her .38 and the shotgun. She was ready.

They'd made a pact, she and Eli. Eli would take the back door, past experience having already shown that to be the likeliest and preferred point of entry for the outlaws. January had argued a little. After all, they were attacking her house, her friends, and the heirs to the

Flowers fortune, as well as herself. This was a fight she needed to win.

Eli had argued he was most experienced. As a former bounty hunter, his reputation alone served to make criminals think twice before taking him on. Plain facts.

So January had conceded. The front door remained hers to guard. She neglected to remind Eli the biggest threat they'd faced so far had come from the man she'd had to kill when he had entered through the front. She moved now to take up a position just to the side of the fireplace, sliding into the inglenook in which she planned to build a bookcase someday—if she lived long enough. From there, she had a decent field of view and a dark place to take cover.

Jem settled in the open space under the stairs, where they'd setup the noisemaker that shot out lead balls. The machine, placed on a swivel, could be turned in an 180 degree arc.

January hoped it didn't come to that, with her new house taking a beating.

Eli stood directly in the middle of the kitchen. Together, he and Jem had turned the worktable over on its side where he could use the heavy maple top for protection should the outlaws break through.

Though Jem had hooked Pen's leather leash around a table leg in hopes of keeping her out of the way where she wouldn't get hurt, the wily old girl had already gotten loose. January could've told him using the usual tie for a horse's reins didn't work for her. The dog knew how free either the horse or herself.

Pen shook, settling her fur, and joined January,

sitting at the front of the inglenook. Not ideal as it made January's presence obvious.

"Stay where you are," January whispered to Jem, who'd moved to break from his spot to reclaim the dog.

They settled back. January was aware of Jem's breath coming in uneven little jerks, loud in the overall silence. Not a sound came from Eli, almost as if he'd fallen asleep. Pen panted. As for herself, she didn't know. Maybe she was holding her breath.

Right up until something loud and heavy thudded against the back door. Then again. And again.

Pen raised her head and bayed.

"Hush," January said, without effect.

The door broke from its latch and burst open. Starlight glinted in the night sky, revealing two men spilling into the kitchen, their forms black shadows outlined briefly in the open doorway.

And exactly as had happened with Gus and Vern on that previous night, the net fell from the ceiling. Only this time, it draped over a single man's head and tangled in his gun. The gun went off, roaring loud in the enclosed space.

Upstairs, January heard one of the girls shriek. Wren, she thought. Hattie wasn't the kind of girl to scream. Not unless her ordeal when kidnapped had changed her.

When January tried to see into the kitchen through the wide arch separating the kitchen and front room, she couldn't place Eli. But then she had to turn away because, in an identical sequence as before, thuds from her side of the house announced the front door was under attack.

This door, heavier and larger, withstood three of

those thuds, before it slammed open. The knob struck the wall and rebounded, only to be thrust out of the way by another two men.

"Jem, now," she shouted, but Jem, perhaps overwhelmed by what was happening in the kitchen, delayed knocking away the spring's catch to set the lead balls flying.

A man, his form massive, placed her location from hearing her shout. He turned and ran toward her. The other headed toward Jem and the stair. In the kitchen, a man cried out.

Eli?

Jem finally got the machine activated. Balls flew across the room, thudding into walls, a couch, a man's body. Not lethally. His yelp showed more anger than pain.

A window shattered.

Pen continued to howl.

Bedlam.

# CHAPTER 17

"Shoot that damn dog," the outlaw who'd spotted January's position in the inglenook yelled out. Pen leaped forward and nabbed the man by the pantleg—her sharp teeth taking a good-sized chunk of skin along with it—as he lunged toward January.

January, her revolver poised, hesitated. Afraid to shoot for fear of hitting her dog. Afraid not to shoot for fear of letting the man get to her. The dim room didn't help. Movement was indistinct. A blur. Too fast.

They should've left the lights on, she thought.

Fists pounded into flesh. A voice cried out. A shot from the kitchen carried into the front room and the same voice as before hollered, "Watch it, bug brain. Kill the dog."

"January!" Jem called out, his young voice scared, and suddenly weak. "He's headed for the stairs."

Pen and her battle with the loudmouthed fellow had distracted January. Somehow, the second man had gotten past her. And Jem. He sounded hurt? Had one of those shots hit him?

She didn't have time to finish the thought as Pen's foe fought loose from the dog's grip on his leg. He lunged forward, crashing into January and taking her down beneath him. She felt the stitches under her arm give way as she brought the arm up to block his hand when he groped for her throat.

He was a big man, going to fat. His weight pressed down on her, squeezing out her breath even as his hand smashed down across her mouth. The fall knocked the revolver from her hand, where it skidded just beyond reach. Grunting, he left it lay, attempting to hold her still long enough to strangle—or suffocate—her. His indecision as to which was, for the moment, saving her as she shook her head from side to side, her hair whipping up into his eyes.

Though not a large woman to begin with, and lean from the work she did, January was strong. And determined.

Aware of the hissing of her breath, she fought free long enough to gasp in a gulp of air. The man outweighed her by a good seventy-five pounds. She couldn't hope to outfight him. Or even outlast him. She needed help.

Where were the others? Eli? Jem?

Writhing, she got one leg free, and though her muscles protested, she used the hard heel of her boot to batter at the back of his knee. He cursed her, using words whose meaning she didn't understand.

He took his hand away from her mouth long enough to snatch at her leg, trying to catch it and hold her still. What he did was open up enough space for her to lift the knee still under him, jerking it into his male parts.

"Bitch," he howled as her knee thrust upward, hard, with a good six inches behind it.

January, dizzy with the effort, didn't know how much longer she could fight. She felt herself fading, right up until help arrived.

Not quite the help she expected.

Pen.

Only this time her brave old dog leaped on the man's back, inadvertently adding another sixty pounds to the weight already crushing January, but baring the man's neck to Pen's gnashing teeth. One hard nip broke into his flesh. Another sank in deeper, drawing a messy flow of blood. The man screamed, struggling now to rise to his feet. He'd dropped his gun, she saw, and was drawing a skinning knife from a belt scabbard.

Pen, flung to the floor but still game, rushed him again. January cried out to the dog, and at the same time, grabbed for the knife. Faster than the outlaw, faster than she'd ever moved before, she seized the hilt and snatched the knife away. The blade pointed outward, held steady in front of her.

Enraged, as if he didn't even sense danger, he bared his teeth and came at her. Most likely, he expected her to run, but she didn't. Bracing herself, she stood her ground. Under his own momentum, the blade slid into his gut a few inches beneath his belt.

It happened fast. Even in the dimness, she could see the surprised look that came over his face. He jerked back, pulling free of the knife and muttering, "Whaaa..." His blood, hot with the heat of his body, gushed over her hand in a flood. Slowly, he sank to one knee before falling forward onto his chest.

Sickened, she dropped the knife and kicked it spinning into the fireplace cavity where darkness hid it.

She hated knives.

"January," Jem, his voice shaky, called out to her again. "Hattie. The stairs."

Her .38 lay where she'd dropped it. Wiping her hand on a blouse already saturated with blood, some hers, some the outlaw's, she picked up the gun and stumbled toward Jem and the stairway. Only half-aware of the noise of battle ongoing in the kitchen, she heard the table scooting along the floor, pans rattling on their shelf, boots thudding, pained grunting, men cursing.

Eli must be holding his own.

"Jem! Are you hurt?"

She thought he shook his head no. Though too dark to see much, she knew the boy had curled himself around his stomach and he breathed wheezily.

He waved a hand toward the stairs where a man carrying a sawed-off shotgun was inching upward.

Leaving Jem and trusting he only had the wind knocked of him, she followed the intruder. His head was cocked upward where enough light came through the hall window to show the empty second story landing.

He looked back once and spotted her weak attempt to catch up. Lifting the shotgun, he fired. Supremely confident, without waiting, he continued up the last few steps.

For a second, January thought she must be hit. She should've been hit. But she wasn't. Maybe he wasn't used to shooting at such an acute downward angle, because his aim had been off. A scatter of buckshot pounded into the single tread in front of her.

Swallowing hard, she went on.

Above her, a girl—she wasn't sure if it was Hattie or Wren—squeaked out, "Now."

The man above her stopped short, though not, she realized, of his own accord. He tripped, his arms swinging as he teetered for a moment on the stair's edge. His shotgun dropped to the floor as he tried to catch himself. A pair of small hands thrust out at him from each side as he began a backward tumble down the stairs. Barely in time, January sprang aside to let him fall and though he reached out to grab her as he went past, she kicked his hand aside and gave him a boot in the rear to help send him down.

He reached the bottom and, moaning, lay still.

"Girls?" she said softly.

The girls, still invisible, giggled. An overwrought giggle, not one of amusement.

"It worked," one said.

"Told you it would," said the other.

The house had gone quiet. Shots faded, moans muted, voices stilled. And yet, January couldn't hear her own heartbeat. Lord knows she could feel it, hammering away inside her chest like a mad blacksmith at his anvil. She shook all over as panic surged, faded, surged again.

This was her home. Who inside it was alive and who was not?

*I will resign.*

The thought popped into her head where it met no argument from her brain.

*I will resign as a county deputy.*

She would put the Flowers Trust into the hands of an executive committee. Maybe she'd change her name.

Have Jem and Hattie become known under their mother's maiden name.

She couldn't bear to move from The Falls and her old family homestead, but she planned to become a hermit like she'd been before she met Shay Billings.

*If anyone comes calling and asks me for help in finding lost kinfolk, kidnapped girls or stolen horses, I will say no. Never again. No more bringing killers to justice. I'm done.*

She was tired. In pain. Again.

She'd had enough of fear, of risking her life, of getting shot and shooting others. Folks would need to fight their own battles from now on. Or find other qualified people to do it for them.

Just as soon as Bethany returned to prison to serve out her sentence—and more, or by glory, she'd know the reason why—and Headmaster Harold Bitters received his just due.

Then she would resign. And maybe Eli...

\* \* \*

ELI FIGURED he'd have all he could handle when they made their rush. *They* meaning however many hardcases Bethany and Headmaster Bitters had rounded up to go after January and the kids. It probably depended on who they hired. Skid Road derelicts, while bad enough, were apt to run at the first resistance. Newly released convicts, and Eli was certain there'd be some, would do their job, the bloodier, the better.

He snorted. Not loud. He didn't want January to hear him. If she did, she'd realize he didn't have great hopes of surviving this. One man, one woman, three kids, up against a gang bent on murder.

When the door flew open under a length of log probably taken from January's own woodpile and used to batter the lock to pieces, he still wasn't ready. And when January's trick—or trap—caught only one of the men rushing through the doorway and allowed him to get off a shot besides, he'd guessed the fight had already gone sideways. The bullet whistled past his ear and lodged in the heavy maple table he sheltered behind.

During all this distraction, the man not encumbered by the net lurched around his partner, tripped, and fell almost on top of Eli.

Eli's Mauser was not the best close-up gun. Hand-to-hand seemed the best he could do. Without hesitating, he lashed out at the second man, punching for the gut but too late to avoid a fist that felt more like the aforementioned battering ram when it landed on his cheekbone. Hard hit, he stumbled back.

A brawler. They'd hired a backdoor bully.

Eli dodged the man's follow-up blow, which gave him a couple seconds to shake off the dizzying effect on his eyesight. Not the best result, it also gave the net guy a moment to rip the burlap from his face and his gun and push his way farther into the kitchen.

Eli, ducking under another blow from the brawler's hammer-like fist, shoved the table into the net guy. Shoved it hard, straight into the man's hips. He howled as his leg went out from under him.

By then the brawler was on Eli again. He got his forearm up in time for it to take the worst of the next punch. About then he realized Brawler mostly used only his left hand. So far, he hadn't thrown a punch with his right. Which meant that for some reason, he must be weak on that side. Or else he saved its power to take an opponent off guard.

Skipping, if that's what one could call the slide Eli took to Brawler's off-side, he threw out a short punch with first his left hand into the lower part of his ribs, then his right, also low.

Brawler grunted, bending some, but not stopping. Not by a long shot.

Eli stepped back, right onto the table just as the Net guy managed to rise from under it. The man went down again.

After that, Eli had no thought except that he had to best Brawler. Best him, or be beaten himself, and Eli did not care to be beaten. They exchanged blows, one after another at first, then more slowly. A lot of blows. Brawler clubbed him hard, more than once, with that lethal left hand.

But Eli used both of his hands. And his feet, once, when he had the chance, and after what felt like a long, long while, he discovered he stood alone and simply stopped. When his legs gave out, he dropped to the floor to find Brawler had got there first. Only Brawler was unconscious, and Eli wasn't. He'd won.

He spotted the Net guy lying motionless under the upside-down table, his nose squashed and his leg bent at an unlikely angle.

Eli wasn't aware of when that happened, and not sure he'd been the one to do the damage. He thought it might have been Brawler during one of his advances, when he'd plunged after Eli, who'd been on the other side of the sink.

Wiping blood from his abused mouth, he felt a tooth wiggle in its socket and resolved to be careful what he ate for the next few days. Give the tooth time to tighten up. A bloody gash above his eyebrow dripped into his eyelashes and blurred his vision, while his cheek had swollen high enough he could see it.

Leaning his back against the wall, he closed his eyes and let the world spin around him.

# CHAPTER 18

HATTIE AND WREN CREPT DOWN THE STAIRS HAND-IN-hand, Wren's eyes so wide she looked like a blue-eyed owl. Hattie barely glanced at the man they'd tripped with the clothesline she and Wren had rigged at the top of the stairs. They'd laid the line across the landing, anchoring it on the railing posts, then yanked the line up at just the right moment to send the outlaw sprawling backward down the stairs.

He lay moaning at the bottom where he'd fallen, on his back with one leg still on the stair. "Help me," he was saying. "Help me." At least he'd lost all interest in the shotgun that had fallen almost within reaching distance. Hattie dragged the gun farther away as she passed.

Neither of the girls showed him any sign of regret. As for January, well, neither did she.

"You girls all right?" Having managed to regain her feet, she hurried to light a lamp, not easy the way her hands were shaking. She set the lamp on the fireplace mantle and examined first one, then the other girl, thankful not to find any visible wounds.

Not the same story for her.

"You're bleeding again," Wren said, pointing at the spreading red stain under January's arm. "Did the stitches pull out?"

"Yes." Although she hadn't felt anything much before Wren called attention to the old wound, she was fully aware of it now. "Not the fault of your stitches, Wren. It couldn't be helped. Things got a little rowdy."

Wren blinked. "Rowdy?"

"Um-hmm." January didn't know how else to put it.

Hattie made a sort of growling sound and rushed to kneel beside her brother when Jem managed to crawl out from his spot under the stair. January saw he was breathing more or less freely again and that he managed to sit up straight as soon as he cleared the stair.

"Are you all right, Jem? How badly did he hurt you?" January hunkered down on the other side of him. Judging from the way he pressed a hand against his side, the outlaw had clubbed him good.

Jem met her eyes. "Busted a rib I think. Winded me pretty bad." His voice was level and matter-of-fact, but he couldn't keep the pain from showing in his face. "He clubbed me with the butt of his shotgun."

"I'm so sorry." Impossible for her not to feel guilty. He was her ward, for pity's sake. She should've taken better care of him. Kept him away from the fight. Only fourteen, he was too young to take part in a situation like this.

And yet, she knew that wasn't quite true. When

someone tried to kill you, you defended yourself, no matter how old you were.

"We'll wrap your ribs," she said. "Not too tight. You have to have room to breathe." She meant the advice for Hattie in case the girl took a notion to play nurse.

And then, although wobbling a bit on unsteady legs, she went on to the kitchen, pausing a moment before entering.

The dead silence from the other room terrified her.

Eli.

She paid no attention to Wren. The girl tagged along behind, saying something about January should sit down, that she looked like a ghost.

Well, and a second later, January did sit, mainly because her legs refused to support her any longer. She'd found Eli, his head leaning back and his eyes closed.

"Eli?" Sinking onto the floor beside him, January pressed her fingertips to the side of Eli's neck. His pulse beat strong, though faster than she thought was right. Relief made the space around her spin.

At her touch, his eyes opened, dark and fathomless, before he blinked and his gaze sharpened. "Don't worry. I'm alive." And then, more softly. "Don't cry, sweetheart."

*Sweetheart.*

She hadn't known she was crying, just like she hadn't been sure he was alive until she felt the beat of his heart. She leaned toward him. "You look terrible." Her voice caught.

He tried to grin, but only managed a wince as his lip split open and blood oozed. "So do you," he said, then a moment later, "Looks like we ought to put Doc LeBret on retainer."

January, figuring the recommendation summed up the situation quite well, didn't even try to argue with that.

Meanwhile, Wren hovered. "What should I do? Should I sew you up again?" She was wringing her hands and though she'd accused January of looking like a ghost, she wasn't much better off. But speaking drew Eli's attention.

"Glad to see you're in one piece, Wren. And Hattie?"

The girl nodded. "She's fine. But Jem..."

"Jem?" He started to pull himself up, bracing against the wall and using the edge of a cabinet for support.

"Jem may have a broken rib," January said quickly. "He got slugged by the butt of a shotgun and is in pain. He'll be all right as long as he doesn't stir around too much." She refused to think of the other things that could still go wrong.

By this time, Eli had managed the climb onto his feet. He stood scowling mightily as he surveyed the destruction of January's kitchen. The door off its hinges, the dining table knocked askew and damaged by bullet holes—let alone the man still crushed beneath the heavy maple workstation—chairs overturned, implements scattered. Dishes broken. The stovepipe knocked askew. No telling how that had happened.

And then there was the bruiser he'd managed to outlast; no small accomplishment considering his beat-up condition.

None of the outlaws, January realized, was the man from the chicken coop. She must've hurt him more than she'd thought. Enough to make him quit.

"This place is in shambles." Shaking his head, Eli turned to January. "Sorry about this."

She shrugged. Her eyes were dry now, swiftly dabbed while his back was turned. She didn't think there was anything to say.

"Got a rope? Or handcuffs?" Eli glared down at the unconscious bruiser. "We'd better get this one under control before he wakes up and goes on another tear."

An understatement. She knew a fight with an ordinary opponent wouldn't have meant ruination like this. From the look of things, their battle had been a near thing as to whether Eli won or lost. Lived or died.

"Handcuffs on the coat rack." She nodded toward a hook by the back door. Or, she amended ruefully, where the back door had once been. It hung open, a cold breeze pouring through that gave her a chill.

Without being asked, Wren skipped over, retrieved the cuffs, and handed them to Eli.

"Thanks."

While he went about the business of cuffing the prisoner's hands behind his back, January had Wren build up the fire in the cookstove as soon as she got the stovepipe back in place. Getting out her tools, she set about the painful task of reattaching the door. Enough to swing it closed, at least. Neither a permanent, nor a perfect job, but enough to hold in some of the heat. And keep the bogeymen out.

Calling Hattie to help, it took the four of them to lift the heavy maple work block off the fellow beneath it, and then to move him from the center of the floor. His chest appeared crushed. His breath came in spasmodic gasps. January thought he might be dying.

Jem, left to guard the hooligan who'd gone after the

girls, was on his feet by now. He stood a few feet away from the injured man, his face expressionless. Jem's prisoner leaned against the lowest stair step, one leg outstretched, the other bent at the knee in an awkward looking position. His main problem was a dislocated shoulder, the hump easily seen beneath his shirt. He was whimpering and trying to call to the man with the knife wound in his belly.

January stared at the live one, frowning. "That won't do any good. He can't hear you. He's most likely dead, by now." Just to verify, she went over to check, looked up quickly and nodded. "Yes. He's dead."

"You kilt Eddie?" the prisoner's eyes blinked shock.

"He killed himself. Ran right onto the knife I was holding. His own knife, in fact."

"Good riddance," Jem said, and January nodded grimly.

Hattie, practical as always, already had questions. "What shall we do with them? Are you going to bury this one up by your grandpa, January?"

"No. I don't want him on my property. We'll hitch up the wagon come morning and take all of them, the dead and the alive into town. If they have friends—" she paused, her lip curling "—or employers, *they* can take charge of the bodies. Otherwise, if they don't have the money on them, the county can send them to boot hill."

The Falls didn't have a boot hill as far as she knew, nor even a potter's field. She was thinking they ought to start one and place it on the cold side of the cemetery where the bodies wouldn't offend the normal folk in their final rest.

\* \* \*

THE REMAINDER of the night passed in restless fashion. Eli and January took turns keeping watch over the prisoners. In the darkest hour before dawn, the inept gunman with the crushed chest drew his last halting breath and their job became just that much easier. The dislocated shoulder kept the one fellow whimpering, whereas the bruiser woke up fighting against the cuffs around his hands and cursing.

Cursing not only Eli and January, but the people who hired him. Though he cleared up a couple things puzzling them, there were no surprises. He only confirmed what they already knew. But maybe, so January thought, they owed him. He solidified her vow to put Bethany, Joe, and their new accomplice, Headmaster Harold Bitters in the place they belonged, whether that turned out to be prison or hell.

A few minutes after sunrise, Johnny Johnson showed up at their door. January heard him first, muttering something she couldn't really hear as he tied Brownie to the rail out back. But when he mounted the steps onto the porch, she heard him clearly. Something to do with holy bodily excrement. Well, nothing strange about that considering the use the porch had been put to.

Rummy from lack of sleep, the corner of her mouth curled up as she went to lift the bottom of the door where it sagged to low to clear the floor.

Holding a finger across her lips, she whispered, "Everyone else is still asleep. Come on in. I'm glad to see you." The truth. They were going to need his help.

He stood in the doorway peering first inside, then peering over his shoulder. "Holy hell, January. What's happened here? Who is the dead man? I don't recognize him."

He meant the unmoving soul lying covered by an old tarp. The body lay on the porch, his shape under the canvas obvious. They'd moved the dead man out there last night, all of them unwilling to leave his body splayed on her floor. And now another waited to join the first.

"Nor do I," she said dryly, "but that didn't keep him from trying to kill us. It just didn't work out for him. Nor for him." She gestured to the man with the crushed chest, whose body lay where he'd fallen. He'd screamed when they tried to move him, and it had seemed kindest to leave him be.

"Another?" Johnny shook his head. "Another."

Johnny had been too loud. Eli, who'd fallen asleep with his head resting on his arms while sitting at the table, stirred.

January nodded. "You can see we were attacked."

Johnny's eyes shifted. "Looks like a howitzer shell went off in here. Are you all right, boss? Is he?" He meant Eli. "The kids?" Glancing back at Eli's bruised face, he shook his head.

By the time she reported on everyone's injuries, Eli's eyes were open.

"Can we make coffee?" he croaked, his voice sounding ragged.

With Johnny seeing to the fire, January filled the pot and got the coffee going, and, moving slowly, started breakfast.

Eli sat back with his first cup of coffee. "Is it possible to heat some water for a hot bath?" His mouth quirked. "Every muscle and bone in my body is stove up."

She could see as much from the way he moved—or didn't move. "Johnny?"

Ever agreeable, Johnny ran down to the cellar to start the boiler.

January guessed Eli had been hurt a lot worse than he wanted to show, especially when he leaned on Johnny's shoulder to make it up the stairs to the bathtub. Later, when he came down, his joints seemed to move some easier.

But maybe, January thought with a secret smile, it hadn't been only the bath. Maybe it was because, as she put out a fresh towel and washcloth for him, he'd caught her around the waist and drew her in close.

She'd looked up, startled.

"You and me, we're going to have a talk when this is over. Agreed?" His voice was soft as velvet and his dark, dark eyes intent on her face. Her bruised and beaten face.

She stared at him. They were touching, belly to belly, her head tilted to his. A moment passed, then his mouth dropped down onto hers and it was as if the world went away. For how long? She didn't know. She only knew it felt good. It felt right. It felt...exciting.

Too soon, his head lifted, and he smiled his crooked smile. "Agreed?" he asked again.

She had to think. What had he said? Oh, yes. A talk. Maybe not a thing to look forward to. But sure to settle whatever lay between them.

So she nodded. "Agreed."

Johnny was left with the chore of milking the cow, hitching Mollie to the buckboard, and with the girls and Eli helping, schlepping two bodies and some unwilling prisoners into the wagon bed.

Funny, January reflected, how squeamish the bruiser and the other one were about sitting beside the dead men.

The sunlit morning was half gone before they got underway to town, Johnny riding behind and guarding the wagon. January rode beside Hattie who held the lines, but trusty old Molly hardy needed guidance, instead following Eli and Jem who rode ahead. Pen, who'd had to be lifted into the bed of the buckboard rode in back, snarling every time one of the prisoners glanced at her.

By then, January had her plans made. Bethany and Bitters had to be dealt with. Today. She didn't figure there was time to waste. When news spread, as it was sure to do, of what had happened here last night, Bethany would have to give this up. Even Bitters must not have unlimited money to pay a gang of cutthroats like he'd been doing.

She had to smile, suspecting men willing to join Bethany's enterprise might be harder to find when they learned how many previous hires were either dead or in jail.

To give the woman credit, she was not only ruthless, but clever. January had no doubt this whole scheme and been plotted in such a way as to leave her in the clear, leaving Headmaster Bitters to take the blame should things go wrong. As they had.

Not but what Bitters deserved whatever happened to him. January just wanted to make sure the blame got equally shared. And she meant to see it done.

# CHAPTER 19

MARSHAL ADAM SOUTHBROOK, WHO'D APPARENTLY BEEN on the look-out for them, hustled outside onto the building's stoop as Hattie called out "whoa" and Molly stopped.

Southbrook's expression was not exactly welcoming. January judging it held more than a trace of dread. Dread that only grew as, mouth twisting, he studied the group who drew up at the hitch rail.

January wondered what would've soothed those frown lines. For the females to appear less beaten and helpless, or the menfolk, meaning Eli and Jem, less worn. At least Johnny appeared his regular self.

Or maybe, she decided, the bodies he spotted in the wagon bed had something to do with it. Those and more prisoners for his already overcrowded jail.

"Good morning, Marshal Southbrook," she said. "I saw you looking at us through the window. I imagine you're wondering what happened."

His mouth worked, as if figuring out what to say. "More dead men," he finally got out. "I oughta be used to it." And, when nobody else spoke, he studied them through narrowed eyes, which widened in increments. "Gawd Almighty, Deputy Billings. And Pasco, you—" He stopped and gusted out a heavy sigh.

*He should have seen us before we all cleaned up and ate our breakfast.* Amusement lightened January's solemn expression. He'd have been convinced the whole bunch of them were a disreputable stain on the community— as if he didn't already. She managed not to grin.

"Gonna need Doc as well as Mr. Hannon from the mortuary," she said. "And the use of a jail cell."

Southbrook sighed. "I figured." He cocked a finger at youngster who happened to be riding his pony past them at just the right—or wrong—time. The boy, his mouth wide open, stared over at them. "You, kid. Go fetch Doc LeBret. And the undertaker."

The kid whoaed the little nag. "Mr. Hannon? Are those people in the wagon dead, marshal?"

"They are. Go on, fetch Mr. Hannon. We need an undertaker and he's the onliest one we got. Hurry up now, there's a good boy. And tell him to bring his wagon."

"Yessir." The kid, face red with excitement, heeled his pony into a trot.

Maybe they really were a disreputable bunch, January thought. Or she was. Look at all that had happened in The Falls since she'd returned here a couple years ago. A land grab, kidnapping, horse stealing, outlaws trying to take over the town. And maybe the most disquieting of all had been the discovery she was heir to the Flowers fortune. And all the trouble that brought.

Not a day went by but what she regretted answering

the mysterious letter from Joseph Flowers Senior's attorney last year. Until she considered Jem and Hattie and the way Joe III and his wife had been—and still were—willing to murder anyone who stood between them and the Flowers inheritance. Including Jem, Hattie, and herself.

Blowing out an exasperated breath, she dismounted, flipped Hoot's reins over the rail, and allowed herself to pace back and forth on the boardwalk in front of the jail. Loosening her joints felt good. She'd been knocked around enough to put a freeze on all her muscles.

And Eli. She was surprised he could even move.

After a while, both Hattie and Wren joined her, leaving Eli, with a few asides from Jem, to tell South-brook about the goings-on at the ranch.

It was a relief when, not very many minutes later, Hannon himself drove up in the mortuary utility wagon —not the fancy ceremonial hearse—to pick up the dead men. He greeted January with a hearty handshake, declaring her his "best customer." The designation didn't exactly please her.

With the bodies disposed of, they all crowded into the jail.

About the only pleasing aspect of the whole business, or so it seemed to January, was seeing Marshal Southbrook place the bruiser in a cell and turn the lock on him. On the off chance of discovering anything interesting, he looked through the "wanted" posters stuck in his mail tray. He found a reward offered for the man's capture, no real surprise, considering. Not a big reward, as he wasn't a top-tier criminal, but, as Southbrook said, enough to pay Eli's horse feed bill for a while, even when he shared out a portion to Johnny.

"You should be happy." Southbrook scowled at Eli. "Makes all this look more...more..."

"Legitimate?" January asked.

"Yeah."

Eli glowered at the marshal. "Well then, if you question the legitimacy, give it all to Johnson. January doesn't need the money, and neither do I. And I'm out of the bounty business."

Johnny tried to refuse any part of it. "Thanks Eli, but I wasn't even there when you was getting pulped."

"You've been picking up the pieces we leave laying around. You've earned it."

Southbrook found paper on one of the dead men farther down in the stack, but he wasn't sure the money was still viable. He waved the poster over his head. "I dunno about this one. Could be he served his time and already got out. I'll have to look into it."

Eli laughed and wincing, stood up. "If there's reward money, give it to Squirt." He reached a hand to January, helping her rise. "We've got a train to catch."

"A train? To Spokane?" Southbrook's gaze sharpened. "What're you folks up to now?"

"It's past time to settle this thing. We can't allow it to go on any longer." January answered. "I don't plan on dying because of my relatives, and neither do Jem and Hattie. Or any of my friends. Someone has to finally deal with Joe III, Bethany, and whoever else she's drawn into her plot."

The marshal shook his head. "Can't say as I blame you. Just...you don't want to get on the wrong side of this. And, Mrs. Billings, you watch your back."

"I will. Count on it." Gathering the two girls and Jem around her like a mama quail and her chicks, January picked up the saddlebag she'd stowed beside her chair and started out the door.

Across the street, Squirt emerged from the livery and waved at them. "What's the news?" he hollered. "Who're them corpses you brought in?"

January shuddered and stopped. Did he have to yell for all the town to hear? Ten minutes later, leaving their horses at the livery, they set off for the depot.

Johnny, once more in charge of the ranch while she was gone, drove the wagon back home. January had no worries about her stock. Even so, at the last moment she called Pen to come with her. Tail wagging, though limping on a back leg, the old black dog trod along at January's side.

* * *

ELI PULLED his hat low over his eyes, shading the afternoon sun shining through the train window to keep it from blinding him. Right off, sleep began to overcome him and he let himself drift. From The Falls to the depot on Havermale Island in town left just enough time for a badly needed nap. And the hat over his face sheltered him from other passengers' wary looks. His battered state did nothing to instill confidence in his respectability. As they'd boarded, he'd been conscious of side-eyed stares.

January sat beside him, Pen at her feet; the girls and Jem took places across the aisle. Hattie, unlike her usual unflappable self, sat straight, her gaze darting from here to there in a disturbed manner. Eli worried she might be reliving her time on the train when the Pinkerton was murdered. He hoped she'd settle down before the next trip. If there was a next trip. If they could stop Bethany before her schemes got anybody—or everybody—else killed.

The whistle blew, announcing their departure. Eli hadn't noticed anyone suspicious who boarded with them, and he'd been watching. Even so, he was relieved when the conductor closed the door on any latecomers. The train, its wheels clacking on the rails as they gained traction, soon left the station behind.

He awakened only once, when the train stopped on a siding where they waited for the east bound train, which had precedence, to go in front of them.

Then still drowsy, but never incautious, he tilted his Stetson and peered out from under the brim. Hattie, he saw, was still awake—barely. But nothing in the car seemed changed, except that January, sound asleep, pressed against him, her head resting on his shoulder with the scarred side of her face on his chest.

Smiling a little, he shifted her weight into a more comfortable position, putting his arm around her to keep her from slipping. It was funny, he thought as he looked down at her, how once he'd been appalled by the contrast of the letter S carved on her cheek, and the other, unblemished side. Nowadays he never gave the scar a thought beyond thinking it a badge of courage. She was beautiful anyway he looked at her.

Maybe aware of his regard, January murmured, "Are we there?" and he replied, "Not yet. Go ahead and sleep."

And she did.

So did he, but only until they reached the outskirts of Spokane and the train slowed to a creeping pace. He was wide awake and uneasy when the train finally halted in front of the depot. Ever cautious, Eli stopped the youngsters when they would've gotten in line to disembark.

"We'll wait." He put a hand on Jem's arm. "Let the crowd thin out. It's too easy to miss seeing a man bent on trouble if he mingles with a lot of other folks. If there is anybody waiting for us, the longer we delay, the more obvious he'll be."

That put two of them on guard as Jem took up a watchful post.

January nodded her agreement, though her dog became restless. In fact, it was Pen's growing distress that made her decide they couldn't delay any longer. "She's got to go." She took a position behind a squat little woman to where the conductor was offering a hand to help the ladies on the steep step.

A lot happened all at once.

Eli, keeping watch behind January, spotted movement at the edge of his vision. A gun barrel poked around the corner of the depot just as she stepped through the exit onto the step. Pen, eager to get to the ground, bounded in front of her.

Eli shouted.

A shot rang out, pinging off the metal side of the rail car and ricocheting into the gathering dusk. Men yelled. Women screamed. A kid or two cried out.

And January tripped over the dog who, startled by the noise and the strangers all around her, hesitated on the step.

The conductor reached for January, and he, also unbalanced, fell on top of her as she plunged off the last step and went to her knees.

Eli, leaping over the two of them, bounded flat out

toward the shooter who wisely abandoned his try for a second shot and took off running.

Pen went after the shooter, baying harsh and loud, and leading Eli by a few yards. The two men and the dog headed into the train yard, avoiding the trains slowly traversing through a maze of tracks. First the shooter, then Pen, then Eli, they leaped in turn over couplings, dodged between cars, stumbled over rails.

Still aching from the fight the previous night, Eli saw the man gaining ground and urged himself to greater speed. Pen, he remembered, had also been hurt in the fight last night. She'd taken a severe kick to the hindquarters as she fought the man manhandling January and was still hurting today. Her limp grew into a three-legged hobble. Always game, she kept going.

Ahead of them, Eli saw the shooter raise his pistol and take a wild shot before dodging around a huge locomotive making its ponderous way through the yard. The bullet whistled past.

Pen was only a few jumps behind the man when, at the last moment, Eli caught up with her. Heart in mouth, he snatched the dog by her collar and dragged her back just in time to avoid the wheels of the idling machine. They could do nothing but wait for it to pass. Both dog and man panted.

Eli heard the shooter yell something triumphant at them and laugh. When the locomotive finally passed, he was nowhere in sight.

"Whoa now, dog," Eli told the dog, hanging onto her though she struggled to be free. "Enough. Looks like he's gotten the best of us. For now."

Pen must've agreed, for she squatted, awkward on her sore hip, and emptied her bladder.

* * *

JEM CAME TO FIND THEM, most probably figuring to join the chase. Eli wondered how the boy had gotten away from January. Disappointment showed on the kid's face when he saw they were headed back and by themselves.

"Couldn't catch him? Not even Pen?"

Eli shook his head. "Look at her. She tried her best. So did I. She's only got three working legs." He didn't mention the pain in his back. Jumping over the couplings had damaged kidneys already aching from the pounding the bruiser had given him.

Jem reached down to caress the dog. "January don't like her dog getting hurt. That's for sure."

"Don't I just know it." If anybody didn't know January loved that dog like a mama loves her child, he'd be surprised.

They took their time getting back, allowing Pen to set the pace to the station platform. As they approached, he spotted the womenfolk through the open doors. They were huddled in the office while the conductor told his story to anybody who'd listen. The stationmaster for one. A loading dock worker for another. Eli didn't try to join them, preferring to remain on the platform outside the building.

January, maybe sensing him standing outside, caught sight of him through the open doorway. Their eyes met over the others' heads. He nodded, pointing toward the lot where the cabs waited. She'd know enough to be ready to move when he gave the word.

A smile touched her lips. Without saying a word, she turned Hattie and Wren in his direction and moved them unobtrusively away from the others. Nobody seemed to notice, listening instead to the conductor's tale.

Somebody, probably the stationmaster, had called for the police, he heard someone say, but so far, no one had showed up. Eli figured that was just as well. The women were safe enough for the moment, surrounded as they were by the crowd. Someone there, who evidently kept up with the society page, had recognized January as the Flowers heir and word had spread.

He soon found a cab with enough room for all of them. While he stayed with the vehicle, Jem went to collect the girls.

Once free of the station, Jem hurried them into the cab. Hattie started to say something, but Eli hushed her. "We'll talk later."

"The Flowers apartment or Hotel Spokane?" he asked January, thinking she might prefer a hotel where there'd be people around. Not to mention the luxurious accommodations, maybe someone to wait on them hand and foot.

"Apartment." A majority chimed their opinions, which left himself and maybe Wren as outliers. Shrugging, Eli gave the driver the address.

For the first time, the man showed interest. "Say, isn't that the Flowers—"

Eli cut him off. "Yes," he said, and got in beside January. Pen had already curled up at her feet.

In the dark, her cold hand sought his. She grasped his fingers. "You didn't catch him. Are you all right?"

"I'll live," he said.

"I skinned my knees." She sighed.

"He'll try again, you know."

"Yes," she said. "Better at the apartment than at a

hotel where bystanders can be hurt." She laughed, short and hard. "Besides, I wouldn't be at all surprised to learn that's where Bethany is staying. A pleasant change from a prison cell."

He supposed she was right. That didn't mean he liked the notion of any kind of shooting. God knows there'd been enough already to last a lifetime.

The Flowers building was dark when the cabbie drew his horse to a halt. They all got out while Eli paid the man and sent him on his way. January handed Eli the key.

"Keep your eyes peeled," she told the kids. "Hard telling who might be around."

The only movement they saw was a pesky raccoon waddling toward the empty—except for some scrubby trees—lot at the back side of the building.

Quietly, they filed inside, remaining silent as they passed through the outer area to the wide stairway. They even managed to walk softly. At the landing on the second floor, Eli stopped and reached over to whisper in January's ear. "You and the kids go on up to the apartment. I'm going to check if your troublesome tenant is still here. If he is, I'll throw him out."

Her smile struck him as being forced. "It'll be fine with me if I never see him again."

It suited Eli, as well. They didn't need Joseph, or Bethany's, stooge watching their every move. Morning, he decided, would be plenty soon enough to take up the chase.

# CHAPTER 20

JANUARY KNEW SHE SHOULD'VE BEEN MORE WATCHFUL AT the train station. Hadn't she warned Hattie to stay back when she tried to get in line? Apparently, she should've listened to her own advice. But the girl been pale and sweating, though the rail car wasn't overly warm. January took Hattie's impatience and the sweat as signs that being closed into the tight space frightened her. Well, that and Pen's need to get out.

But January didn't blame Hattie a bit. She suspected the girl might carry the fear of trains with her for a good long time. Those things had a way of sticking with you.

For instance, she still had horrors— But she'd resolved never to think of some of the past events that colored her own nightmares.

The fact remained it had been her fault for all the trouble at the station. Her's and Pen's, when the poor dog needed out badly enough to take matters into her own...paws.

If it hadn't been for the conductor, she, and maybe

Pen, would be dead by now since Eli's warning had come a short second too late.

She should be grateful the conductor had been a slight sort of fellow. Otherwise, she would be in worse case than suffering from a pair of painfully stinging knees and a couple skinned palms when he landed on top of her.

But, mostly due to Eli taking charge, at least they'd made it in one piece to the Flowers Building and the safety—hopefully the safety—of the penthouse apartment. January figured some of that safety depended on just when Bethany and the school's headmaster got together to plan another attack. If things worked out right, her own party would be ahead of the game.

And she had no doubt this wasn't finished. All signs pointed to Bethany not being the type to give up. Not where money was concerned. A lot of money.

"Where are we all going to sleep?" Hattie's question broke into January's reverie. The girl stood in the middle of the front room blinking around as the light came on. She sounded uncharacteristically cranky.

There were only two bedrooms in the apartment, aside from a small maid's room. January hadn't really thought that far ahead, but it seemed a simple enough matter. Not much different than when the deputy from Cheney had stayed the night.

"You and Wren in your room. Jem and Eli in mine. I'll take the maid's room." January knew she sounded short. Impatient. She needed some time alone.

"Oh," Hattie said.

Wren, her brow puckering at Hattie's tone, looked uneasy. "I can stay in the maid's room."

"Do as you're told. Both of you." Spinning away from

them, and wincing from the twinge in her knees, let alone the pain from her plaguy bullet wound, January went back to the foyer and stood with the door half open. She'd watch for Eli until he got back. For Eli, or for whoever else might come up the stairs.

Five long minutes passed while she waited there. Girl's voices came from within, but she only listened with half an ear. They seemed to be arguing, and she huffed out a breath. Just what she needed. More battles. Jem, at least, knew enough not to join in.

Footsteps sounded on the stair at last and Eli came into sight. He smiled when he saw her. "All clear. I went down to the basement. Your caretaker is gone for the night, but everything appears safe and sound. I checked the offices on the first and second floors. They're locked up tight." His grin quirked as he came close to her. "I picked Granger's lock and looked around the office. One thing I can tell you, the man is no investment broker. The only items in his office are a table and chair, a telephone, and a cot. Oh, and a pad of paper, two pens, and three dime novels. That's it."

January opened her eyes wide, but in truth, she wasn't surprised. "That's all? Not even a desk? Or a file cabinet?"

"No desk; no file cabinet. The man must've been bored out of his senses, waiting to report something."

"So he's only ever been here to spy on me. Funny, really, since I'm only here when I have business. Hence the novels you found, I suppose. He needed something to occupy his time."

Eli's eyebrows rose. "I can't say much for his taste in literature. He didn't bother to make the room appear a place to do business." Eli locked the door behind him and added, "Unless it's to take on more jobs like the one he's doing here."

"Huh. A professional snoop." January led the way into the front room. "Just don't ask me to feel sorry for him."

She heard the smile in his voice when he said. "I won't."

They found Jem in the kitchen opening cupboards in search of food. Not a successful quest, judging by his scowl. "Ain't there anything here to eat, January? It's past suppertime."

For the first time in hours, it occurred to her that she was starving. The girls, and Eli, must be as well. She stared at Jem. "Sorry. I had Wren throw out anything perishable when we last left. I didn't want the place smelling like rot the next time I opened the door."

"I'll go buy something," Jem offered. "Tell me what you need and how much."

January caught Eli's shake of the head.

"I'll go." He'd unbuttoned his coat, but now he did it back up, hiding the Mauser in the holster across his chest. Except for a bulge, anyhow. He thought for a moment. "Any of you like that noodle stuff the Chinese cook? That's quick."

Jem grinned. "Hattie and me, we do. And it's cheap. Dunno about Wren."

"She'll eat what is put before her," January started, and Jem finished with, "or she'll go without."

Eli turned back at the door. "I won't be long. Lock up behind me."

"I will."

January suspected Eli had more on his mind than simply getting food. He'd looked too thoughtful for such a simple chore—unless he expected the man at the train to make another try. But then, while she would make sure to seal the kids in, she had other ideas in mind, as well.

The girls were still chattering in Hattie's room, although they sounded more amiable now, and Jem went off to have a bath while the boiler was still delivering hot water. That suited January fine. The second she was alone, she went out onto the landing, twisted the lock, and pocketed the key. She stood there a long moment, listening. Getting a feel for the building. It felt empty, she decided. Just like Eli had said.

While Eli had searched, he didn't know the building like she did. Like Joseph and Bethany did, for that matter. They'd often been honored guests here, visiting Joseph's grandfather before he died.

She started her exploration in the cellar. While there, she made sure to stoke the boiler. She'd be wanting a bath in the magnificent claw-foot tub herself after supper. Uncomfortable in the chill and dark of the large below-ground space, she hurried. Her chore was made harder by the single electric bulb, which did a poor job of acceptably lighting the large room. She often wondered how Jem and Hattie had fared during the time they'd lived down here.

Eli knew about the secret passageway leading outside from the apartment, but she didn't think he knew about the cellar's second door. A point in her favor was that she doubted Joe or Bethany did either. She couldn't imagine either of them, with their sense of superiority, coming into a cellar to examine the bones of the building. But if Granger had been thorough enough, he might have found it when he stayed after the building was supposed to be closed and the janitor gone home.

She slipped behind the boiler to where a two-foot wide chute entered from the outside. Unlike some places, coal storage here was in a shed easily reached by the delivery people outside but connected to the building via the chute. What she was interested in right now was whether anyone had been accessing the place through a narrow door between the shed and the building. Most men would have to turn sideways to get through it if they ever saw it at all. January could manage easily and did.

As far as she could tell, no new tracks had been left in the coal dust on the ground aside from the caretaker's. He wore boots with a self-administered tread design she easily recognized. Her anxieties relaxed just the least little bit.

From there she went through the same motions Eli had earlier, only January went a little slower and took her time. She found, just as he had, nothing of importance.

Until she stood in front of Granger's office. Opening the door required only the use of her master key. Carefully, she closed it and, switching on the light, waited for it to grow brighter.

As Eli had reported, there were only those few things inside. At first glance, at least. What Eli hadn't mentioned, was the odor of a man who neglected his personal hygiene. Which struck her as odd since Granger had always appeared prosperous and well-dressed for his position, his beard trimmed, his shoes polished. She'd never noticed an smell around him on the rare occasion she'd seen him before. The cot. Had it indeed been Granger using the cot at night, or had it been someone else?

She stepped forward and pulled the blanket covering the cot out of the way. The sleeper had left an imprint there. Definitely a larger man than Granger. A chill swept over her, leaving goosebumps on her skin. Did that mean he—whoever he was, whatever his intention—would be coming back? Or might he have been one of those in the fight last night? If so, was he one of the dead? Or... She stopped herself. Chances were, he'd be someone different.

*Steady.* January didn't know exactly why, but she pulled the pocket pistol she routinely kept in her boot and set it on the table when she picked up the books. Shaking them out revealed nothing, except the stub from a railway ticket indicating someone had traveled to The Falls from Spokane and back again on the afternoon train yesterday. The person who'd nailed the note to her door, she suspected. The evidence didn't surprise her.

Her ears had a peculiar buzz in them. At least this was proof Granger had taken the room on a pretext. Certainly enough to get him removed from the picture. Drawing a breath, she looked down at the tablet.

At first, all she saw was a blank page. But then, when she accidentally drew a finger across the surface, she felt an imprint there. Something that made her hold the page up to the light.

Whether Granger or the unknown person, whoever last used the pad had written with a heavy hand. And Deputy January Billings most surely wanted to know what it said. She tore the paper from the pad, folded it, and stuffed it in her pocket. More evidence.

Figuring it was time—past time—to go, she replaced everything as she'd found it, retrieved her gun, and headed for the door.

She had her hand on the knob when she heard a shuffling movement on the other side. Then the sound of a key inserted into the lock. That's when her heart began beating harder and faster.

*Damn.* She hadn't turned off the light. Whoever this was, they'd have seen a glow shining from under the door. She didn't dare turn it off now.

A quick glance around told her what she already knew. No place to hide. She'd have to get the drop on whoever entered and bluff her way out of trouble.

As the door opened, nearly catching her in the nose, she backed up behind it until she stood hidden against the wall.

A plea flashed through her mind. Be Granger. I can take him if I have to.

But of course, it wasn't Granger. She might've known. It was the larger, stinky guy. And when the door slammed shut again, she stood in plain sight.

He, whoever he might be, walked past her across the room, headed, she presumed, for the table and chair. He probably intended to keep an eye on the road outside.

*Waiting, watching for us.* Then, *he'll see Eli when he returns. He'll bushwhack him.*

Seeing him from behind, she thought he had the same shape as the man who'd shot at her at the train, glimpsed as he ran away. Same broad, but rounded shoulders. Same odd, narrow-brimmed hat on his head.

January's heart sank even further. The breath she took carried to the man as he pulled the chair from under the table.

He whirled. Eyed the gun she had leveled at him. "Sir," she started, "you are under arr..."

"Son of a..." His curse overwhelmed her citation. But then his upper lip lifted in a sneer. "Well, by gawd, this is right handy. How'd you get here before me?" Without waiting for an answer, which she didn't intend on providing anyway, an easy twist of his hand on the chair back picked it up and flung it across the room at her. As she dodged the scarily accurate throw, he lunged toward her.

January hadn't expected him to be so fast. He was halfway across the room when she came to her senses and fired. The bullet took him in the same arm he'd used to throw the chair.

He bellowed, blood leaked, but he kept coming.

She fired again. This time he howled. A bullet hole showed in the front of his coat. A hole that instantly filled with blood.

And then he was on her, reaching for her with his undamaged hand, but particularly for her gun. He grabbed for the pistol's barrel, thrusting her hand upward.

But even as he pushed up, her finger tightened on the trigger. If he'd thought to stop the little S & W from firing, he was mistaken. The hammerless .32 barked.

The bullet ripped through his hand taking three fingers with it. The impetus slowed, the bullet came to rest in his thick neck, somehow missing the artery there, but hitting a nerve or something that caused him to drop to the ground as if pushed from a bluff.

January, her ears ringing, hadn't heard anything but the gunshots, but when a man's voice said, "Is he dead?," she spun to face the new threat, the gun already coming to bear.

"Eli." She breathed again. The revolver lowered. "I almost shot you."

"I noticed." He stood in the doorway holding a covered basket she supposed contained their supper. He gazed into her eyes as if looking at a stranger. "Is he dead?" he asked again.

"I don't know." She swallowed. "I don't think I care. He's the one who tried to kill me at the train, isn't he? The one you chased?"

"Looks like it."

Upstairs, the girls were making noise almost like the clucking of hens. In seconds, a light moved on the staircase showing one—or all—the kids on the move. Slowly. Cautiously, but coming to her assistance.

Eli called out, "We're here. You can come on down."

Jem, fresh from the tub and barefoot with a towel wrapped around him, was the first to reach them. He carried the shotgun generally found almost hidden in the elephant foot umbrella stand in the foyer. Aimed out ahead of him, he was taking no chances.

Hattie came next, toting the big Colt .45 Joseph Senior had kept in his office.

And Wren held the iron poker from beside the fireplace. She looked scared, but very determined.

They crowded into the room, staring down at the man on the floor. Same as Eli had done, Jem said, "Is he dead?" then paused. "He doesn't look dead."

"No," Hattie said. "He hasn't got that gone away look dead people get."

They both had some experience with death.

Wren startled them all with a soft shriek. "He moved. I seen his eyelids twitch."

If she hadn't been discomposed herself right at the moment, January might have laughed. Or at least smiled. But having shot a man three times and he still refused to die, well, she could sympathize with Wren.

Heaving a sigh as though the weight of the world pressed upon her shoulders, January turned to Eli.

"Would you call Milt Ferguson? We have to report this. I'll keep an eye on this one. Make sure he doesn't recover and hightail it out of here."

Eli walked around the fellow sprawled on the floor. "Telephone is right here. If it's connected, and I figure it is so the watchers could call their bosses, it'll save a little time. I'll make the call."

He gestured toward the basket, which emitted smells to tantalize her hunger. Jem was already heading toward it.

"He can wait. Let's eat first," Jem said.

So they did.

# CHAPTER 21

ELI ATE FAST. TOO FAST, PROBABLY, TO EITHER MIND HIS manners or honor the efforts of the Chinese chef who'd packed the basket. Having left the wounded man on the floor where he'd fallen, he warned them it would be a mistake to be absent too long. A short examination had left him marveling over how the man had survived this long, but he said he was worried that if Bethany's hired killer was subject to miracles, he just might get up and walk out if nobody kept an eye on him.

A ballyhooing from the front of the building alerted them Milt had arrived, bringing with him an ambulance from the Deaconess Hospital and a couple more policemen.

January, having followed the kids upstairs and helped portion out the containers of food, soon discovered her appetite had faded to nothing. She sat looking down at the plate on the table before her, her stomach jumping in protest. A few bites told her it'd be best if she left the rest. Shooting a person, she'd discovered, tended to upset her. It was almost a relief to follow Eli down to the second floor as he opened the door and led the policemen to the wounded man.

Milt hunkered beside the "victim," as he insisted on calling the man and eyed him with an unsurprised expression. January, standing back, thought she wouldn't have called the would-be assassin a victim, unless as a victim of his own stupidity by underestimating her.

"Howdy, Dave," Milt said as the man's eyelids flickered open. "Can't say as I surprised to see you here."

Dave's mouth moved. "Milt," he said. Or at least he mouthed the word. No sound passed from his mouth.

January shot the copper a narrowed glance. "You know him?"

"Yeah. One of the toughs who hangs around old man Piper's bar. There, and sometimes out at the junction." Milt stood up and shrugged. "This is what he does; loiters around the saloons and picks up odd jobs terrorizing folks. Beats 'em up usually, but I reckon it depends on the pay."

Eli huffed. "Paid him well enough to try shooting us at the train when we came in. He's the one I chased through the train yard."

Milt turned to January. "Somebody told me you was the target. That right?"

*Somebody, huh? Was that somebody Eli, by chance, when he went after the food?*

She nodded in answer to Milt's question. "And he tried again, just now. He broke in to the building."

Eli shook his head in denial. "Actually, January, I think he has a key."

Her eyes widened. "A key?" She thought a moment.

"I'd say that proves Bethany is at the head of this. No one else should have a key."

"By rights, she shouldn't, either," Eli gritted, "but since he rents an office, Granger does. And this *is* his office."

"Well, if it is Missus Flowers, she don't have one now." Eyes narrowing, Milt squatted again as one of the ambulance men laid a stretcher down beside Dave and prepared to roll him on to it. He pressed a thick forefinger into a spot on Dave's chest, and when the man's eyes flickered, asked, "That right? Is Missus Flowers the one who hired you?"

Dave turned his head to the ambulance fellow. "Get me outa here." His voice, barely audible, sounded as if he were gargling blood.

The ambulance man stepped forward. "Ferguson, we gotta take this man now. He's bleeding out. I doubt he's gonna make it as far as the hospital."

Milt rose, eyeing first Eli, then January. "Anything more you want to ask this feller?"

"Yes," January said. "Where is Mrs. Flowers hiding out?"

But Dave was either stubbornly reluctant or beyond the capability to answer.

Milt directed one of the extra patrolmen to accompany the ambulance to the nearby hospital and keep his eye on the prisoner. Then he pulled the chair from the corner where it had landed when Dave threw it at January, and sat himself at the table. He pulled a tattered tablet and a pencil stub from his uniform pocket and stared at her.

"So. Let's have your version of the story."

He stopped her when she got to the part about

opening the office with her master key. "Is that legal? Say somebody rents a place, don't that mean he's got a right to privacy?"

January was ready. "To a certain extent. According to the lease he signed, I have the right to inspect the premises if I suspect he's using it for purposes other than business. Nefarious enterprises, for instance."

Milt mouthed those words. "Nefarious enterprises, eh. How do you spell that? And did you? Suspect them, that is?"

"I did."

"Why?"

She held up one finger. "Because he stayed late, after the building is locked, almost every night. There's even a cot, which is entirely against the rule of no one staying here overnight." She held up another. "Because I never saw anyone visit his office to do business." Yet another finger. "And because he accosted young Miss Flowers whenever he saw her. As he did when she stayed in the apartment."

"Accosted?"

January set her arms akimbo, then quickly changed her mind and put her elbows back down as her over-stretched stitches pulled. "I'm sure you know what I mean."

"Uh." Milt licked the tip of his pencil and wrote something on his notepad. "He ever accost you?"

She snorted. "He didn't dare—and he knew it."

He snickered, then wiped his hand across his mouth as if to still the sound. "That don't surprise me none. You are a wee bit scary, Deputy Billings." He took another look around the room, taking in the sparse furnishings. And the cot. "Speaking of Granger, when did he leave?"

Eli answered. "We don't know. We came directly from the train station and he was gone when we got here."

"So as far as you know, Miz Billings, you shot a burglar tonight."

He was giving her a way out, she realized. Well, she'd take it and be grateful. "Yes," she said.

Milt got up. "Guess that's that, then." At the doorway, he paused. "I'm leaving an officer here to watch the place tonight. You folks take care. Pasco, I get off shift along about midnight. You need somethin', just holler. I'll be at Moseley's Saloon for a spell after that."

Eli nodded. "Do my best not to drag you into this."

"I'll be at Moseley's," Milt said again, then he was gone.

In the silence, January gazed down at the blood on the floor, thankful the wood had a finish that would keep the stains from going too deep.

"I'm going to sell this building." She shivered. "My dad may have done a lot of the construction on it, but frankly, it's a burden. For me and for Jem and Hattie. I'll close up the secret stairway, first. Nobody ever needs to know it's even there unless they tear the place down."

Eli reached for her hand and pulled her into his arms, cradling her with a gentle rocking motion. "Will you come home full time then?" He stared down at her, his dark, dark eyes holding her in warmth as welcome as his embrace.

It was as if he were sending a message beyond what his words said. She couldn't think of anything but him. *Come home, he'd said.*

Behind them, Jem spoke, his voice gruff. "Are we going after her? Her and Headmaster Bitters? We aren't letting them go, are we?"

"Of course not." January drew apart from Eli, feeling cold when she stood alone again. "Although it would help if we knew where they are."

"The school, I bet." Jem huffed. "Good old Bakewell Academy. That's the first place I'd look."

"You would? Why?"

Eli appeared to be thinking it over and Jem bobbed his head in agreement when he said, "He's got a point. Home ground for Biggers. His wife is there to give excuses for him." Then another idea occurred. "But I don't think so."

January raised an eyebrow. "No? Where do you think? The brothel?" The brothel was her choice.

Eli nodded. "Seems more likely. That little junction is notorious as a place to hire men who aren't choosy about how they earn a buck. A lot of ex-convicts gather there. And Bitters might think his involvement is still undetected. As far as he's concerned, his only connection is the persecution of Jem. He won't want to bring the conflict to his home ground."

Jem blew a scornful raspberry. "Doubt if he's worried about Mrs. Bitters finding out. She ain't no sweet pie herself. She's probably in on the whole deal. But yeah. The junction is closer to town anyway. More convenient."

January had to think back. When they'd rescued Hattie the other night, she'd only seen the shed and the back of the house. She had no idea what the rest of the place looked like, but she was ready to find out. "Bethany," she said, hesitating, "she's used to being a society lady. Would she countenance being there for more than a single meeting?"

Eli shrugged. "After her time in the prison I doubt you'll find she's as particular as she used to be. She won't be bothered by the...the sin she sees there. You can expect prison to change a person, and for a woman already of uncertain character, the change is not always for the better. Like Bethany, Ruby is a case in point."

"Who's Ruby?" Jem wanted to know, but Eli just shook his head.

Ruby Pasco, Eli's father's wife, although they were divorced now, was also serving a couple years in the state prison. January had personal experience with Ruby and believed Walla Walla a fitting institution for a woman of her propensities. She had to wonder if Ruby and Bethany had met. Possible, she figured. There weren't so many women there they could remain unknown to each other. Unless they wanted to, what with both thinking they were the queen bee.

She gritted her teeth, just thinking about these women. Sometimes she felt as though she'd known more bad women than good ones in her life.

Sighing, she said, "There's only one way to find out. Let me talk to the girls and we'll go see."

"I'll go down to the livery and saddle the horses." Eli cast a final glance around the room and urged the other two out before turning off the light. "Jem, you walk January over when she's ready. I don't want her out by herself."

Almost as grim as Eli, Jem narrowed his eyes. "Saddle three. I'm coming with you."

Eli hesitated, then said, "All right. I'd rather have you along with us than following on your own."

Opening her mouth to speak, January hushed herself in time. Eli was correct. Jem had a right to see justice done. After all, in a way, Bethany's vendetta had started with him. Him and Harold Bitters. Jem might be a boy in years, but as an orphan charged with taking care of his younger sister, he'd grown up fast. He became capable beyond what most adult men ever did, especially when they had people, relatives, willing to kill for their inheritance.

In the apartment, January explained the plan to the girls. "If we're halfway lucky, this will all be settled tonight." She put her arms around Hattie, who shook with dread. Wren just looked hopeful.

"Watch out for Jem," Hattie whispered.

"I will best I can." A promise January meant to keep.

"I wish he'd never done that," Hattie burst out. She looked through the open door into Joseph Senior's old office where Jem was digging more ammunition out of the gun cabinet and filling the belt he'd latched low on his waist.

January heard all movement go silent. "He? What he? Done what?" she asked, but she knew.

"Our father. I wish he'd never come and brought us to live here after Mother died. I wish Jem and me could've stayed on the ranch and just been anybody. Or nobody. I don't want to be rich."

"You don't?" Hearing this, Wren's mouth dropped open, then her eyes filled. "Well, I guess you don't know how it is, Hattie Flowers, when you ain't got enough to eat and your ma has to let awful, stinking men do stuff to her. She hates it, but she has to. Was you ever hid away so's nobody could see you? Did other women laugh and say your time was a comin' and pretty soon you'd be just like them?" She paused. "And know it for the truth."

Hattie stiffened. "Yes. Not the women part so much, but we were hidden away all the time. We had to act like we weren't even there and hope nobody noticed us. And then people wanted to kill us. If it wasn't for January and Eli, we'd be dead already. I'm tired of being hunted. I'm tired of worrying about Jem and him worrying about me and both of us always having to be so careful." Her voice rose loud enough for Jem to catch the last part of her tirade.

He froze. Glanced at January, who tried to wipe what she knew was a stricken look off her face. Then he closed the office door behind him and stood with his back to it.

"Hattie," he said after a few seconds, "I'll be all right. Count on it. We'll talk about this when I get back. Not now."

"Yeah?" she said. Tears stood in her eyes. "*If* you get back. If January gets back."

"We'll be back." January said in unison with Jem, and he added, "I promise."

"See that you do." Hattie spun, stormed into the bedroom and slammed the door.

Wren stared after her. "I'd get my butt whomped if I acted like that."

Joseph Flowers senior had a lot to answer for in January's opinion. From the constant indulging of his outlaw grandsons, to siring a son and a daughter in his old age and leaving them—sink or swim—to settle things on their own. She didn't bother to put herself into his schemes. If he hadn't gotten worried about the kids at the last moment, she doubted she—or they—would ever have known each other existed.

She sucked air into her lungs, then let it out on a gust. "Wren, lock up after us. Do not let anyone in until we get back. And keep Hattie here. Wrestle her down if you have to. Can you do that?"

Wren stared at her. "Sure."

"Jem, get a move on. Eli will be waiting for us." January turned on her heel, grabbing up Eli's coat from the tree in the foyer as she went out.

The two of them didn't speak as they traversed the few blocks to the big Model Livery Stable. Which didn't mean January neglected to watch for suspicious characters. A single drunk, the air around him reeking of cheap hootch, stumbled toward them, his hand groping out at January. Jem started to draw the .45 Colt that had belonged to Joseph Senior, but January stilled him.

She pushed the past the man, looking back once as he mumbled something after them. Nothing to worry about, she decided, as he sank down under a bush in someone's yard and retched.

A scare over nothing. It was becoming habitual, she thought wryly.

They found Eli, when they finally reached the livery, standing out of sight inside the huge barn holding the reins of three horses. "Took you long enough," he muttered, when he handed the reins of the black mare to January.

Jem swung up into the saddle and clicked his tongue to the horse Eli had chosen for him, heading east without them.

Accepting the coat she'd brought him with gratitude, Eli nodded after Jem. "Trouble?"

She made a face. "Trouble."

Minutes later they caught up with Jem, and a couple hours after that, they arrived at the cut-off where the road led to the settlement at the junction. Lights, they discovered as they approached from the rear, were on in only two buildings. Both were brothels, but only one showed signs of life.

Vera's House of Women. A catchy title.

A two-wheeled buggy drawn by a single horse stood hitched to the rail. A saddle horse lazed hip-shot beside it.

# CHAPTER 22

BIRDS NESTING IN THE TREES FILLING THE ACRE OR SO behind the brothel went still as they passed beneath. Light was dim here, overhung by the canopy of pines. Clouds moving across the sky complicated matters. Snow melt coming down from the mountains kept the river full, and the pounding of water tossed over the rocky riverbed pulsed loud. It smelled like clean earth.

Eli thought the night, though downright cold for this time of year, would've been beautiful if it hadn't been for their destination and what he knew awaited there.

He'd drawn his horse to a halt and sat studying not only the main structure, but the outbuildings, as well. After a time, he dismounted. January, stiff from her tussles with men opponents these last few days, groaned a bit as she followed suit. Jem, already down, tied his horse to a low branch and took January's reins. Theirs appeared to be the only horses tethered among the trees. Odd, Eli thought, from what he'd heard of the place. The grove usually sheltered several saddle horses

"I'm not staying out here," Jem said, low-voiced. "You ain't leaving me behind."

Eli, whose intention had been to do just that, hesitated, but January was already giving permission. "We won't. But understand. You're not in charge, Jem. Listen to Eli. Do as he says. Or as I say."

A bulldog expression crossed the boy's face, but he nodded. They were ready then.

"Spread out," Eli said. "One at a time, get across the open yard to the back door. I'll go first. Next Jem. Last January. Be quiet."

Then he was gone. Since he wore dark clothing, he melded well with the shadowy dark as he crossed. So did Jem. January, though, wore a pale yellow blouse. Though mostly covered by her jacket, the blouse flashed briefly when some feathery clouds cleared as she ran. But she was fast, her time in the open brief.

They crowded onto the small porch. Eli tried turning the knob and to his surprise, the door opened. "Too easy," he muttered. *Another trap?* But they had no choice. He went in. "Stay alert."

Knowing he could rely on January, he meant the warning for Jem.

As before, on the day he paid for Madeline's burying, the kitchen was warm and smelled of cooking. Yeast bread, for one thing. Onions and slightly charred beefsteak for another. It appeared Vera didn't starved her workers, at least. The only point he'd found in her favor.

Soft-footed, they passed through the kitchen and entered the dining room restyled into a reception room. Empty now, one of the telltale lamps they'd seen from outside burned here, the flame flickering as the kerosene burned low.

The room beyond was the one that interested him. Vera's private meeting room. Voices came from behind the closed door, rising and falling as a woman spoke. Apparently, Vera had an important customer in there with her.

Or maybe more than one. Eli didn't figure to take anything for granted.

It appeared Vera wasn't happy. "You owe me money," she was saying, her gravelly croak perfectly audible even through the closed door. Although in fairness, it was a cheap door, thin and ill-fitting in its framework.

"You'll get your money when I get mine," a second female said, her tone nasty. "I told you that going in. You were fine with the deal at the time. I'll remind you. A deal is a deal."

"That was before that half-witted scum you hired beat one of my girls to death." Vera made a half-sob; one that sounded almost as sincere as a politician's promise. "She was a fine lookin' woman before he messed her up. A real money-maker for me. And that's on you. I heard you tell him to go ahead with whatever he wanted to do long as he kept her quiet."

A pause, then the second woman said, "But she is quiet. Quiet about your part in this, as well, don't forget. He did the best thing. She's just another dead whore. It happens all the time. I'm sure it's not the first time here."

"Yeah? Well, don't you forget you cost me the young girl. A regular little beauty. She'd a made a small fortune for me if she kept her looks for a few years. I was just ready to break her in."

Vera hadn't, he observed, denied Bethany's claim.

Beside him, Eli felt January shudder. Rage, sorrow? All of that and more?

"Not my problem," Bethany Flowers said carelessly.

"You think not? You owe me, missus. It's time for you to pay up and get out."

"Watch how you speak to me, you ugly old whore, or you'll soon find yourself with nothing."

Vera's voice rose higher. A screech, in fact. And a great deal louder. "A least I don't pretend to be nothing but what I am. You, you're no better than me. You just don't get paid for it what with that weak, scraggly man you got with you. Using him for muscle. What a joke. Why, I'd be surprised if he can even—"

Bethany shouted. "Shut up. Shut your mouth you worthless…"

The women were becoming more heated by the moment. Eli had his hand on the doorknob, thinking he ought to intercede, when behind him, January gasped, hard and sudden, and Jem dropped onto the floor, his head thudding against the wooden floor.

His hand on his Broomhandle Mauser, Eli pivoted.

"Entertaining to hear them going at it, isn't it, Mr. Pasco?" Harold Bitters stood in a doorway between the front hall and reception room holding a cocked revolver in his hand.

The gun didn't concern Eli so much. It was the other that did.

Eli froze. *How the hell?* How could Bitters gotten in without him being aware. Had the headmaster been out front, hiding, waiting, all the time? They—no. He—he should've checked the front. In a hurry, he'd gotten careless.

The noise the women made with their quarrel had

covered any sounds, Eli supposed. Had it all been deliberate? Had they known when he, January, and Jem rode up? Well, too late to matter.

Right now, Bitters' face was set in sour lines. He couldn't have helped hearing Vera's opinion of him. Could be he hadn't appreciated it.

The headmaster took a step toward him, pushing January ahead of him. Bitters held her against him with one arm locked around her throat. His other hand held a small revolver, the barrel jammed against her temple. This close up, it held plenty of firepower.

"I'm afraid neither woman is as ladylike as one might prefer," he said. "To tell you the truth, I'm sadly disappointed in Bethany's behavior. Perhaps we should join them and have a close-up view of the proceedings. Granger? Disarm him. The boy has a gun as well. Get it."

Paul Granger stood to Bitters' left. Facing her, Eli could see the fury flashing in January's eyes. On the floor at Granger's feet, Jem stirred. Eli saw one of the boy's eyes open and look directly at him. As for himself, he could do nothing as Granger sidled up to him and snaked the Mauser out of his chest holster.

"I believe I'll keep this," he said, holding it up and wagging it in Eli's face. "I hear they're a damn good gun. And expensive." His finger was on the trigger.

Eli knew just how much pressure it required for the gun to shoot. Not much. He expected to die right then and there. Determined not to go without a fight, he shifted his weight onto his left leg and prepared to jam his boot into Granger's crotch. The opportunity was lost when Granger ducked away and gathered the Colt from Jem's belt. Jem remained flaccid as a pile of old clothes lying on the floor, even when Granger toed him with his boot.

"He's out," Granger said, satisfied.

"Good. In we go," Bitters said, cheerful as a grasshopper in September. Then to Eli, louder, stronger. "I said *in* we go, Pasco. Now."

The inner room had gone quiet.

Granger stepped back but kept the gun on him as Eli pushed the door wide with the flat of his hand and entered. Bitters pushed January in ahead of him. The women, who stood one on each side of a fireplace containing a couple smoldering wood chunks, went silent.

The women stared, taking in the parade as they filed into the room. Then Bethany laughed, though her face remained red with rage. "Look at this. We've got them. How clever of you, Harold. I'm so proud of you."

"Thank you, dear heart." Her approbation evidently gave him courage. Bitters preened before glaring at Vera. "Weak? Scraggly?"

"Finally grown some balls, have you? Maybe you oughta put this one in her place like your men did to Madeline." Vera stood her ground, arms akimbo, and glared right back. In fact, she stepped forward a pace, the better to look at January.

"So you're the one the old man left everything to. That's some scar you got there, girlie." Vera chortled into January's face. "I'd give a dollar to know what kinda man did that to you."

As it turned out, her curiosity would forever remain unsatisfied. In fairness, she did get some warning when January, looking behind the woman, drew in a sharp breath and her eyes widened.

Vera whirled. Too late, as it happened, because Bethany, who'd picked up the heavy iron fireplace poker standing so conveniently on the brick hearth, used it to whack Vera on the side of her head. Whacked her hard, the thud landing with a crack of bone and a spurt of blood. The poker's hooked edge sank in deep. Whatever Bethany had been working at in prison had given her muscles.

Even as Vera sank to the floor, Bethany dropped the poker and made a move as if to dust off her hands. "Old sow," she said. "So, there's one loose end cleared away." She looked meaningfully at Bitters.

He, as taken aback as anyone by Bethany's action, went limp. His hold on January loosened and, at the same time, he ignored Granger just a second too long. Then Bitters's senses returned and his revolver went from aiming at January to coming around to point at Granger. A little late, as it happened.

Granger must've sensed danger, but what with the gun in his right hand held on Eli, and fumbling with the Mauser in his left, he got a bit flustered. His gun wavered.

January wrenched out of Bitters' slackened hold and skipped aside. Toward Bethany. In a single glance Eli knew Bethany was in trouble.

As for Granger, Jem, who'd come awake—if he'd ever been anything else—grabbed him by a pantleg and yanked him down as Bitters fired. The bullet went over Granger's head into the wall. Meanwhile, Jem grabbed his ears and banged his head repeatedly on the floor.

Which left Bitters to Eli. First, his right fist came down on Bitters' forearm, knocking the pistol from his grip. His left fist smashed into Bitters's jaw.

Bitters threw up his hands, an ineffectual effort to guard against further blows. He doubled up a fist and poked at Eli's eye. He even tried to run, equally as useless.

Eli didn't even feel the slight jabs. He fell into an alternating rhythm of left and right until the headmaster lay on the floor beside his intended victim. His face a ruin, only half-conscious, he groaned.

Eli stood over him, his anger finally cooling. Jem, he saw, was staring at him. "Sorry," he said to the boy. "You shouldn't have seen that. But I gotta say he scared me. I thought he was going to kill January."

After a moment, Jem nodded, though not as if he thought Eli had been scared. Not for even one minute. "So did I. I thought he was going to kill us all. Including him." He looked down at the man he'd both saved and conquered.

"He was." January, the only one not breathing with a sound like the bellows on a bagpipe, had already snatched the rope curtain tie-backs from the windows and secured Bethany. And stuffed a cloth in the woman's mouth.

\* \* \*

As MUCH AS she disliked the necessity, January sent Jem back to town by himself. With him, he carried notes to both Milt and Delbert Avery. The one to the attorney she figured was as important as the one to the policeman. Maybe more so.

"Follow the road," she told Jem. "It's faster. And hurry, but not so fast you kill your horse."

Jem looked appalled. "I won't," he said. "I would never. You can trust me. I know what to do."

She smiled, bent forward and, reaching up, gave him a peck on the cheek. He'd grown taller now than she was. "I Know you do. And I do trust you."

Eli, she noticed, stopped the boy on his way out, and after a few brief words, Jem rode off into the night.

One thing January had insisted on. The sheriff needed to come here himself, not simply send deputies to collect Bitters, Granger, and Bethany and, as he was wont to do with important people, let them go.

January, in the past, had spent a winter studying procedures the sheriff's—any sheriff's— office was required to follow. Eli, as a bounty hunter, had not been bothered much with so-called due process. She was. And she knew just what to do.

Ruthlessly, she disgorged the doves from their rooms and herded them all downstairs, bidding them to be seated in the reception room. The two who hadn't already come downstairs to investigate the shooting and noise, that is. The other two were witnesses, of a sort, having bravely gathered in the hallway when the commotion started and not only seen Bethany kill Vera, but January's close escape. The women's chatter rose like the clucking of January's hens. None of them appeared terribly upset by their madame's murder. Just a bit shocked when one of the women talked about how easy it had been.

Speculating, it crossed January's mind to wonder why one of them hadn't done the same before.

She and Eli placed each of their prisoners separately in an upstairs room and tied them to a bed. She didn't want them colluding with each other and making up stories about their innocence.

As for Vera, Eli said they'd might as well leave her to lay just as she'd fallen and closed the door.

They were finished. All of them.

# CHAPTER 23

THREE MONTHS LATER, ON THE DAY OF BETHANY Flowers's execution, January rode over to her old house and walked down to the stream where another of Hoot's brethren, a silver yearling, stood splashing in the slow-moving water. She still hadn't finished making a place for her horses at the Kindred Creek house. Too many interruptions, what with trials, cleaning up a whole lot of legal matters with the Flowers Trust, and the regular spring work of ranching.

She'd received an engraved invitation to the hanging scheduled to take place in the courthouse courtyard, but she'd ignored it. The very idea made her sick. In fact, as the hour of the execution came and went, she found herself trembling. Did the hanging really occur? Or had Bethany somehow, at this late date, managed to get her execution transmuted, maybe into a long prison sentence. Her attorney had been trying.

Taking off her boots, January plunged her feet into the shallow water beside the colt, savoring the swirl around her ankles and wishing the motion could wash away all of these dismal thoughts. The colt didn't shy away from her, accepting her palm on his velvety muzzle and the pat on his cheek. She hadn't named him yet but would soon. Something suitable, maybe a little mystical, because this one had an uncanny sense of what she said to him. Just like Hoot, but an ability lacking sometimes in the others of his line.

Meanwhile, she tried not to think.

She didn't want to think. Not about Bethany and the rest of the Flowers clan, anyway. Joseph would serve out his prison term of several more years. John B would be released next year. She profoundly hoped she'd never have to see either of them again.

As for Jem and Hattie, well, they'd grow up under her care, but they were pretty independent already. They were going to be just fine. And the waif Wren, enrolled in the same school as Hattie, would be all right too. January would see to that. She'd promised, and she always kept her promises.

Giving the colt a final pat and leaving him to his splashing, it occurred to her that all her troubles should be over as of today. Or so one would think. She, with Delbert Avery's serious help, had already put the transfer of the Flowers Trust into motion. Soon she'd be done with it, except in a supervisory position. A *slight* supervisory position.

So, she told herself again, all her concerns were almost laid to rest, settled and sure.

*Except.*

Except for the new one, an offer she'd received just this week. It wasn't the offer she'd been dreaming of for the last year. Dreaming of and trying to believe happiness could happen twice in one life. It could, couldn't it? Other times... Well, maybe not.

The unexpected offer was something to dwell on. She needed somebody to discuss it with.

She needed to talk to Eli. Her answer to the offer might depend on what he had to say. Maybe. If he said anything.

Her old dog had followed along with her to the house she still called Shay's, and decided to paddle her feet in the creek as well. Standing midstream now, Pen gave a short "ruff," jumped out of the water, and shook herself off.

Droplets splattered onto January, making her laugh. "Stop." She held up her hands in defense. Then she saw someone riding up the trail to the house and knew Pen's bark had been a warning. She was good that way. The somebody soon became clearer and a moment later, January knew Eli had arrived.

An answer to a prayer, or something else?

As usual, a trill of pleasure swept through her at the sight of him, overriding her tension. Pulling on her boots, she went to meet him, Pen trotting beside her. The moment of laughter had gone.

They met at the gate into horse pasture, a wide meadow where half was dedicated to pasture, half to a hayfield. The tall timothy grass Shay had first planted there three years before was almost ready for mowing. Over at the gate, Eli dismounted and opened it to let her out. Pen just ducked underneath the poles.

But why was she even thinking about hay? Or gates?

His face serious, Eli held a hand out to her. "You okay?"

Nodding, she took it, wondering if she looked pale. She felt pale. "Well? Did Milt get back to you?"

"He did. I came as soon as the telegram arrived." He drew a breath. "It's done." He took a yellow flimsy from his shirt pocket and handed it to her.

Her fingers shook as she fumbled the paper out of its folds. Her eyesight danced for a moment before clearing.

### BETHANY FLOWERS DEAD AT 10:30 A.M. MOURNERS FEW. THE TOWN QUIET.

THE LAST PART about the town being quiet must be Milt's way of telling them the city had made its judgment and she and the kids would be welcomed into the fold. Or perhaps, in society's silence, they were hoping people would soon forget they'd supported Joseph and Bethany, rather than her and Joseph Senior's young children.

She looked up at Eli and forced a hint of a smile. "I'm glad its over. Jem and Hattie can finally stop looking over their shoulders all the time. Maybe they can get back to being kids again."

"They're lucky to have you, January. You know that, don't you?"

January shrugged. "I've wondered, though, if my cousins, and Bethany, of course, would not have been so ruthless if Grandfather Flowers hadn't left everything to me."

His expression showed doubt. "And maybe they would have. Pieces of work, sweetheart, all of them."

He'd done it again, called her sweetheart. Her dad had called her that a time or two. Shay had called her sweetheart—and a few other loving names. What, exactly, did Eli mean when he used the word? Why did he say it in a way that sent shivers up her spine? Time to find out. Past time.

She took a breath as they walked together toward the rail where she'd hitched Hoot. Eli's horse followed him without reins as docilely as Pen followed January.

"A fellow from California called on me yesterday afternoon," she said. "Startled me some when he told me what he wanted."

Eli stopped and looked down at her, a crease forming between his dark eyes. "What did he want?"

"The ranch at Kindred Creek."

"What? Your ranch? He wants to buy your ranch?"

She nodded, smiling slightly. "Took me by surprise, I can tell you. And he made what I believe is a fair offer. Cash money, so he says."

"Who is he?" he demanded, his voice grating. "Where'd he come from? Besides California, I mean. What made him come to you?"

January leaned against the rail, Hoot's nose whuffling against her back. "I don't know. I didn't ask. He said he'd been traveling around the area for a week or so, looking for just the right place to set up. Which means the right acreage, the right site, and the right house. Seems he recently got married and plans on having a family soon, but wants his wife to have a good, modern house. Most of the places he's looked at are old. He mentioned a problem when it comes to outhouses. His new missus demands her house have a bathroom."

"A bathroom?"

She nodded. "You can't blame her, can you? I can't. He said my place is a little far from town, but he expects automobiles will be showing up in the country before long, and it won't seem so distant. And, there is a bathroom."

"So you said."

January heard an odd tone, like someone searching for what he wanted to say. "Yes," she went on. "Apparently someone in town told him I'd built a house with a bathroom, so he decided to approach me after he'd looked around a while."

"Do you trust him?"

"I trust that he wants to buy my ranch. And he has the money. He showed me the bank's credit slip."

Eli went silent, and stayed silent for several moments, looking off into the distance as if trying to see ahead.

January, judging by the way his jaw muscles worked and his feet shuffled, would've said he was angry. Or nervous. Yes, maybe nervous.

"What are you going to do, January? What did you tell this fellow?" he asked at last.

"I told him to give me a day and I'd think about it."

"You did?" No mistaking his discomfiture. "But—" He stopped.

"Yes. I told him it depends." She swallowed hard at the knot forming in her throat. If Eli said—"

And he did. "Depends on what?"

*On you.* But she couldn't say that. She just couldn't. Women didn't ask men to marry them. *Did they?*

She realized she'd been silent for too long. And he was waiting for her to speak, his gaze sharpening. Turning from bewildered to...to something else.

"If I can find something a little closer to The Falls, for one thing," she said in a rush. "A place with good water and room for the Belgians and the brood mares and all my critters. And...and...well, most any house can be fixed up. I know how, and I'm good at it. I can always build another bathroom."

He'd gone a little pale, but no one would ever say Eli Pasco backed away from a challenge. His mouth set. "I might know of a place like that. The animals, the house to fix up. It's a good house."

January's gaze flew to meet his. "It is? You might?"

He nodded. "You'd have to share it though. You'd have to share it with me."

Now her breath caught and she felt a little dizzy. Quite suddenly, she just couldn't stand it anymore. She had to have this settled, once and for all. "Eli, are you asking to marry me? Or just offering to let me come live with you?"

"Let you? Sweetheart, when we're married, I insist you come live with me." He hesitated. "If you will marry me."

The answer on her face must've been obvious. His eyes glinting, he grinned then, and let out an uncharacteristic whoop that made Pen howl and the horses jump.

There seemed to be only one thing left to do. It went without saying she loved him, so she'd thought she didn't need to say the words, not even to herself, but did she? She wanted to. So she did. "I love you, Eli Pasco."

Well, what else could he do besides wrap her in his arms, declare that he loved her too, and kiss her until she trembled? And, finally, considering all those kisses, he got around to a real proposal.

And she got around to saying yes.

## A LOOK AT:
## THE SPEAKER OF CLOVIS CREEK

**Fighting to keep her past a secret, one woman struggles to preserve the future she's worked so hard to build.**

Ocean Galliard is trying to blend in as best she can in her new home of Clovis County. But when a prisoner is brought into the cafe she's working at, unkempt and rambling in Polish, she can't help but take action. Growing up with her Polish grandmother, Ocean knows enough to understand that this prisoner's life—and the life of his child—are in danger.

Working with the Clovis County Sheriff and his deputy, Ash Joes, to translate the man's pleas, the case progresses. But Ocean's knowledge of foreign languages attracts attention of the worst kind, and she's soon thrust into the criminal underworld of cattle rustlers, kidnapping, and lynching.

As tensions build, Ocean begins to develop feelings for a certain tall, dark, and quiet deputy. And while Ash has never been a stranger to conflict and unrest, she can tell his limits are being tested as he struggles to keep her safe and protect his county.

*Will Ocean forsake her own happiness to safeguard hidden truths...or will they unravel one translation at a time? Buy your copy today and dive into this western romance, full of danger, love, and intrigue.*

*AVAILABLE NOW*

# ABOUT THE AUTHOR

2019 Spur Award winner for *The Woman Who Built a Bridge* and 2020 Spur Award winner for *The Yeggman's Apprentice*, C.K. Crigger lives in Spokane Valley, Washington, where she crafts stories set in the Inland Northwest.

She is supervised by a feisty little dog with a Napoleon complex and ignored—except when he wants to lay on the keyboard—by a reclusive cat. Not satisfied to write only of the historical west, she also writes contemporary mysteries and dabbles in the speculative genre.

A member of Western Writers of America, she reviews books and writes occasional articles for *Roundup* magazine. *Buried Under Books* also features her book reviews.